M000042272

Alex in Deutschland

A Novel by Roger Neumaier

This book is a work of fiction. Any references to real people are used fictitiously. Other names and characters are products of the author's imagination. Any resemblance to actual persons, living or dead, is entirely coincidental.

Copyright 2021 by Roger Neumaier

Published in Paperback and eBook, December, 2021.

All rights reserved, including the right to reproduce this book or portions thereof in any form whatsoever. For information, address Bratman Publishing; PO Box 415; Edmonds, WA 98020-0415.

Cover photo, Frankfurt Opera House, 1935, by Dr. John J. (Hans) Neumaier

Printed in the United States of America

Library of Congress Control Number: 2021925217

ISBNs: 978-1-956920-02-4 (paperback); 978-1-956920-03-1 (eBook)

In memory of my father,
Dr. John J. (Hans) Neumaier,
who witnessed the Kristallnacht burning
of Frankfurt's Westend Synagogue.

Prologue: A News Article

The Oklahoman; August 4, 1962

Shot of Drug Kills Indian Bull Elephant

Shaken with Seizure, Tusko Dies in Short Time

OKLAHOMA CITY—Tusko, a young Indian bull elephant, the subject of psychiatric research here, was shaken with a gigantic seizure and died an hour and 40 minutes after an injection of 297 mg. of LSD, lysergic acid diethylamide.

"We were very dubious that we would see any reaction at all." Said Dr. L.J. West, head of the Department of Psychiatry at the University of Oklahoma Medical Center. "But we discovered the nervous system of the elephant is fantastically sensitive to the same drug to which man shows a fantastic sensitivity and that it is markedly different from other animals."

The LSD experiment at Oklahoma City's Lincoln Park Zoo on Friday, August 3, was to help define the nature of the periods of the naturally occurring *going on must* that male elephants experience once or twice a year after reaching sexual maturity.

The drug, approximately 100 micrograms per Kg. of the estimated body weight of 7,000 pounds, was delivered by means of syringe fired from an air gun aimed at the animal's rump from a range of 25 feet. Dr. West expressed surprise that such a small dose could kill the massive beast.

Within three minutes, the beast's knees buckled and it "went into the most peculiar state of excitation of the nervous system—a thunderstorm of spasms," Dr. West reported.

Dr. West believes there is a significant similarity between the elephant and human brain that makes the animal a promising research subject. Dr. West said he and Dr. Chester Pierce, chief of psychiatry at Veteran's Administration Hospital had taken LSD prior to Tusko's injection.

Chapter 1: Oklahoma; September 1962

Alex was waiting in front of the Student Union Building when a black 1949 Ford coupe rumbled up to the curb. A student jumped out and pulled the back of the passenger seat forward. Alex climbed into the car's back seat. As the car chugged off, Judy, who had invited Alex to go swimming, introduced him to Steve, the driver and to John, seated in the passenger seat. Instead of acknowledging Alex, they continued a conversation that had been going on before Alex got into the car.

"This is big stuff Steve," said John in an authoritative tone. "Professor West told me LSD will give mankind the opportunity it has been looking for to understand what goes on in the brain when someone is mentally ill."

Judy looked at Alex and rolled her eyes.

Steve scowled. "Invite me to Stockholm, Dr. Einstein, when you accept your Nobel Prize."

"Steve, our minds are complex. There is more we don't know about how humans behave than we know. Your labeling Professor West's experiments as stupid proves you're just an ignoramus."

John and Steve continued to toss insults back and forth. Judy took out a pencil and wrote something on her notepad, then showed it to Alex. In bold letters she had written *John is an arrogant doofus. Ignore him!*

Then, Judy added in a whisper, "But he sure is right as rain about LSD. It's really super. Last term, when I read *The Doors of Perception,* I memorized an Aldous Huxley quote about LSD. 'Each person is at each moment capable of remembering all that has ever happened to him and of perceiving everything that is happening everywhere in the universe.' LSD might teach us how this could be! Isn't that amazing?"

Alex was feeling disappointed he was wasting his Saturday morning going swimming with these science jocks. He simply responded, "Yup, it sure is."

Judy didn't seem to catch the sarcasm. "But you know why they're off on it this morning, don't you? Did you read the *Oklahoman* article last week about the experiment where the elephant died at the Lincoln Zoo?"

"Yah. I saw it."

"Well, all three of us work in Dr. West's lab. We were there with West when that experiment went way beyond weird. West injected a bunch of LSD into this African bull elephant named Tusko to see how the LSD would affect the elephant—all, of course, in the name of science. Well, after Tusko died, John slipped a little bottle of the LSD into his pocket. He's been doing his own personal research ever since."

For the rest of the ride to the lake, Judy chattered about the dead elephant while Steve and John went back and forth on John's getting high. Half an hour later, the Ford Coupe turned off of the county highway onto a gravel access road. After bouncing down the dusty road for about a mile, they parked next to a small lake. The four students got out and stripped down to their swimsuits. John opened a brown paper bag, took out a small bottle and brightly announced: "It's time for LSD."

After loosening the bottle's black rubber eyedropper cap, John pinched it, drew clear liquid into the eyedropper and then squeezed a single drop onto his outstretched tongue. He offered the eye dropper to Steve but Steve just scowled. Judy, on the other hand, opened her mouth and

John squeezed a drop of LSD onto her tongue. She smiled, waded into the water before diving into the lake.

John held the eye dropper out toward Alex. "Wanna get high, pal?"

Alex paused. He'd smoked marijuana a couple of times since starting college. Those experiences had been OK. But this seemed much more intimidating. "Oh, what the hell," he thought to himself. He opened his mouth and a moment later, it felt like two drops—not one—hit his tongue. Alex wondered if that was a second drop. He decided he'd probably just imagined it.

*****

Alex stood knee-deep in water. The LSD had had a slightly metallic taste but he didn't feel different at all. He just was enjoying the water. It was so warm and comfortable. And the rocks and pebbles on the bottom of the lake. They felt good on the soles of his feet.

Steve waded up to Alex. "John is such an asshole. The only reason he works in Dr. West's lab is so he can score drugs and get high. I'm a little worried about you, Alex. I don't know if you noticed, but I think John gave you two drops—not one. You might get really high. If you begin to feel weird—don't panic. After LSD hits, everything'll seem strange. You'll be high for about ten hours. Let me know if you start to flip out."

*****

Alex stood still, watching the others swim. He didn't feel different than he had before getting the drops. Maybe he just wouldn't react to the LSD? He watched a small fish swimming a few feet away. He walked up to it, but it slithered away. Alex was taken aback by the clarity with which he could see the bottom of the lake; all the different colors; all of the unusual shapes of rocks around his feet. It all seemed so beautiful. The day was getting hot. Alex had never seen the sun shining this brightly. When he looked up, he was stunned to see individual rays of sunlight coming towards him. He felt the warmth of the sun on his shoulders. As he thought about it, he realized he had never appreciated how different the sun, water and rocks are from one another. He reached down into the clear water of the lake and picked up a stone. It was grey granite with streaks of white quartz in it—how incredible! That rock had probably been around for millions of years.

Alex forgot the morning's car ride to the lake. He even forgot he was with other people until John swept his hand across the water's surface and splashed him. It was stunning how the droplets of water moved through the space, from John's hand to Alex. They moved in slow motion—each drop a small liquid prism emanating all the colors of the rainbow. As each drop floated through the air, it left a silver trail.

Steve walked up to Alex. "You're really high and your shoulders are getting burned. You need to get out of the lake. Judy is having a bad trip and John is off in la-la-land. We need to get out of here."

Steve shepherded the three hallucinating students to the car and drove them back to campus.

*****

Alex woke up in his dorm room. He had been sleeping deeply. His thoughts were all jumbled. "Did I oversleep? Am I late for work? Do I have a class?"

Alex paused, trying to figure out what was happening. "Wait—I was going to go swimming. I better hurry."

Alex hopped out of bed; then froze in place. "No—I went swimming already and I'm still in my swimsuit. But why was I in bed?"

Alex looked at his clock radio. It was 7:15. "Is it morning or is it evening?" Shit! I met those crazy science jocks at the Student Union. Then I rode to that lake with them. What happened next?"

Alex sat down on his bed again as he tried to figure out what was up. Then he sat up straight. "My god," he thought to himself. "I think I took some LSD. Then, we went swimming and I became really high. It was amazing—strange, but beautiful. I remember seeing the small fish, feeling the stones on my feet, splashing water; watching the drops move in slow motion. And while we rode back to campus in that old beat-up black jalopy, I told the others how much I hate being a student—how awful it was to have to go back to the dorm. I told them I felt caged—trapped inside the university—just like that elephant, Tusko, that got killed at the zoo."

*****

Half an hour later, while he was eating breakfast in the dining hall, and not enjoying a single bite of it, Alex continued his internal monologue. "What the hell am I doing here at the University? In fact, why am I in college at all? What I said to those others. It's the truth. I don't want to be a student. I hate it here. The only reason I'm a university student is because Papi is scared that there'll be another Holocaust—here in the United States— that I'll need to escape just like he had to leave Nazi Germany. The only reason I'm here is because Papi's afraid that someday I'll need a PhD to get a visa—to be able to escape to wherever-the-hell I need to escape to. But I've had it. I hate living in fear. I hate the sciences—and I don't live in Nazi Germany."

Alex paused and took a deep breath. Then he broke through his silence and shocked the others at his student dining room table by saying angrily and out loud. "Damn it. This is my life. I'm moving to New York."

Chapter 2: Getting to Know Alex

Alex phoned his parents Monday morning saying he would visit them on Tuesday. Papi asked suspiciously in his heavy German accent, "What is the occasion for this visit?"

"I have something to share with you. I'll fill you in tomorrow when I get there."

After he hung up the phone, Alex let out a huge sigh. This was going to be really unpleasant. But he shook his head sadly as he thought to himself, "It has to be done."

*****

Early the next afternoon, Alex phoned from the Wichita bus station. "Papi—Can you pick me up now?"

Alex's luggage was already stashed in a bus station storage locker when his father drove up in front of the Greyhound bus station. Alex got into the two-tone blue '56 Dodge Coronet. Nothing was said and the ride home was steeped in tension. Klaus Schwarz's eyes were focused on the road and Alex was totally focused upon how he would inform his parents of his decision. A few minutes later, Klaus parked the Dodge in front of the Schwarz family's red brick bungalow. Alex's mother came out onto the cement front porch to greet her son. She was wearing her blue apron with red roses; one she often wore when she was busy in the kitchen.

"Hi Mutti. You look well."

"Alex. It is good to see you. I hope everything is ok. I am preparing your favorite dinner."

Alex gave his mother, Anna Schwarz, a hug. The family went into the house. Klaus and Anna Schwarzs' home had a joined living room/dining room. Alex looked around. Nothing had changed. On one interior wall in the living room, there was the series of framed photographs that had always been there. Several were of his father's family. They had been taken in Frankfurt in the mid-1930s. There were two photos of Mutti's family in front of their Wichita home. They had been photographed years after their immigration from Germany, at about the same time as his father's family photos.

The living room had no television. Alex thought about his father had always said that televisions were "a means of destroying civilization, not a means of improving it." more than once, Papi had said, "There will never be a television in this home." Alex's mother returned to the kitchen from which Alex soon heard the familiar sound of her pounding veal cutlets into the thin pieces of wiener schnitzel he loved so much.

Klaus Schwarz's voice interrupted Alex's reveries. "Alex. We play chess?"

*****

Klaus Schwarz's well-worn chess pieces were already set up on a wooden chess board on the dining room table. As he approached the table, Klaus closed the swinging wooden panel door to the kitchen. Alex knew his father was signaling to his wife that he did not want to be interrupted during the chess game—or during the conversation that would accompany it. Alex reflected on the sacrament that chess games had become in the Schwarz home. Klaus had taught his son to play chess when Alex was only five. Father and son had played at least once a week since then—except when Alex attended the University. As they sat down, Alex thought about all of the years of chess with his father—all of those games he had lost. His father had explained this with a simple logic. "It should not be easy for a person learning chess to win. It makes them soft."

Alex knew that today, his father wanted to play chess because of the conversation that would accompany the game. The game had become the designated occasion during which Alex must inform his father of his plans.

Alex sat down at the table. Today, he had the white pieces. He would move first. Alex took a deep breath and slid his king's pawn two spaces forward to E4. Klaus said nothing. He looked at the board for a moment; then responded by mirroring his son's move: King's pawn to E5. It was once again Alex's move. Alex's father had deferred the opportunity to speak. Their protocol was that one only spoke during their own turn. However, this day's game turned out to be different. Apparently, Klaus was too anxious to wait for his turn.

"Why the unexpected visit, son? What is the bad news that you are here to deliver?"

Alex did not respond. Papi would have to wait. He had had no right to ask a question during Alex's turn. Both Alex and Klaus knew what Alex's next move was going to be— the first five or six moves in each of their chess games were always identical. Still, Alex took his time. He needed to rehearse, in his mind's eye, exactly what he would say to his father—how he would explain his decision to quit the university. Finally, after two or three minutes, Alex made his move: Knight to F3. Alex knew his father's next move would be King's Pawn to D6. But his father did not move a chess piece. It was his father's turn—he commanded the stage.

"Why are you here, Alex? What terrible news do you intend to share with your mother and me?"

Then the father made the expected chess move. The responsibility of responding to Papi's question was now upon Alex. "Papi. What the Nazis did to you was most horrible. But..."

"Alex. It was not the most horrible for me. I escaped. It was the most horrible for my mother, my father, my brother—for the six million other Jews who died in concentration camps."

"I know that, Papi. But I do not live in Nazi Germany. What you faced—what your family faced—the terror that was unleashed on you—I do not face it. I am not you."

There was quiet. Alex looked at the chess board. But the nature of the chess game—of their conversation—had changed. Klaus took a handkerchief out of his pocket and wiped his forehead. He pursed his lips, then bit the back of his hand, an action Alex knew meant that his father was becoming angry. Klaus stared at Alex. Alex continued to look at the board. The only sound came from the kitchen where Alex's mother continued to pound delicate pieces of veal into wiener schnitzel.

It was still Alex's turn to move a chess piece. By their convention, Klaus should not have spoken. But their chess standard had been broken. This time Klaus spoke in German. "I now know what you are about to announce. You are going to inform your father that you have decided to leave the University. You are going to say he is an old man—afraid of something that no longer exists. You are going to tell him you do not need an education in the way that he did. Am I right?"

Alex nodded.

"Well, my belief is that you are a fool. I cannot understand how Mutti and I could have failed so completely in raising you. How could you have become so outrageously ignorant?"

Alex stared back at his father. When he responded, it was also in his father's native tongue. "Yes, Papi. I am not you. And yes, I am leaving the university. I face different challenges in my life than you did when you were my age. I do not face a political system that wants to kill me. My challenge is that I have a father who wants to control every aspect of my life. You fear that the terror you faced as a young man will find a way to destroy my life. I do recognize that you and Mutti love me. But you have no understanding—none whatsoever—of how I feel about my life. And the worst thing is, Papi, you don't care."

Alex was about to continue speaking. But his father stood up, took a deep breath and bit the back of his hand one more time. Then he pushed the door open and went into the kitchen. Alex heard what was said. He knew it was said for his benefit.

"Anna—our son knows it all. He is quitting the university, disregarding everything we have striven to give him—everything we have ever done to help him—to protect him. Go ahead. Cook his favorite meal for him. Then, the two of you enjoy it. I am not hungry. I cannot sit down at a table with someone who shows so much ignorance—so much insolence toward a father who has always provided for him— who treated him with the utmost love. I am going for a walk. Then I shall work at the office."

A moment later, just before Alex heard the back-door slam shut, he heard his father say, "Enjoy your dinner with the ingrate."

Alex slowly and carefully put the light golden boxwood and black ebony chess pieces back into the birch box in which they had been stored ever since Klaus Schwarz had received the set as a bar mitzvah gift in 1924.

Anna Schwarz entered the dining room. "Alex. I am sorry your father is being so—so hard on you. He can't help himself. He loves you very much. He is concerned—afraid—for you. We both are."

She paused and looked at her son.

"I am sorry too, Mutti. But it is my life, not his. Mutti—I have withdrawn from the university. I love you. I love Papi. But it is my life. I must live it in the way I think it should be lived. Papi must accept that. Mutti—I am going to live in New York City. I need to be on my own."

Anna Schwarz paused, shook her head, and looked down. Then she took a deep breath and raised her eyes to her son's face, smiling sadly.

"Come Alex. Fill your plate. Dinner is ready."

Chapter 3: The Big Apple

The temperature was in the high eighties and the humidity made it feel even warmer. A short, slightly built young woman in a dark blouse and white skirt approached the lower-eastside New York City tenement building in which she lived. Her brown hair was simply cut—somewhere between a buster brown and a bob. Her name was Lucy—derived from her Russian given name—*Lyusya*. Lucy had just walked home from her job at an upper-eastside investment bank. She glanced briefly at a tipped-over garbage can and its spilled smelly contents. Then she walked up the six concrete steps to her building. Before entering, she opened the unlocked door of a small mailbox and put its contents into her purse. As she climbed the three flights of wooden stairs to her apartment, she heard the Costas' baby crying and smelled the rich garlic and oregano of Mrs. Vittorio's marinara sauce.

Lucy unlocked two deadbolts and opened her apartment door. She turned on the lights and looked around her home with satisfaction. She was pleased with the brilliant array of color. Each wall, each piece of trim, each stick of furniture was painted an intense red, blue, yellow, purple, orange or green. She turned on the kitchen faucet. A trickle of water ran into a copper bottom tea kettle. When the kettle was half full, she placed it on the hotplate and turned it to high. Sliding aside a purple paisley cloth hung in front of kitchen shelves, she took out an earthenware mug and sat down on a sky-blue wooden chair at a fire engine red dining room table. She put a pinch of Constant Comment loose leaf tea into the mug. Then she waited for the water to boil.

A few minutes later, the tea kettle whistled in the midst of a loud squeak of wheels and shaking caused by a subway train passing beneath her building. Lucy poured hot water into the mug and inhaled the tea's sweet scent of orange rind and spices. As she sipped the tea, she looked around the room. A roach ran across her counter top. Lucy laughed silently.

With a thick Slavic accent, she said aloud, "Grandfather's words true. It not fancy, but it home."

Lucy took her mail out of her purse. There were a couple of bills and an advertisement for furniture rentals. Her attention was drawn to a handwritten envelope with no return address. She recognized the handwriting. It was from her old boyfriend, Alex. She paused, wondering what Alex had written. Then taking a deep breath, hoping for the best, she opened the envelope.

August 31, 1962
Lucy,
I haven't written for a couple of months. Sorry. I hope you're doing well. I'm doing ok—not really. I've been thinking about my life. I finally made a few decisions. You know how much I hate the university. Same issues as I wrote to you about in the past. Well, I've made a decision. I decided to drop out.
I hope your invitation for me to visit still stands. Because I'm coming. I don't know if you have a phone. So, I can't call you. I'm just hoping I'm still welcome.
Tomorrow, I visit my folks and give them the unpleasant news—the prodigal son is going to

disappoint them one more time. Then I board a Greyhound for the Big Apple.

I will probably get to NYC around the 7ᵗʰ of September. I'll go directly to your apartment. If there is a problem with my staying with you, I'll go to the YMCA or find some other cheap place to stay. If you're not home, leave me a note on your door with any special directions.

I miss you a lot and look forward to seeing you.

Love, Alex

Lucy smiled. She spoke out loud once again. "American boy finds courage to visit his Russian."

Looking at the calendar hanging over the kitchen sink, she continued to speak aloud. "Today is Thursday—sixth day from September. Alex arrive tomorrow. I make Borscht—welcome him. Fix broth tonight—finish Borscht tomorrow, after work."

She grabbed her purse, threw a strapped burlap shopping bag over her shoulder and headed down the stairs. She crossed the street to Matteo's butcher shop. Matteo wrapped the five chicken legs she purchased in brown paper. Then she was on her way to Cecil's Corner Market. There she bought onions, carrots, celery, cabbage, two potatoes and a large red beet. Satisfied she had all the ingredients required to make the next evening's dinner; Lucy returned to her apartment.

*****

Lucy—Lyusya Simonov—was born and raised in Vladivostok. In 1957, when she was sixteen years old, her father, a career Russian diplomat, was assigned to the Soviet Union's United Nations delegation.

15

New York was a big change from southeastern Russia. Lucy had looked forward to returning to the Soviet Union. But a year after her family arrived in New York, when Lucy's father was ordered to return Russia, he announced to his wife and daughter that he had requested and received diplomatic asylum in the United States. Lucy's parents told her college would be a great opportunity to see a different part of the United States. In January of 1959, she enrolled at the University of Oklahoma.

Lucy's family lived happily in the US, but not for ever after. In the spring of 1961, Lucy's parents died in a car crash. It was her sophomore year at the University. Unable to afford ongoing tuition, she returned to the place in America she knew best—New York City. The only person she regretted leaving in Oklahoma City was her boyfriend, Alex Schwarz.

In New York City, Lucy's Russian language skills helped her find a job as a secretary working for a multi-national bank. She continued pursuing her degree, taking evening classes at City College. In June of 1962, Lucy received an undergraduate degree in psychology with a minor in art history.

*****

Alex's bus pulled into the New York City Port Authority Building early on the morning after Lucy received his letter. After leaving the Port Authority Building, he spotted a sign in front of a little diner that read *Complete Breakfasts—99 cents*. It seemed like the perfect welcome to New York City. Alex was hungry and walked into the diner and sat down on a stool at the its counter. He ordered and then devoured a 99-cent breakfast of two eggs—easy over, bacon, hash browns, orange juice and coffee. As he ate, Alex studied a map of Manhattan. He was on 42nd Street and 8th

Avenue. Lucy's apartment was on Sixth Street, just off of Second Avenue. Alex asked his waitress how to get there.

"Sweetie, it'll take less than half an hour to walk there. Do yourself a big favor and save the twenty cents bus fare. Walk it."

That sounded good. Just then, Alex didn't want to have to figure out the bus schedule or learn about the subway system. He appreciated the advice and left his waitress a 25-cent tip. Then he set out for Lucy's—hoping she had received his letter—hoping her invitation for him to visit was still good.

By the time Alex got to 40th and Broadway, he was getting a feel for New York City. "Wow," he thought to himself. "So many different people: men in yarmulkes with side locks walking next to businessmen in three-piece suits; women wearing shawls over their heads next to others in pastel dresses; an assortment of different languages coming from people with such different colors of skin. Toto, I've a feeling I'm not in Kansas anymore."

As he walked, Alex happily remembered how he had met Lucy, how much he enjoyed being around her and how positive and honest she was. They met half way through his freshman year, working as dishwashers at a burger joint just off campus. At first, he'd wondered why she never spoke to him. He soon discovered why she was so quiet. She could read and understand the English language well. But she wasn't skilled in speaking it.

Lucy had a strong Russian accent and was challenged by English's complex grammatical rules—past tenses, future tenses and conditional tenses were unsolved puzzles for her. She rarely used *a, and,* or *the.* She tended to substitute one preposition for another in a random manner. But Alex could easily ignore those language challenges. After all, his father still sometimes had difficulty with English. What was important to Alex was that she was intelligent and interesting. And he liked her looks.

*****

A half hour later, Alex spotted the worn-down tenement in which Lucy lived. It looked like every other building on sixth street. He lugged his suitcase up the cement steps into the building and then up the staircase. By the time he got to Lucy's apartment, he was breathing heavily. Sweat was dripping off of his nose. Alex knocked. There was no answer. Then, he spotted a folded piece of paper thumbtacked to the wall next to the door. *Alex* was written on it in her slanted script. Alex took the paper down from the wall and opened it.

> *Welcome New York Alex. I at work now. Sadie, at apartment 104, give you my keys. She expect you. Go get keys. Make you comfortable. Milk and yogurt in icebox. Bread with peanut butter in cabinet.*
> *See you later alligator. I home at six.*
> *Lucy*

Alex trudged down the steps to apartment 104 to get the keys. His knock was answered a young woman wearing blue jeans and a large white t-shirt while holding a crying baby on her hip. She. In the background, Alex heard another child crying and a blaring television soap opera.

"You gotta be Lucy's friend. I'm Sadie. Welcome to the Taj Mahal. Here are the keys to Lucy's dream apartment."

Alex thanked her, took the keys and headed back up the stairway. After figuring out which key worked on which lock, he got into the apartment. It had a tiny kitchen with a square wooden table painted red that was surrounded by four wooden chairs. Each chair was a different style and was painted a different bright color.

"Yup," he thought to himself, "the Taj Mahal."

Alex quickly found the apartment's bathroom. After relieving himself, then washing up in its wall-hung sink, he explored the rest of the apartment. That didn't take long. The bedroom was the only room other than the kitchen and bathroom. It was only big enough to hold a double mattress and small dresser. An orange curtain hung across the doorway that separated the kitchen from the bedroom. Alex was tired. He lay down on the mattress and was soon deep asleep.

*****

When Alex awoke, it took a moment to remember where he was. He had no idea what the time was. He heard sounds coming from the kitchen. Shaking the cobwebs out of his head, he got up and pushed the curtain aside. There she was, sitting at the kitchen table, busily chopping vegetables. A pot of soup was steaming on a hot plate and the room was permeated with a pungent aroma. Alex smiled at Lucy.

"Alex. You sleep like baby. I here two hours now. Dark outside. I worry you sleep through night—not enjoy borscht with me."

Hearing her speak triggered positive memories. He flashed on the first time he met Lucy and heard those thick Russian rolled *R*s, the unusual cadence of her speech and its musical tones. "I am so happy to see you, Lucy. Sorry I didn't wake up sooner. I was awfully tired."

He gave her a quick kiss, hoping she was just as happy to see him. He had forgotten how soft her lips were.

"Well Alex. I surprised read in letter you be here for visit. But it please me. I hope you stay at New York. We find you good job."

Alex gave a big smile. "That pleases me, Lucy. I accept your invitation."

They both laughed. Lucy stood up and took a stoneware cup from the cupboard. She opened the refrigerator and took out a bottle of Gallo Chablis, unscrewed its cap, filled the cup and handed it to Alex.

Then she lifted her cup of tea and held it up, out towards Alex. "Nostrovia Alex—To our health."

*****

Alex's first order of business was to find a job. He started with the help wanted ads in the Sunday *New York Times*.

"Lucy—Papi would be disgusted with my lack of ambition. I'm going to apply to become an elevator operator at Macy's, a houseman at the Roosevelt and a doorman at a nearby apartment building. The jobs won't require any thought—exactly what I want."

By the end of the week, Alex had been hired as a doorman at an apartment building on 34th Street and Park Avenue.

"It's an easy gig," he told Lucy. "All I do is open the door, close the door, and call building residents when their packages arrive."

*****

Weekends became a non-stop tour of the Big Apple. One Saturday they went to the top of the Empire State Building. A week later, they were at a chamber music concert at the J. P. Morgan Library. New York had so much to enjoy! The couple visited exhibits at the Metropolitan, the

Guggenheim, the Modern Museum of Art, the Whitney and at countless other smaller museums and galleries.

"You know Alex. I study for psychology. But art my love. I find joy in drawing and paint. At New York, we able to enjoy much art—many artists."

"Lucy—Going around this city with you—well, my life's become an art course. Every museum we walk through is a non-stop lecture about the artists we see. But I love it—don't stop!"

"I promise Alex. Not stop."

One of Lucy's favorite museums was the Cloisters, a North Manhattan combination of gardens, fine art and medieval castle, transported stone by stone, from France. "Seeing Cloisters help appreciate how wonderful it be travel at Europe. You want travel Europe with me? I wish visit Italy and France—see painting from renaissance artists, from great impressionists."

"Yes, Lucy. That sounds very cool. I'd want to go to Frankfurt and see the places my father enjoyed as a child."

Alex and Lucy decided to set aside as much of their earnings as possible. In a year, they hoped to enough to travel to Europe.

*****

One sunny Saturday, Lucy suggested going to the Bronx Zoo. Shortly after arriving at the zoo, they stopped at the African Elephant exhibit. Lucy bought a bag of peanuts. She wanted to throw the nuts through the bars to a huge African elephant. When she started to do this, Alex was overcome with uncomfortable feelings. He had always felt zoo animals were treated cruelly, that zoos were like little concentration camps for animals. But seeing the elephant that day made him think of the Tusko—the elephant that had been killed in an LSD experiment at the Oklahoma Zoo. That thought was followed by a surge of unpleasant memories of his LSD experience.

"Lucy, I am sorry but I don't want to stay here. Can we get outta here—quick?"

"Why? I enjoy zoo."

"I feel really uncomfortable."

"Why you uncomfortable? You uncomfortable with me?"

"No. I'm sorry. It'—it's complicated. Can we just go? I'll explain it all later."

"Complicated? Complicated? I enjoy zoo. I enjoy elephant. Why you ruin it? What so complicated?"

"It isn't about you—it's not even about today."

"What you mean—not about today? This is today. You ruin it. Go home. I stay. I see you after."

Lucy turned her back to Alex and continued to throw peanuts to the African elephant. Alex watched her for a half a minute. Then he headed toward the zoo entrance. As he walked, he thought about how Lucy had turned her back not just on him, but on his feelings. It reminded him of how his father always ignored his concerns and that that was why he had come to New York City in the first place! Alex strode out of the zoo.

That evening and the following day, Alex and Lucy did not speak to one another.

*****

Alex occasionally received small gifts from residents of the building in which he worked. Sometimes it was a box of chocolates. Other times, it was tickets to a sporting event or a concert. One evening, a resident at the apartment building gave Alex a marijuana cigarette. Alex put it in his pocket and carried it home. He told Lucy he'd like to smoke the joint with her after supper.

"Alex, I not want smoke marijuana. It illegal. If I arrested, US government maybe send me back Soviet Union."

"Lucy—they wouldn't do that."

"You not know that, Alex. Many Americans not care for Russians."

Alex didn't force the issue. That evening, he decided to smoke the joint by himself. After a few drags from the marijuana cigarette followed by short coughing spells, Alex was high. He told Lucy he was tired and was going to bed. Alex fell sleep immediately.

*****

When Alex woke up the next morning, he was perplexed. He wasn't able to stop thinking about a dream he had had. It seemed so clear. The dream had taken place in their apartment. In it, a woman had lost her temper and screamed at another woman. It was so intense and while he knew it had been a dream, it seemed real. Lucy had already left the apartment to go to work. He looked at the clock, saw how late it was and after dressing quickly, took off for his job.

That evening, after dinner, Alex told her about the dream. Lucy listened intently and then responded. "Alex, woman in dream sound like my friend Ruby. She sublease apartment to me. Ruby have awful temper. Get angry fast. Many times, I hear her scream at other people. She tell me she even scream at parents when she was teenager."

Lucy listed several other instances where Ruby had gotten angry and told someone off. Alex thought it was strange. Maybe Lucy had told him about her before. He wasn't sure. In any case, they didn't talk more about his dream.

*****

A couple of days later, Alex asked Lucy, once again, if she would smoke a marijuana cigarette with him.

"Alex—I tell you before. I not want that drug—or any drug. Marijuana dangerous. Bad to mental health. You ignore me say this."

"Lucy. You ought to try it. Who knows? Maybe you'll like it? And there is no danger from the cops. This is America. But I do understand why you are afraid. I grew up in a home where my father was always fearful the Nazis were somehow going to stage a coup here—in the US. Papi may have been paranoid—but he had some good reasons. However, I am not like that—and you shouldn't be. This isn't the Soviet Union. Police aren't going to rush in and send us off to Siberia. Walk through this building late at night, sometime. You'll smell dope being smoked on every floor. And we would be super careful. I'd put a towel across our door's threshold. That's what we did at the University. No one would be able smell the dope.

"And as far as mental health goes— and here I'm gonna quote Papi. 'The whole world is nuts except for me and you...but sometimes, I wonder about you.'"

As he shared this, Alex reflected on the fact that his father could be a lot of fun.

Lucy enjoyed Papi's quote. "Agah. I try one time. And you correct about hall smell. It always strong. But question of you. It me or you who nuts? Remain be seen."

*****

Later that week, Alex bought a half an ounce of marijuana from a fellow doorman at work. He told Lucy they could smoke a joint together after supper. "I not want smoke marijuana evening before work. Tomorrow Friday. I smoke with you after work."

The following day was Alex's first weekday off of work since he'd started his job. Before leaving home that morning, Lucy added, "If you want, it OK you smoke dope before I home. Then, I do other time."

After Lucy left for work, Alex went to the corner newsstand market to buy the New York Times. Returning to the apartment, he read the sports page's analysis of the Yankees' seven-game triumph in the World Series.

After finishing the article, Alex remembered what Lucy had said just about smoking the joint during the day. But even though she had given her permission, he felt guilty doing that. She had been willing to smoke it that evening. After even more reflection, his perspective evolved. "Oh, what the heck," he said aloud to himself. "She did tell me to go ahead if I wanted to. I'm going to smoke it now. And then, I ought to go out and celebrate the Yankee's success by buying myself a jelly doughnut!"

Alex put a towel across the door's threshold and placed the plastic bag of marijuana, a new gold, blue and white packet of *Zig-Zag* cigarette papers, a can to be used as an ash tray and a box of wooden matches on the kitchen table. Sitting down in front of them, he tried to roll a joint, something he had never done. It turned out to be harder than he thought it would be. The joint kept falling apart. The paper just wouldn't stay sticked together around the marijuana. After three failures, Alex succeeded. He lit the marijuana cigarette and sucked in its acrid smoke, holding it in his lungs for about fifteen seconds before coughing it out and gasping for fresh air. Then he repeated the sequence. He felt relaxed and sleepy. Taking a nap seemed like a good idea. It was his day off, after all. And he really didn't need a jelly doughnut. After crushing the end of the joint into the ash tray, Alex stood up and made his way into the bedroom. He lay down and almost immediately was asleep.

A half hour later, Alex awoke from the nap. He shook his head from side to side. He was disoriented. He had had another dream that seemed real—again, it had been in this apartment—and was about that same woman.

*****

That evening As Lucy walked into the apartment, she carried a paper bag full of groceries and had a big smile.

"Well Alex. We smoke dope now? Then I make solyanka. I buy potato, cabbage, carrots, pickles, dill, sausage, mushroom, onion and tomato at store. Solyanka special. You will like.

"Solyanka sounds great, Lucy. But you remember you told me to go ahead and light up if I wanted to? Well, I did. Sorry Lucy."

Disappointment showed on her face. "That ok, Alex. We smoke another time."

"Sorry, Lucy. But that's not all." Alex hesitated for a moment. "I had another weird dream. After I smoked the joint, I got tired. I went to bed and fell asleep right away. Then I started to dream. It didn't seem like a dream, Lucy. It was so clear. It seemed like I had woken up and was just watching the whole thing—the same woman—in this apartment. She had short black hair, thick dark eyebrows and a really flat face. She was dressed in worn blue jeans and a Yankees t-shirt—and she obviously wasn't wearing a bra.

"She lost her temper—again—worse than in the other dream. This time she was reading the riot act to a man. She gave him a royal tongue lashing. She called him just about every bad name in the book. It wasn't clear what she was yelling about, but boy, was she ever mad. Her last shot at him was that he was *a poor excuse for a human being.*"

Alex took a deep breath, exhaled and then looked down at the floor. "It's really weird. I remember it so clearly. It wasn't like a dream. It was more like—like I was there—watching and listening to her."

"Alex—woman in dream. She not only act like Ruby—what you describe look like Ruby. You play game at me? Someone tell you about Ruby—maybe show photograph? Then you decide play trick? Alex, this not funny—not game. I angry. I not cook dinner. You not nice. Maybe you think this funny. I not. Why you do this? I never speak you about Ruby. How you dream what she look like unless someone tell you? I think you make mean joke. I trust men before—they deceive. This make me fear something wrong for us. First you leave me at zoo. Now you tease around Ruby. Maybe I pick wrong man again."

"Lucy, I would never deceive you—never play a game like that. You're right—that would be mean. But I didn't do that. I really dreamt it and the dream seemed real. I don't know how the person in the dream could be so similar to your friend. But I give my word; I'm not playing a trick on you. I'm just telling you what I saw in my dream. The weirdness of this whole thing upsets me too. And I'm hurt that you question my honesty. Have I ever lied to you about anything?"

Nothing was said by either of them for half an hour. Finally, Lucy broke the stalemate.

"Ok, I believe it dream. But whole thing strange. I call Ruby. I ask her if this happen."

"Look, Lucy. I probably will never have another dream like this. If we call her, she's gonna think I'm really strange. Let's forget about it."

Alex waited for a response. After a couple of minutes of silence, Lucy spoke. "OK, Alex. I try believe."

Alex was relieved that Lucy had given him a reprieve. But he was left wondering about the whole strange episode. "Something is odd," he thought to himself. "Lucy's concerned with the similarity to her friend. But for me, the most bizarre thing is the dream's clarity. I recall every damned weird detail. It's too strange."

*****

The following Friday night, Lucy was washing dishes after dinner. Alex was reading the Village Voice.

"Alex. We smoke marijuana cigarette tonight? I keep promise—I try smoke."

Alex was pleased. Maybe Lucy's willingness to smoke the dope signaled a return of trust in him?

"Great Lucy. Let's finish up in the kitchen. Then I'll roll a joint."

A few minutes later, the two of them sat at the kitchen table, drinking mint tea with honey. Alex lit a freshly rolled marijuana cigarette. Lucy inhaled from it first. She coughed all of the smoke out immediately.

"Here Lucy. Let me show you how you do it. You gotta suck in air around the joint in addition to sucking it through the joint. That cuts down the sting of the smoke."

Alex demonstrated his technique. He held his breath while handing the lit marijuana cigarette to her.

This time, Lucy took a much smaller draw of smoke while mixing it with fresh air from outside of the joint. She succeeded. Ten seconds later, Lucy expelled the smoke and started to laugh.

"Alex. I see. It funny. And table and chairs—they amazing colors. Apartment like cartoon."

Alex laughed. "The room does look silly with all the different colors. Doesn't it?"

Lucy looked at him for a moment, shrugged her shoulder, then inhaled the smoke one more time. "You want vanilla pudding Alex? I want pudding."

"Yes Lucy. Vanilla pudding would be nice. Could you put some chocolate chips in it? That would be really tasty."

A moment later, Alex started to get sleepy. "I'm gonna lay down for a minute. Let me know when the pudding's ready." He walked into the bedroom, laid down and almost instantly fell asleep.

Lucy turned her attention to the pudding—first, she carefully took the milk bottle from the refrigerator. Then she poured milk into the pan, put the pan on the hotplate and turned the hotplate on to high. After the milk had boiled, she stirred in a package of vanilla pudding mix. Finally, she poured the mixture into four small bowls and counted out four groups of eight chocolate chips. She then dropped one group into each bowl. Now, the pudding just needed to cool.

"Pudding difficult," she said aloud. "Each step hard. But pudding done."

A quarter of an hour later, Lucy went into the bedroom and shook Alex's shoulder. "Wake up sleepy-head. Pudding ready. Come table."

Alex pulled himself out of his sleep and followed her into the kitchen. The pudding was still hot. Blowing on each spoonful before sucking it in, Alex focused on the pudding's sweetness, its warmth and its thickness.

"Lucy, the melted chocolate swimming in the creamy vanilla is simply wonderful."

After scraping every bit of pudding from their bowls, the couple sat at the table.

"Good?" Lucy asked.

"Heavenly, Lucy." Alex took a deep breath and then added, "But I got a problem."

Lucy looked up.

"I'm sorry, Lucy. I had another strange dream. When I got into bed, I fell asleep right away. Then the dream started. It was weird—like before. I knew I was dreaming—even though it didn't seem like a dream. The person you told me is Ruby, she was breaking up with her girlfriend. That was weird enough to watch. But they got real nasty in what they said to one another. And once again, it happened here—in this apartment. During the dream, I remembered very clearly you and I had spoken about Ruby—and that I had dreamed about her before. And in dreams, at least in most of my dreams, you are not that conscious that you are dreaming. And on top of that, I hardly ever remember anything after a dream. But I knew it was a dream—it just didn't seem like it—it seemed too much—too much like being awake. And afterwards, now, I remember every single detail. Anyway Lucy, it was super intense again. Your friend—Ruby—and her girlfriend—the things they said to one another were so nasty."

Lucy handed Alex a pencil and spiral bound notebook

"Alex, write every word. This I learn in psychology class. More long you wait before write down dream detail, you remember less."

Given how intensely Lucy had reacted the prior time he had told her about his dream, Alex figured this was a positive response. He took the pencil she handed him and, while sitting at the brightly painted red kitchen table, carefully described in the notebook what he had seen in the dream.

> *October 26, 1962. I had another intense dream about Ruby. I had it after going through the same routine that preceded the other dreams— smoked a joint—became sleepy—lay down—and fell asleep.*
>
> *In the dream, another woman actually called her Ruby. Ruby was screaming at the other woman—told the woman she was a whore—and used a bunch of other mean names. It all took place in this apartment. I remember seeing the colored dining room furniture and saying to myself, "It's taking place in our kitchen again."*
>
> *The two women kept screaming at one another. The other woman threw pans and a vase— the vase shattered. Near the end of the dream, the other woman (Ruby called her Jenny) unlocked the apartment door's deadbolts, opened the door and slammed it as she left the apartment yelling "Bitch".*
>
> *Then Ruby sat down on a chair and wept.*
>
> *That's when I woke up. Lucy was shaking me.*

When Alex finished writing, he looked up. He was disappointed to see Lucy's expression. Lucy was not happy. Alex didn't know what to say. He just slid the notebook to her.

As she read his notes, Lucy sat on her blue wooden chair at the red kitchen table, slowly rocking her body forward and back. "This third strange dream. Each dream of my friend who you claim not know. All here in apartment. Alex—too hard to believe. I want trust. But it difficult. I upset. Not just this. You different person than I know from Oklahoma. First zoo—you leave me—not explain. Then, you say me you dream real things about someone you not know. You believe if I tell you special things? About your friend? About person I not know? It feel good if I walk away from you—like at zoo? I think not."

Alex didn't know what to say.

"Alex. I see you upset. But I more upset."

"Yes, I am upset Lucy. This scares me. I don't know what the hell is going on. And it upsets it me even more because you say you don't trust me."

"You not dream like this before—ever?"

"I don't know what more I can say Lucy. I've been totally honest with you. I have never had a dream like this—even after the two or three times I smoked dope at the University. But I can explain the zoo—why I acted so—so intensely. And now, I am wondering if maybe the event that drove my reaction at the zoo might be somehow linked to these weird dreams."

"You say me, Alex. I sit here, listen."

Then Alex told Lucy about how he had gone swimming with a group of grad students; how one of them had some LSD he had stolen from the laboratory in which they worked after an experiment had killed a zoo elephant named Tusko. Alex told Lucy how he was probably given a double dose of LSD, and how upset he had gotten about being a student after taking the LSD.

"So anyway, Lucy, that whole experience was the straw that broke the camel's back—it caused me to decide to quit school. My life seemed out of my control before then—but hearing about the elephant—then going swimming in the lake with those assholes—and getting so high I didn't know what was happening—all that set me off. I realized I needed to leave the University—get out from under the clutches of my father's fears. And that is what got me to leave U of O and come here."

"Since coming to New York, in addition to all of that, I have started having nightmares. In those nightmares, the university turns into a crazy place that kills many elephants while the student who gave me the LSD chases me around—yelling at me. And after I wake up in a sweat in the middle of the night, I realize that the dreams are also about Hitler—they are about my father's family being murdered—they are about my father's fears—and apparently mine—of it all happening again."

"I wake up in the middle of the night in that sweat. I feel sadness for the elephant that was murdered. I feel guilt for my father's despair at losing his family. I feel lost. And Lucy, seeing the elephant at the zoo brought up all those bad feelings. And talking about it now, the first time I have spoken about it, I wonder if maybe, the double dose of LSD might have screwed my brain royally—so that when I smoked dope at your place, I was able to see your friend. I know that that sounds nuts. But then, I am beginning to feel like—well, maybe I am going nuts."

Lucy looked down. She took a deep breath and sighed. "Alex. Sorry me. Hear this from you make me sad. But you need explain zoo feelings when we at zoo—not now. You not trust me. If we live together, it not fair you not share.

But I add this. Americans crazy. To experiment with elephant not science—it cruelty! Student not intelligent, he selfish little rat. And your father..."

Lucy paused while she gathered herself as she wiped away a tear. "Your father. I understand your father. My mother..."

Lucy let out a big sigh and looked down to her right. Alex asked, "What about your mother?"

Lucy didn't respond to his question. She looked at the table, then at the empty pudding bowls and finally at the joint that had been crushed in the ash tray. She spoke. "You tell me, Alex, you not want me call Ruby—not ask her if things you saw real. But sorry. I call Ruby now. No choice."

Alex said nothing. Lucy walked over to the phone, picked it up and dialed *O*. She gave the long-distance operator Ruby's number. A couple of minutes later, she was speaking with Ruby.

"Yes, things good here. Yes, we love apartment. Thank you much! I still work bank. Alex doorman job—on Madison. Yes—things good. How you?"

Lucy listened to Ruby for a couple of minutes. Alex heard her say *agah* multiple times; adding an occasional *that nice.*

Alex thought to himself, "Boy, Ruby is a talker and Lucy—what a patient listener."

Then Lucy seemed to take control of the conversation. "Ruby—we have curious things happen. Alex smoke weed three times since he live here. Each time, he fall asleep, he have odd dream—dream about you. But I not tell Alex about you—never describe you—never show picture of you. But he see you in dreams. He describe how you look, how you act. I listen when Alex describe. I know it you.

Dreams take place here—in apartment. Each dream, Ruby—you get mad at someone. You lose temper. Today, Alex dream you and woman—he say her called Jenny. You girlfriends. But you stop it—not be very nice. You call Jenny *whore*—other names. Jenny call you *bitch*. You throw things at her. She throw things—even throw vase. Vase break."

Ruby interrupted. Lucy listened for quite a while without saying more. The conversation lasted another half an hour.

*****

After the phone call, Lucy described Ruby's reactions to Alex.

"Yes. Name of girlfriend Jenny. Ruby and she lovers. Jenny flirt with men—with other women. Ruby say she think I speak with Jenny. She think Jenny tell me what happen. Ruby think me and Jenny play mean trick on Ruby. Ruby begin angry at me. After I explain it not trick, Ruby say more. Ruby stop relationship. You see last argument—most bad argument ever. Broken vase in Ruby's family for hundred years—before American civil war. Ruby still upset—losing beautiful vase. I tell Ruby about other dream—argument with man. Ruby tell me it true too. She call man *sexist son-of-bitch*. She say she not want talk about that more. It make her angry just think to him."

Lucy paused, biting her lip for a moment. "Ruby say me, it like your boyfriend in room when arguments happen. Ruby say she feel—her word—*violated*. Her say: *What sort psycho-crazy man you live with?* Then Ruby embarrass. She explain anger—why she yell. I interrupt. I say, Ruby—everyone angry sometime. You need not apologize. What I love about you—your passion! That not what upset. I tell her what upset is Alex dreams see stuff he not see—or hear. I tell her it frighten me."

Lucy got up and poured a cup of tea for herself and one for Alex. She sat down at the table, sipped the tea, and then continued. "At end of call, Ruby say, *Alex lay off weed. If he can't stand heat, he need get out of kitchen.* I think that funny. You no cook anyway. But Ruby show me you speak truth. Now, I embarrass—I apologize—for doubt you. Sorry, me."

Alex smiled. "Lucy—Your doubting me seems more rational than if you had believed me. This whole damned thing has been too strange for any sane person to accept."

"Well Alex, then I sane. Because I not accept."

*****

After the phone call, Lucy grabbed a notebook and started writing down the logical options that might explain Alex's dreams. For ten minutes, Alex watched silently as she pondered, then wrote. When she'd completed writing, Lucy slid her notebook over to Alex to read.

How Alex dream things that really occur?

- *He smoke marijuana before visit New York City. Not have weird dream. Conclude, weird dream not only from smoking dope.*
- *Possible factors:*
  - *Apartment—All three dreams in apartment. Maybe caused by chemical gas or something at apartment?*
  - *Marijuana—Even though two types marijuana from different people, it possible both have similar added chemical. In future, we always make sure get marijuana different source.*

o *Ruby—Ruby maybe have strange power? She affect Alex?*

o *LSD—Alex say this maybe cause. LSD he take at lake affect brain? Idiot give Alex two drop LSD, not one. Cause switch flip in brain? Trigger visions after smoke dope?*

o *Mental health—Alex mental health or brain problem?*

After Alex finished reading the notes, Lucy continued her analysis. "This not normal Alex. You see into past. Not just dream—you have dream vision of truth. I not call these *dreams* any more. They now called *dream-visions*. We need understand dream-visions. We not able explain how they happen. We must treat like psychology experiment—figure out variables; control variables; then analyze dream-visions. Before you smoke marijuana again, we do research. We learn if science literature speak to this. I go in library tomorrow—search for research answer. You not smoke marijuana until we know more. Next time you smoke marijuana, it be different place. But many things we need think through—build a plan."

Alex was surprised at her intensity. Lucy was approaching things thoughtfully. And there was good news. She seemed to have forgiven him. But there was some really bad news. Lucy seemed to be planning an experiment. His role in the experiment felt uncomfortable. He was afraid he was going to play the role of Tusko.

Chapter 4: Working on an Experiment

"Lucy—are you awake."

It was the middle of the night. Lucy groaned, indicating she had been asleep, but wasn't any longer.

"Lucy. I came to New York to escape the University. Being a student made me feel like I was in a cage—like I was the one being kept at a zoo. Everything I did was to satisfy others—my father, my mother, my professors. I escaped the University and came to New York City to live with only person I knew who did not try to control my life. I felt so good about that! But these dreams—these dreams have put me into another sort of confinement. It feels like I traveled back in time—and had to deal with the anger of a person I never met. Then, on top of that, you accuse me of lying to you."

"So sorry. This scary for you."

"Thank you, but what is most upsetting is seeing you so excited about turning this whole thing into a research project—me being the subject of the experiments. Did it ever occur to you that I might not want to be a guinea pig?"

Lucy didn't respond. Alex looked over at her. She hadn't heard his last statement. She had fallen back asleep.

*****

Lucy and Alex were sitting at the kitchen table drinking tea. It was Saturday morning. Lucy shared her plan for the day in a matter-of-fact way. "We go library research psychedelics. Something like dream-visions occur for someone sometime. It probably studied and studies available. We be patient in our look. We find studies."

"Lucy. Did you hear anything I said last night? I don't want to do this anymore. I'm out of it. I want to forget it ever happened. I won't smoke marijuana again. We need to move forward from this."

"It important understand what happen to you, Alex. This truly special. We need understand."

"You are doing to me what those awful people did to Tusko."

"Oh Alex. Don't be scaredy-cat. Be man."

"Lucy—you're wrong. This is my life. I say we drop it."

"I sorry Alex. I need understand what happen. You wish not help. That your choice. I see responsibility to science. I do research."

Lucy didn't look at Alex as she finished her statement. She just picked up her notebook and purse, put on her jacket, and was out the door.

*****

During the week that followed, Alex didn't see a lot of Lucy. She spent all of her free time at the Main Branch of the New York Public Library on 42nd Street and Fifth Avenue. It was the largest public research collection of books and papers in New York City.

Each evening, when Lucy arrived home after her research, she refused to discuss what she had found. "What I do, Alex—it my business. You choose not help. That your choice. You wish not explore? You afraid? You not curious? That your business. I study psychology. This unusual. Famous people search—never find anything like this. God give you something special. But you afraid to explore. You want ignore. That your decision. I do research."

Alex had no one other than Lucy to speak with about the dreams. And now, she not only refused to discuss them with him, she had stopped speaking with him about anything. He considered his options. It wasn't like he could call up his dad and ask for advice. He imagined how angrily his father would react if he had tried. *Papi. This is Alex. Hey—I was just wondering—what you would think about the fact that I travel back into the past every time I smoke dope? I realize, it might be caused by the LSD I took at the University. Could you give me some advice?* Sure—that would have gone over well.

A couple of times during disagreements, Lucy had criticized his lack of flexibility. She sarcastically used the phrase *Alex's way or highway.* Now, it was clear to Alex that it was Lucy's way or the highway. The only alternative he had to going along with her was ending their relationship. But she was his only friend in the world. What choice did he have?

One evening, after Lucy returned from the library, he addressed the issue head on. "Lucy, can we talk?"

"You wish speak? I listen."

"Lucy. You haven't been very nice to me recently. "

She shrugged her shoulders while looking him directly into the eyes.

"I've given it some thought. I will explore the research with you. But I make no promises. And—it isn't fair for you to get angry at me just because I tell you I'm uncomfortable being the subject of an experiment."

"So. What you say?"

"Go ahead. Include me in the research. Include me in the planning. But I am not gonna commit to anything more than research and planning—at this time. If I decide this is dangerous or stupid—well—I'm out of it. But I am saying I will at least consider participating in...your experiment. I just want to be treated nicely."

Lucy gave a big smile, looked up at him, and delivered a nice soft kiss. "This good Alex. You have concern. That fair.

But not let fear control you. Thank you for listen me. We work together."

Then Lucy updated Alex on her library research. In a nutshell, she had found nothing even faintly similar to his dream-visions.

*****

Over the next few weeks, the couple visited the library each evening pouring over diverse scientific and not-so-scientific works. Their efforts produced no success.

Lucy didn't want to give up. "Alex. Somebody, sometime, experience this. I certain."

"Yeah Lucy—someone did—me."

They found studies of hallucinogenic experiences; memoirs of people who had become addicted to drugs; anthropologic papers focusing upon peyote, mushrooms and other natural hallucinogenic substances in primitive civilizations; essays and books speculating about what might cause a person's mind to deviate from reality during drug experiences; moralistic analyses that condemned drugs as the devil's tool; and a series of books and essays Lucy referred to as *gobbledygook.*

"*Gobbledygook* is noise idiot make on paper when take drugs—think they profound."

Alex laughed and agreed.

*****

While they were in the library one evening, Alex recalled that Judy had shared a quote about LSD that might be relevant. It took him a few minutes to remember the name of the author she quoted during the ride to the lake to go swimming. Then it hit him. The quote was from the author of Brave New World. He looked up that book and saw the author was Aldous Huxley. Then he found Huxley's book *The*

Doors of Perception. While Lucy continued to go through the book stacks searching for a paper on hallucinogenic drugs and sleep, Alex went through *The Doors of Perception* and found the quote Judy had shared. 'Each person is at each moment capable of remembering all that has ever happened to him and of perceiving everything that is happening everywhere in the universe.' That quote seemed hauntingly relevant to their search and to his dream-visions.

Alex brought the book over to Lucy and showed her the quote. She pondered it for a moment and then expressed approval with a single statement. "This man smart."

They checked *The Doors of Perception* out from the library that evening. A day later, Lucy had finished it. "After he take peyote, Huxley decide human brain not collect data. It screen out data so person able function. Mental ill peoples not able screen out that much data. Flood their mind. Overwhelm their thinking. Huxley summarize this in quote from Cambridge philosopher name of Dr. Broad."

Lucy opened *The Doors of Perception* to a bookmarked page and read. "We should do well to consider much more seriously than we have hitherto been inclined to do..... that the function of the brain and nervous system and sense organs is in the main eliminative and not productive. Each person is at each moment capable of remembering all that has ever happened to him and of perceiving everything that is happening everywhere in the universe. The function of the brain and nervous system is to protect us from being overwhelmed and confused by this mass of largely useless and irrelevant knowledge, by shutting out most of what we should otherwise perceive or remember at any moment, and leaving only that very small and special selection which is likely to be practically useful."

Lucy gave a big smile. "This book explain everything that happen is out there for all—it always available. But brain block out access. Dream-visions you have let you see things other minds screen out. Door in your mind unlocked by LSD. Now, when you smoke marijuana, your door swing open. We finally have explanation for dream-vision!"

*****

During the period they had searched for relevant research, Alex did not smoke any marijuana. In fact, he was so distressed by the dream-visions, he hoped he would never smoke dope again. But he didn't tell this to Lucy figuring there was no point in upsetting her. One evening after Alex returned from work, Lucy let him know that the status quo was about to change.

"Alex. Research not give us much. We need change approach. We learn whether dream-vision cause could be this apartment. We go different place. You smoke marijuana, sleep, maybe dream-vision. We learn from that. Chelsea Hotel at West 23rd Street rent rooms to artists and writers. My friend at work is artist. This weekend, she away—visit parents. I tell her we want small vacation. She offer us stay her place for weekend. I say *yes*. She say me Chelsea Hotel neat place. It like history of artists museum. Many famous people once stay there. I write names down."

Lucy started reading from a written list she held in her hand. "Mark Twain, Allen Ginsberg, Jack Kerouac, Dylan Thomas, Diego Rivera, Tennessee Williams, Jean-Paul Sartre, Simone de Beauvoir. I not know these people. But she say maybe you know. Anyway, room not fancy, but it perfect to our need. I tell her you smoke marijuana a lot. She say no problem. Everyone smoke there. Her neighbor say so much smoke people get high after one ride on hotel elevator."

Lucy beamed a smile of satisfaction and said, "Now we have place for experiment. Yesterday, I buy hashish from bank mailroom boy. Hashish like marijuana—but more stronger. Tomorrow night, you smoke hashish—we see what can happen. I keep watch—take coffee thermos, sit, stay awake whole night."

"Lucy, aren't you going to ask me how I feel about this? Shouldn't this be my decision? I told you I would participate in research. But I didn't commit to being the subject of the experiment—volunteer to be Tusko for a night. I said I'd consider it."

"No Alex. I not ask how you feel. We just do this. Right? Tomorrow we do experiment. OK? Please."

Alex shook his head and laughed thinking to himself, *damned if I do and damned if I don't.*

*****

Friday night started like a date—Alex and Lucy had an excellent dinner of goulash at a Hungarian restaurant near the Chelsea. After that, they were off to the hotel. The dingy lobby through which they entered had chipped marble floors and worn wainscoting. Across the lobby's walls was a crowded patchwork of abstract and modern paintings and drawings. Two women were squeezed together in an overstuffed mohair chair, smoking cigarettes and listening to a skinny unshaven kid in jeans and white t-shirt singing folk tunes in a quiet coarse voice while accompanying himself on a well-worn acoustic guitar. Occasionally the skinny kid stopped singing and played a harmonica that hung from a holder near his lips, all the while continuing to play chords on his guitar.

Lucy and Alex listened for a moment, then walked up the art deco stairway and turned down a grimy hallway toward Lucy's friend's room. The walls of the hallway were full of black and white photographs of sea shells and charcoal sketches of nudes. Alex noted that Lucy's friend had been right about the smell of marijuana. The hall reeked of it. He thought to himself that he might get high there without smoking anything.

Lucy stopped in front of room 205, put a key in the door lock, turned it and opened the door. They stepped into a small studio apartment. It was furnished with worn-out mahogany furniture—a desk, dresser and bed. Hung from its walls were large prints of brightly colored comic book characters.

Lucy seated herself on an upholstered rocker. Alex sat down across from her on the room's single bed. Lucy pulled out an unfiltered Camel cigarette and a straight pin from an envelope in her purse. She broke the cigarette in half and used the head of the straight pin to create a small cavern in one end of the cigarette. Then, she took a small chunk of hashish out the envelope and stuffed it into the space in the cigarette. She handed the half cigarette and a box of wooden matches to Alex.

He lit the cigarette with a wooden match, inhaled deeply and held his breath for a short while before coughing out the smoke. Alex said, "This is very harsh hashish." A moment later, he repeated the phrase *harsh hashish* and giggled.

"Focus Alex. This serious. Try not cough."

After more efforts to inhale deeply (each of which ended in fits of coughing), Alex put out the cigarette in an ash tray on the floor. He lay down on the bed and looked around the room. His gaze stopped at a large print with a title printed beneath it: *Popeye the Sailor Slugging Bluto.* Alex laughed softly. "It was good of you to get me into a place with such fine art. I didn't realize how sophisticated my taste was as a kid—I often read an entire Popeye comic book—in one sitting!"

"I not understand what you speak about Alex. You need focus now."

Alex shut his eyes and was soon asleep.

*****

A moment later, when Alex opened his eyes, he heard the slurred speech of a drunken Irishman. He was in the same room in which he had fallen asleep. It was the same furniture—though the mahogany pieces were less shabby. But instead of the bright comic prints, the walls displayed black and white photographs of fashionable women from the beginning of the century.

The speaker was a red-faced man with thick, curly, combed-back hair. He wore baggy pants and a cardigan sweater over a white open collar shirt. He had a filter-less cigarette hung from his lower lip as he poured whiskey from a half-pint bottle into a depression ware glass.

The man gave a deep intense cough, took the cigarette out of his mouth for a moment and drank a swallow of whiskey. Then he spoke to a woman who was standing in front of him. "Liz. I am in love with you. But I am also in love with Caitlin and always have been. My problem is that Caitlin and I can't live together—we can't stand one another. I drink—she drinks—and we fight—wicked battles in the day and enjoy the rapture of one another's bodies during the night. And yes—I do bed young women—and Caitlin explores similar delights with her cacophony of lovers—but that is how it is! My life—one mistake followed by another—goes forward and backward. The only things that make any sense are the sweet and sometimes tumultuous words that happenstance and whimsy allow to fall into my almost unblemished poems. My sweet poison, this devilish whiskey, is the only real medicine that fully responds to my melancholy."

At that point, the man stopped speaking as he was overcome by a fit of coughing. The slender woman to whom his words had been spoken had a thin angular face and long straight black hair. She was wearing dark grey slacks and a black sweater. She listened intently with an anxious look on her face.

"Dylan—you need sleep. You drink too much. You smoke too much. And you always hurt the people who love you."

Then, she gave the drunken man a pill—which he washed down by finishing his glass of whiskey. Alex moved away from the bed as the man stumbled across the room toward it—wheezing and coughing the entire way. After reaching the bed and then falling into it, he turned his back to the woman and fell into a deep sleep. The woman took off her slacks and sweater and quietly climbed into the bed behind him, pulling the covers over them. She gently put her arms around him, closed her eyes and fell asleep.

*****

Alex awoke. He began to tell Lucy about his dream, sharing many details he had noticed as Lucy wrote intensely into a spiral-bound notebook.

"I am surprised to still be resting on the bed. In the dream-vision, I moved away from it when the drunken man got in the bed."

Lucy continued to write while he described what he had seen and heard—an intense interchange between a drunken Irishman and a young American woman.

When Alex finished describing the dream, Lucy peppered him with questions. "How was the room decorated? Can you remember the face of the Irishman? What was on the desk?

Alex answered each of her questions. The dream-vision was crystal clear in his head. He did not feel high. "Watching—and then telling you about the exchange between that man and that woman—it has totally drained me. I'm exhausted."

It was Lucy's turn to surprise Alex. She took a paperback book out of her purse and showed Alex the back cover of the book. It featured a black and white photograph of a man's face. Alex immediately pointed at the photo of a full-faced man wearing a white shirt and a polka dot bow-tie.

"That's him! How the hell did you know I would see him in my dream? What is happening here?"

"I make admission. Friend tell me she live in room poet Dylan Thomas stay. I research at library. He here October, November of 1953. I learn that when he here, he have pneumonia—but do nothing cure it. He always party with friends—drink liquor—have sex with many women. Friends give him sedatives. He go into coma—here in this room. They take him to hospital. But coma never end. He soon dead. You familiar—Dylan Thomas before today?"

Alex shook his head from side to side. "I had no clue who either of the people in the dream were; who this Dylan Thompson was or what was going on. I just saw a drunk Irishman whose life was way out of control."

"I also not know him—not know poetry from him—before this week. I hear him on LP recording at library yesterday. When you speak his words, tell of dream-vision, you sound like recording."

"The dream-vision still seems awfully clear to me—the words I quoted were pretty close to what I heard. When he spoke, he spoke with so much expression—yes, and that thick Irish accent."

"Experiment answer questions. Know dream-vision not tied to apartment—not to Ruby. You not know Dylan Thomas. So, we learn dream maybe linked to person from where you sleep. Thomas passionate. Many people live in room 205 before Thomas. Many people after. But you not dream them. Why else but passion of him you dream Dylan Thomas? This my theory."

Alex paused for a moment. "Ok—I see your logic. But you overlook one other possible explanation. There was one other person in the room who had strong expectations for what I would dream."

Lucy gave a quizzical look. "Who that?"

"That person was you, Lucy. Given we are shooting in the dark, isn't it possible that your expectations could have been the driving factor?"

"Agah. Not think of that. Darn."

"Lucy—there is a lot you are not thinking of. For example, what just happened to me? My nerves are shot. It may seem real cool to you that I traveled back a decade to see some drunk Irish poet who was about to die. But I don't feel that way. My nerves feel so ragged. The terrible thing is that I really want to be with you. But if being with you means I must continue to subject myself to this insanity—well, then I gotta ask myself—Is it worth it?"

Chapter 5: Grand Central Number I

Alex and Lucy said little as they walked home from the Chelsea the following morning. Each was focused on their own thoughts.

About half way home, Alex broke the silence. "What I just went through, Lucy, it sort of makes all the rules of how the world fits together seem a little tentative."

"Alex, we just begin learn about dream-visions at Chelsea Hotel. Now, we need learn more."

"I am impressed with your scientific enthusiasm, but I'm more than a little afraid I'll end up like Tusko. You're treating this whole thing like a high school science project. How would you feel if you were the subject of the experiment rather than the scientist? I'm feeling like I never want to smoke grass or hash again."

He looked at her. Seeing a tight lipped, almost angry look, he added, "unless and until we figure out how to proceed."

They walked in silence for a while.

"What happen defy any recorded event—more interesting than any science I study in university. We on edge of something special, rare, unique, Alex. I know it frighten you. But it opportunity for you—for me—for science—for world. We must try understand. This urgent we continue. But I understand you afraid. I not push."

Alex's shoulders relaxed for a moment when he heard those words.

Then, she concluded her thought. "Until we find excellent plan."

*****

Much to Alex's relief, Lucy did not bring up a new plan in the days that followed the Chelsea dream-vision. They went back to their routine. Most of their time together that wasn't spent eating, sleeping or working was spent exploring the art museums and cultural locations of New York City. But Lucy had not dropped her desire to explore Alex's dream-visions. She often visited the library on her way home from work. She just didn't mention it to Alex.

*****

About a month after the Chelsea Hotel dream-vision, Lucy and Alex were finishing a dish of savory Kung Pao chicken at a Szechuan restaurant on 14th street. While trying to capture the last morsels of rice from her plate with her wooden chop sticks, Lucy said calmly, "We need expert—someone who explain what science know about drugs—how affect mind. We not able ask government help. They arrest people for use marijuana. If they learn about dream-vision, we have no say. Government do experiment—not care about you or me. We lose everything. We need professor we trust for explain things. Professors from Oklahoma not competent. This they display when they murder Tusko. If you not want be my victim, you certain not want be their victim. Professors from City University—I not trust—too close government. I now try find researcher we trust. Person speak authoritative for what science know about dream-visions."

"Thanks so much for bringing it up, Lucy, I wasn't worrying about anything. So, I really appreciate your giving me something to worry about. We have a phrase in English: *There is an elephant in the room*. In our case, the elephant in the room happens to be dead."

Lucy gave a quizzical look. "What you mean?"

Alex thought about explaining what he had just said, then decided it would be its awfully complicated to explain.

*****

The couple continued to go out for dinners, explore Manhattan art galleries and see films. The subject of dream-visions did not come up.

Their apartment was only six blocks away from the Bleeker Street Cinema, one of the best foreign film theaters in New York. Once a week, Lucy and Alex had an inexpensive dinner at a small Italian, Chinese or Yugoslavian restaurant and afterwards went to see a film by Francois Truffaut, Claude Chabrol, Orson Welles, Federico Fellini or some other avantgarde director. During the next few months, Alex smoked no dope and had no weird dreams. Lucy continued to visit the library and read articles about the effects of drugs on the human mind. But nothing she found shed any light on Alex's dream-visions no one came to mind from whom she felt comfortable requesting advice.

*****

One evening in early February, after watching a Jean-Luc Godard film starring Jean-Paul Belmondo, Alex and Lucy went to a coffeehouse to hear a folksinger. In between sets, Lucy reopened the can of worms. "I think much about dream-vision. Tonight, we talk about what next. OK?"

Alex looked up from his tea and said nothing. He knew she was not going to take *no* for an answer. So, he might as well listen. He looked at her—unsure of what was coming.

"All dream-visions were in bedrooms. We need try public place. We buy used wheel-chair. You fall asleep in wheelchair. Then we able go somewhere else than bedroom. If someone upset, I say you have sick mental problem."

Alex chuckled. Then spoke. "So, let me get this straight. Now you're proposing telling anyone who asks what I am doing that I'm nuts? This makes me think I am not coming out on top."

Lucy ignored his comment. "Also, I worry about thing you speak after Chelsea Hotel—me know it Dylan Thomas room maybe affect dream-vision. That awfully good point. Me know about place maybe affect what you dream-vision. We need discover if knowledge of you or me cause what you dream. I decide plan for answer question. It require three separate dream-visions."

"Oh—you're now planning to do three dream-visions at a time. How'd I get so damned lucky?"

"Here plan. You choose place we not know. Must be public place we able roll you into or out of in wheelchair—place with history—place we able research. First dream-vision, no research on place by you or by me. You try have dream-vision at place. We see what happen. Before second dream-vision, I research. Find past event, same place. Very important—I not share what I find to you. Then you have dream-vision. Third dream-vision. You do library research before. You learn much about event. Tell me nothing. Then, you have dream-vision. We learn from set of dream-visions. Answer if you or me aware of event—how it affect what you dream. We learn if we steer dream-visions to specific event—or not."

"What if I don't have any more dream-visions? What if we go there and I just sleep—or don't even fall asleep? Who knows—maybe this whole thing won't happen any more—or maybe I have to be in a bed to have a dream-vision? I'll be straight with you Lucy. That is what I hope happens. I want to be with you. I know you are excited about these dream-visions. So, I have been going along with it. But I gotta be honest. I would rather forget about the whole experiment. It frightens me. When you talk about experiments, it sounds like you are playing Professor West and my role is the elephant. I'm at risk. I hope I have no more dream-visions. If that happens, if we try a couple more times and there are no more dream-visions, can we stop playing science? Can I return to be a normal guy living with a woman he likes?"

"OK Alex. You not dream-vision. No more experiments. Then you not worry. We live life."

Alex was quiet. He turned to listen to listen to the young Hispanic woman singing folk songs. She was singing Spanish ballads. Alex focused on her. Her voice and demeanor were soothing. Lucy was focused on Alex—watching him intently. The ballad ended. Alex looked back at her.

"Ok. It's a deal, Lucy. It seems like a pretty smart plan. But it still makes me feel like a mouse in a maze. However, based upon what I know about Tusko's experience, it may be way better to be this mouse than that elephant."

*****

Alex's assignment was to find a safe and secure place where Lucy could watch over him as he slept in a wheelchair. The location had to be a place where there would be little risk that anyone would inquire about what Lucy and he were doing—and no one would demand that they leave. Alex got on it. He spent the next few days considering the many sights he had visited in Manhattan. Each one that came to mind presented a problem. He ruled out Central Park because of weather uncertainty. If it started to rain while he was having a dream-vision, it could be problematic. Based on that insight, Alex decided to rule out all outdoor locations.

He excluded the Empire State Building because there wasn't a location in that landmark building where he and Lucy could sit for hours without standing out like a sore thumb. In the same vein, security officers at the United Nations would not have allowed them to stay in one spot while Alex slept.

After a couple of days, Alex selected Grand Central Terminal in the center of Manhattan—at 42nd Street and Park Avenue. He judged that since Grand Central is always busy and crowded, no one would question a couple who waited in the Terminal. "And think about it, Lucy—all of the different things that must have happened at Grand Central Terminal that could be a basis for an interesting dream-vision."

Alex and Lucy walked up to 42nd Street to check it out. Commuters and tourists quickly passed through the terminal as they rushed to their trains. While there was not a lot of seating, since Alex had already purchased a used wheelchair at the Salvation Army Store, lack of seating was not an issue.

"Alex—you right. Grand Central Terminal perfect site for experiments."

*****

The following day, Lucy purchased a half-ounce of marijuana from a co-worker who had gotten it in New Jersey. Alex agreed that the chances that marijuana would be similar to the weed Alex had already smoked were slim. Alex would smoke a joint from this half-ounce in each of the three attempted dream-visions. As Lucy put it, "Not want difference between what you smoke be possible explanation why difference dream-vision results."

The following Saturday, they were ready for experiment #1 at the Grand Central Terminal. Per Lucy's plan, they didn't do any research on the building before attempting the dream-vision.

Alex agreed with Lucy when she said, "Bryant Park best spot for you smoke dope. It like little garden—just blocks from Grand Central."

*****

On a cool morning in late February, Alex and Lucy walked from their apartment to Bryant Park, pushing the empty wheelchair. They moved at a fast pace to stay warm. As they approached the park, Alex was full of tension. He wasn't sure why—the other dream-visions hadn't been that terrible. They had just been exhausting. But he couldn't help himself. As he walked, he repeated a thought to himself— almost as if it were a mantra: "I hope I don't have a dream-vision."

In a quiet corner of Bryant Park, Lucy sat down on a bench. Alex, sitting in the wheelchair, casually pulled out the joint and lit it. He inhaled deeply a couple times before speaking in a pattern of speech that imitated W.C. Fields, "This should do the trick. And remember, a dead fish can float downstream, but it takes a live one to swim upstream. Now, darling, off to the Grand Central."

Alex got out of the wheelchair. It took less than five minutes to walk to the Terminal. Throughout it, Alex continued to make wisecracks using the same poor imitation of the old vaudevillian. "The best cure for insomnia is to get a lot of sleep. If you can't dazzle them with brilliance, baffle them with bull. A rich man is nothing but a poor man with money."

Lucy did not seem to enjoy any of his comments. When they arrived in front of the imposing Greek revival columns of the Grand Central Terminal's main entrance, Alex gave one last Fields imitation. "I'd rather be in Philadelphia."

"I not know why you say these strange things, Alex. But maybe, after I listen you, I too wish you be in Philadelphia."

*****

A couple of minutes later, they were in the center of the main terminal concourse, right next to terminal's famous information booth crowned with a large golden timepiece. Scores of people scurried past them and across the terminal concourse—each going to their own unique destination.

Alex looked up at the light streaming into the concourse through the Terminal's tall cathedral-like windows. Gigantic chandeliers hung from a ceiling that was decorated with a massive mural of a starry sky. Alex sat in the wheelchair, looking up at that illustration of the constellations. Then, he closed his eyes as he leaned his head forward and fell asleep. For the next hour, Lucy stood next to the wheelchair watching Alex. Commuters, hurrying to their trains, speaking with companions or reading newspapers, paid no attention to the man sleeping in a wheelchair or the woman standing nervously next to him.

*****

Alex woke up. Lucy pushed his wheelchair across the Terminal floor to a corner of the Terminal. He got out of the wheelchair and they walked out of the large building. Once out of the Grand Central Terminal, they had a chance to debrief.

"You dream-vision Alex? What you see?"

"I did—and this dream-vision was different, Lucy. It wasn't about anger or sadness. It was a dream about—well, it was about happiness. It was the same Terminal—lots of people rushing to destinations—the flow of conversations echoing throughout the building. And based on what people were wearing, I think it must have been sometime in the 1930s. I know it was winter because the commuters wore overcoats. I watched a young woman looking around. She seemed a little lost. Then the she spotted a guy across the concourse and called to him. The woman was almost six feet tall—several inches taller than the guy. She had dark hair tied in a top knot and wore a long dark red coat with a white scarf. I distinctly remember how the gold pin on the lapel of her coat sparkled. She looked financially well off—as opposed to the guy who was wearing a shabby navy pea coat, dark blue stocking cap and patched denim trousers. His laced-up leather work boots were worn and he obviously hadn't shaved for a number of days."

Alex stopped speaking. He smiling softly while visualizing his dream. Then he shook his head, realizing that he needed to continue describing his dream-vision to Lucy. "They rushed together—into each other's arms. She was sobbing. He was working at holding back his tears. She told him she'd been afraid he wouldn't come back—that he'd stay at his work in Kansas City. I gathered they hadn't seen one another for a couple of years and they had planned on getting married a few years before. But her parents never liked him and after he lost his job as an illustrator for a New York magazine, her parents wouldn't allow her to marry him. They used to refer to him as *the loser*. But he was now working for the WPA and he told her it was enough to get by. It let him do his art. He told her—her name was Beatrice—how happy he was to be doing what he loved—painting stories about America. He talked about how much he had enjoyed creating the mural he had just completed in the Kansas City Municipal Building."

Alex was beaming as he continued to describe what he had seen and heard. "Jimmy—that was his name—told her he had two weeks off before he was gonna start another mural—one that really had him excited. It was going to show the history of working people in the Midwest. He told Beatrice the mural was going to take a year to complete. Suddenly, I saw worry flash across her face. She said: *Jimmy—You are not going to go away again. I couldn't stand it. You can't do that to me. It's been such hell. My parents keep pushing me to marry someone they approve of. They just won't give me a break.* Jimmy looked her in the eye and said: *Screw your parents, Bea. We need to live our own lives. Let's get married today. Come back to KC with me. Never let your parents separate us again. We'll start our own family. We'll stay together forever.*

Alex's smile expanded to a grin as he finished describing the dream. "Beatrice broke down crying in his arms. It was pretty emotional, Lucy. I watched them hug, kiss and then they wept. When they walked away—out the same doorway that we passed through when we came into this building, he had his arm around her waist. She had her arm over his shoulder. Lucy—they were so happy! And then I woke up. You were here. I don't know for sure if they really existed—or if I just made them up in a dream. But I gotta tell you, Lucy, it seemed as real as any of the dream-visions. I was just as awake and it felt like it wasn't a dream—but me seeing something as it happened. The emotion was just as intense in the other dream-visions. But this time, Lucy, it was all positive. Nothing but positive! It was so wonderful to be there—to be able to see it."

*****

Minutes later, as Alex and Lucy were walking down Madison Avenue, pushing the wheelchair, as they made their way home, Alex said, "The dream-vision turned out so positive, Lucy. I am so relieved. My other dream-visions— Ruby's arguments at the apartment—the poet's rant at the Chelsea—they were actually really painful to observe. This— this was an upper. The couple was so cool—so inspiring."

"I pleased everything good, Alex. Wheelchair work nicely—you sleep. No one bother me for stay in center of Terminal. First experiment, new series—we can call success."

A block from the apartment, Alex asked, "Don't you wonder what happened to the couple—I mean Beatrice and Jimmy?"

"Maybe. They sound nice people. I happy for them— they marry. But that not my issue. I worry during wait— something go bad for us. You speak you fear dream. Me too. Stand in center of Grand Central—next to wheelchair—you sleep—I not know what happen to you—not know how you react—if you in danger. I not worry about Beatrice or Jimmy. I worry about Alex."

Alex looked and saw Lucy bite her bottom lip, then casually wipe away a tear. They stopped walking. Alex put his arms around her. He hadn't understood she was afraid for him. She seemed so organized, so cool, so analytical. He thought it was all about the experiment for her. They stood there, embracing on Madison Avenue, as busy people walked around them on that sunny Saturday afternoon.

"It's four o'clock, Lucy. I'm hungry."

"I hungry too. Take wheelchair home. Then go out eat—Chinese?"

*****

They ordered pork and lobster egg rolls, a garlic snow pea stir fry and Chongqing Mala chicken. Alex had his journal with him. He wrote down the details of his dream-vision as they waited to be served. Lucy was writing into her notebook as well. She wrote out an analysis of what she referred to as *#1 Grand Central Experiment*.

Their dinner was served and received all their total attention. After they had completed their dinners, they finished their day's entries into their journals.

Alex asked, "What did we learn today?"

"This I speak to in journal. You listen? I read?"

"I am all ears."

What we learn today? First—after Alex smoke dope, he fall asleep wherever. He not need bedroom. Wheelchair great. Event again full of passion. But today different—no sad or anger. Today full of joy. We not know anything about people Alex see until dream-vision. They from past —maybe real—maybe not. No connection to us. We not know why Alex dream these people—must be reason. We need learn why.

Alex say he feel awake during dream-vision. He know it not regular dream while it happen. Alex analyze situation during dream. He make judgment during sleep. Example: Alex hear about Beatrice mama and papa—but they not in dream-vision. During dream, Alex decide parents are mean people. This subjective—not unreasonable deduction—but not usual dream thought.

One thing more: Each dream—Ruby, poet, and today—all about love. Big difference—today positive. Lovers not separate—no anger, no jealousy. Why love part each dream? Necessary or coincidence? We not know.

Lucy finished reading aloud and looked up from her journal. "Next, I do research. I need discover event from Terminal before you do next dream-vision. Until then, you not think about Grand Central. We learn if I affect dream-vision."

*****

Before they left the restaurant, Alex opened his fortune cookie. He laughed and read it aloud: "Your dreams will be fulfilled sooner than you had hoped. But be careful what you wish for."

As Alex walked home that evening, he thought to himself, "How incredible this whole thing is. The good news is that Lucy and I are on the same page. The dream was so positive."

But as Alex continued his thoughts, he began to worry. "I had hoped I wouldn't dream anything at all—that it would all be over—no more dream-visions. I wanted to live my life with my girlfriend and not be the subject of an experiment. Now, not only are the dream-vision experiments not over, but I liked this last one. Before, it was Lucy pushing me forward. Now, I've been sucked into it too. Will I know when to stop? Will I know how to stop? Where will this all end?"

Chapter 6: Grand Central Number II

The following morning, Lucy was off to the library. Three hours later, she returned with two books about the history of New York City. All she said to Alex was: "I find what I need."

*****

The following Saturday, Alex and Lucy were once again on their way up Madison Avenue to Bryant Park. It was raining hard. Alex pushed the wheelchair while Lucy held an umbrella to shield both of them from the rain. At the park, Alex smoked a joint and their experiment moved forward. Upon arrival at the main concourse information booth, Alex said he was sleepy. Lucy wiped the rain off of the wheelchair seat with a small towel brought for that purpose and Alex sat down. Within a couple of minutes, he was fast asleep.

*****

Alex looked at the far end of the Grand Central Terminal. Its massive wall displayed a mural of military might. Spread across the wall, reaching the curved arch of the Terminal's ceiling, was an illustration of a naval ship surrounded by World War II fighter air planes. On each side of were massive drawings of Army tanks. Printed beneath the ship, the jets and the tanks was *That Government by the People shall not Perish from the Earth.* In addition to travelers hustling between trains, Alex saw armed military guards at each door with rifles slung over their shoulder.

Across the room, four men in trench coats stood under a sign that read *Baggage Check.* Suddenly, a half dozen men wearing dark double-breasted suits converged around those four men with handguns drawn. They were followed by a dozen military guards who aimed rifles at the trench coat wearing men. A hush spread across the terminal. The trench coat wearing men raised their hands. One by one, they were handcuffed. Another group of soldiers arrived and pointed military rifles out from the group, across the terminal. They alertly scanned the entire concourse.

One of the men in dark suits spoke in German to the four handcuffed prisoners. He informed them that they were being arrested by the FBI for being Nazi agents. Within minutes, the handcuffed prisoners, still surrounded by FBI agents and some of the soldiers, were hustled out of the Grand Central Terminal. The remaining uniformed men continued to hold their rifles in a ready-to-fire position while surveying the terminal. Finally, those soldiers lowered their weapons, left the Terminal and the concourse began to return to normalcy.

*****

Alex awoke. He started to tell Lucy what he had seen. Asking him to wait until they could get away from the crowds, she pushed him in his wheelchair to a quiet corner of the Terminal. There, Alex excitedly told Lucy what he had just seen.

She listened to him calmly, then responded. "You saw failed Nazi sabotage. It occur June, 1942. Four Nazi men come to United States in German U-boat. Mission was sabotage economic targets. First target was hundreds of feet beneath Grand Central Terminal. Place called M-42. It secret large electric transformer. Transformer convert alternating electric current to direct current to run electric trains. If Nazis succeed, all train traffic for New England stop. But FBI find Nazi agent explosives at baggage storage in Terminal. Nazis come retrieve explosives—you see this. They arrested. When I at library to find event at Grand Central Terminal, learn about this Nazi plot. It was big deal. Today we learn my conscious awareness affect your dream-vision. I cause you dream this today. We also learn people in dream-vision not need be in love. But scene is intense with much emotion."

*****

Lucy and Alex walked back to their apartment. The rain had stopped and the sky had cleared. Not a word was spoken. Alex was lost in thought of all that was transpiring—the magnitude of what was happening—how much was available to him personally that perhaps had never been available to anyone—ever. When Alex looked at Lucy, she had a furrow on her brow. He had never seen her look so serious.

She spoke slowly. "I think about what we learn. We both amazed. Wish it safe I write paper about dream-visions. They one of most unusual things anyone ever experience—anywhere—anytime. But two reasons I not write paper. Reason one: If we announce what happen, you become next Tusko the elephant. Scientists put you in cage. Destroy you—call it science. Reason two: Nazi sabotage failure help me realize bad use for dream-vision. Government, military or capitalist would use dream-vision go back in time—get secret information. Example—someone go back in time—spy on meeting. They invisible—hear what discussed. Privacy never occur again—on anything, anywhere. Someone always able go back in time—steal whatever said. Dream-vision like weapon. Weapon of war and economics."

Alex considered what she had said. She was right. But now, he was the one who was intrigued. One more dream-vision couldn't hurt. "Lucy, it's my turn to do the research, to identify an event. Next week, when I do another dream-vision...."

He stopped speaking and laughed aloud at himself—how much his attitude had changed. Lucy looked at him intently. She had a confused look—obviously waiting for him to finish his thought—which he did.

"Next week, when I do my dream-vision, I'm gonna find out if I can guide myself through time as skillfully as you just did—doing what you did to me today. Monday during lunch, I'm off to the library—got to know the itinerary—got to know the itinerary."

"Alex, we make mistake. I wrong. Change mind. Experiment bad idea. It not occur before—how much we play with fire. We discover most dangerous thing. You in serious danger. We both in danger. We find something—I think—terrible."

"Relax Lucy. We'll do it one more time. Then maybe we quit. One more time isn't going to put me in a whole lot more risk. And now I am curious. I trusted you when I was uncertain. You need to trust me now. If it was fair for you to ask me to follow through on the experiment, then it is fair for me to ask you to let us finish. Trust me a little."

Lucy was silent as they walked up the stairs to the apartment. She did not respond until after they got into bed. "Ok Alex. You right. You promise me you do three dream-vision experiment. If a deal, then I need follow through. One more dream-vision. Then maybe we quit. Ok?"

Alex didn't say anything. He tenderly kissed her.

Chapter 7: Grand Central Number III

During the week that followed, Alex spent his lunch hours doing research at the library. Thursday evening, Lucy asked him about his research.

"Alex—I know I not supposed ask. But I curious. What you learn at library? Give small hint? Please?"

She turned her head at an angle and gave him an imploring look. Alex smiled. He wasn't used to Lucy being impatient—but he was going to have some fun. "Lucy, I wish I could tell you. But our protocols don't allow me to do that. Mustn't break the protocols, you know, especially since my lead investigator, who is such a stickler for following a plan, is standing in front of me."

Lucy punched him in the shoulder. "You correct, but lead investigator not happy with answer. Maybe sometime soon she make you suffer a little for be so cute."

*****

The following Saturday began with the familiar routine. By eleven in the morning, Alex and Lucy were in front of the Grand Central Terminal's information booth. The Terminal was as crowded as they'd seen with families taking advantage of New York City's public-school spring break. Lucy paid no attention to the crowds. Alex was already asleep in the wheelchair. She watched him closely. Alex's face gave no clues regarding what he was dreaming. It was as inexpressive as it had been in each of the prior dreams.

After sleeping for almost an hour, Alex woke up. Shaking his head, he gave a big sigh. Let's get out of here."

The moment they reached the sidewalk outside the Grand Central Terminal, Lucy said, "Ok. Speak me of dream."

Alex, had a serious expression on his face. He took a deep breath. Then he spoke. "First, I gotta explain what I pursued in this dream. I was fired up about that cool couple— Beatrice and Jimmy—the ones I saw in my first Grand Central dream-vision. I know I was supposed to come up with a unique event. But I couldn't stop thinking about them—what could have happened to Beatrice and Jimmy? Once I decided I was going to pursue them, I realized I didn't know their last name. I was searching for a needle in a haystack. I decided the best way to find them was to find Jimmy—I researched WPA murals painted in the late thirties in Missouri and Kansas."

Alex took a deep breath and let it out slowly. He frowned, then continued. "I found several WPA artists named James. I had to do more research on each of them. Finally, I found an artist named James T. Logan. His wife was named Beatrice. So, I researched them. I learned they were married in New York in February of 1936. That must have been right after I saw them in my first Grand Central dream-vision. Anyway, they did move to Kansas City. Jimmy continued to work for the WPA. They had two children—a boy and a girl—Thomas Hart Logan and Jessie Hull Logan. Each of the kids were named after other WPA artists— probably Jimmy and Beatrice's friends. Anyway, the last thing I learned from my research about Jimmy's WPA work was from 1941. He was partnering with another artist— creating a post office mural in Eldon Missouri. I even found a picture of the mural they painted. It was a picture of working-class folks coming together at a picnic in the Ozarks."

Alex and Lucy had started to walk back to the apartment.

"As an aside, I learned why people get into studying family histories. Histories like this are a puzzle. You look for clues—and then, if you're lucky—presto—you discover so much! I really got into it. My dad would have been impressed. In fact, it was frustrating that I didn't have time to continue researching. That period of history—the depression and WPA art—it's so fascinating. The artists turned out to be such interesting folk. And I also got some insight into why you like studying the history of art so much—art is such a window into a culture's soul."

"Alex—dream-vision. Speak me about dream-vision. Other stuff, say later."

"I woke up, I was facing the same World War II mural I had seen in the last dream-vision. The concourse was crowded with soldiers. But the war must have just ended. Uniformed men carrying duffle bags were embracing family members and lovers. Many people were weeping and smiling at the same time. I studied the crowds. Were Jimmy and Beatrice out there? Maybe Jimmy was coming home from the war. Or maybe he already had arrived—Beatrice and the kids were coming in from Kansas City. I was so excited to see what would happen next. They were such a sweet couple. Then I saw Beatrice holding the hand of a little dark-haired girl in a royal blue coat. They walked behind a little boy—he was wearing a grey wool coat with a matching cap. Beatrice and the kids were followed by an older couple. The man wore a black cashmere overcoat. The woman—she resembled Beatrice—wore a mink coat and hat. A porter trailed the group, pushing a cart packed full of luggage. They all were walking toward me."

Alex sighed, looked down at the pavement, shook his head sadly and was quiet for a moment before continuing to describe what he had witnessed. "Beatrice's eyes were swollen red She had obviously been crying. She held a handkerchief. The woman in mink, her mother I realized, spoke to her. *Come on Bea. You and your kids should stay here with us. Jimmy would have wanted you all to be safe and well cared for. Why go back to Missouri? What's in Missouri? Your family is here. We want you with us. Tell her Frank.*

"The man—he turned out to be her father—had a pained expression on his face. He spoke. *Honey, Bea doesn't want to be with us anymore. I don't know why she wants to go back to being impoverished in Kansas City. Maybe it reminds her of her husband. Maybe she hopes they somehow find him over there in Europe. I don't know. But we can't stop her. She's not a kid anymore. We can't control her. She's grown-up.*"

As Alex told Lucy about the dream, he stopped walking and looking off into space. In his mind's eye, he saw it all happen one more time. "Beatrice's face tightened up. She walked more quickly. All of a sudden, she turned to face her parents and spoke. *I'm sorry mom and dad. It's my life to live—not yours. I don't know if they'll ever find Jimmy. But my life—my kids' lives—are back in Kansas City where Jimmy and I made our home. Maybe he's gone for good. I realize that. But I have to continue to live—I have Tommy and Jess to think about. Our world is in Kansas City—that is where I—where we have to go. Goodbye Mom. Goodbye Dad. I'm sorry it has to be like this. But it has to be like this.* Beatrice took one hand from each of her kids and walked away from her parents who just stood there and watched."

Alex walked for a while without saying anything or looking at Lucy. Then he sighed again and continued. "That was the dream-vision. It was painful—really painful. Lucy, you know how much I like happy endings. I was not prepared for this. It wasn't happy at all. It was just empty. A minute later, the parents started to leave the terminal. At one point, Beatrice's mom and dad turned and looked back. Beatrice and their grandkids were gone. The parents took one another's hands, turned toward the exit—shoulders slumped—not saying a word to one another—and left the Terminal."

Alex stopped walking, turned to Lucy and said, "My dream-vision was over. I awoke—sitting there in the wheelchair—just a moment later but eighteen years after that sad goodbye—feeling sad—not knowing what happened to Jimmy, to Beatrice, to the kids or their grandparents—just feeling regret—such emptiness. You were right. I should not have had another dream-vision. I should have quit after the Chelsea.

"Lucy—It was so sad."

Nothing more was said until they arrived at the apartment when Alex told Lucy he wanted to lie down.

Instead, Lucy handed him his journal. "You still need write dream-vision in journal. So sorry—I know it painful—but you need document."

Alex sat down at the kitchen table and began to write. Lucy filled the tea kettle with water and put it on the hotplate. She pulled out the brown earthenware tea pot and its companion mugs and dropped mint tea leaves into the bottom of the tea pot. Then she sat down with Alex at the table and began to write in her notebook. A few minutes later, the kettle whistled. After the water was poured into the tea pot, the room was permeated with the scent of mint. The only sounds for a few minutes were pencils scratching on paper. They each wrote intently. But they wrote two very different accounts of the day.

Alex narrated the tragedy he had observed. Instead of focusing on the specific actions he had seen or words he had heard, he emphasized the sadness of the event. Lucy summarized the facts—her notes spoke about the significance of what she had learned. She concluded her journal input with the following observations:

- *Not know certain if event occur, but library information Alex find about couple in Kansas City support realness of dream-vision. It probably happen.*

- *Alex guide himself for dream-vision like I guide him last week. It show he able control dream-visions.*

- *Each dream-vision event have passion and occur at place Alex fall sleep.*

- *Is somebody somewhere who can help us understand?*

- *Alex say no more try dream-vision. He done. How can that be? This special opportunity— something never seen before. Alex require space now. I give it.*

- *I need think. But do no more now. Maybe no more forever?*

- *What we try accomplish? What purpose in what we do?*

- *I confused. What to do?*

The scent of mint still dominated the room, but the tea pot and cups were empty. Alex took the teakettle from the hotplate and poured more hot water into the teapot. A few minutes later, each of them had another cup of hot tea. After putting a spoonful of honey into his tea, Alex slowly and methodically stirred the honey as he gazed off into space. What had happened to Beatrice? What had happened to her children? The honey was certainly totally dissolved. But Alex continued to stir.

Moments later, Alex went to bed. Lucy stayed at the table, rereading the last entry in her notebook: *I confused. What to do?*

*****

That night, Alex woke up at two in the morning. He was terribly cold and could not stop shivering. His body shook so intensely from shivering that his teeth chattered and his muscles began to ache. The undershorts and a tee-shirt he had worn to bed were soaked with sweat. So were the sheets around him. Continuing to shiver, Alex took off his wet tee-shirt and shorts. Lucy used a towel to dry him off as best she could. Then she brought him fresh underwear and changed the sheets. They got back under the covers. Lucy wrapped her arms around him and rubbed his back. After a while, his shivering ended, his teeth stopped chattering. Lucy continued to hold him in her arms, rubbing his back. Soon, Alex became aroused.

After making love, they lay together in one another's arms.

"Grand Central today—it upset you—yes?"

He nodded assent.

"You calm now."

He smiled and nodded again.

They both laughed.

"This scary. I not like see you upset. We stop experiments—for now."

He lay there in bed, wondering what *for now* meant. Soon, exhaustion took over and Alex was asleep.

Chapter 8: Holy Days

Over the next few months, Alex and Lucy continued their day-time jobs, enjoyed local ethnic restaurants and explored the city. Alex's dream-visions were not discussed. However, in late May, over a dinner of caponata at a small restaurant in Little Italy, Lucy brought up the topic. "What you think about dream-visions, Alex? We not speak this for months. What you think?"

Alex laughed. "Lucy—remember the phrase in my fortune cookie last February? It said *Be careful what you wish for because you might get it*. Well, that was advice I should have taken seriously. I always wanted life to be an adventure. But the dream-visions turned out to be more adventure than I want. Look—I care for you. I've enjoyed the past nine months more than any period in my life. And, I hope we stay together. But what have we focused on more than anything else since I moved in? What have we worried about? Not getting married—not having a family—not buying a home—not building any sort of future. For most of our relationship, we've just focused on a freaky thing that happens to me—turning my life into a scientific experiment. We haven't been like Beatrice and Jimmy—excited just to be together—willing to take risks for our companionship. Life has enough pitfalls without adding a major goal of traveling through time. I have become more like Tusko than a normal guy in love."

"What you say, Alex. It is truth. I care you too. I want continue become closer."

She paused for a moment. "I not angry, you say you be like Tusko. You have reason say this. We stop thinking dream-vision. Instead, we make serious plan visit Europe. We save money, buy ticket and go. Right?"

Alex and Lucy left the Italian restaurant hand-in-hand; smiles on their faces.

*****

The summer of 1963 was pleasant. Alex and Lucy continued to explore New York City and enjoy all it had to offer. They also made regular deposits into their savings accounts and spent a lot of time imagining, planning and talking about their journey to Europe. Each evening they went for a walk. They got to know one another better. They shared and discussed important details of their lives; telling stories about their families and comparing the cultural dynamics of Russia and the United States.

"There was an awful lot of anti-Semitism in the United States before the war. Some people actually liked Hitler because he hated the Jews. That all changed after Pearl Harbor. The country came together. Then, after the war, in the late forties and early fifties, Americans turned their fear towards communism and the Soviets. People who defended Russia were treated like criminals."

"That wrong. Russia defeat Hitler. But cost horrible—Russia pay big price. Millions die! Every family lose someone. Russians know America think they win war—not Russians. But it not true. Russia win war. Stalin much loved by Russians. He defeat Nazis. But people also fear Stalin—know he cruel. My pop and mom not ever speak bad about Stalin—not in open. That dangerous. Too many people disappear. Still, when Stalin die, fear change—become fear for what come next."

*****

One evening after work, Alex met Lucy at Central Park's *Alice in Wonderland* exhibit. It is a bronze statue of several characters from the story of the girl who fell down a rabbit hole and had extraordinary adventures with the Mad Hatter, the Cheshire Cat and the White Rabbit. Lucy wasn't familiar with the story of Alice. She asked Alex about it. He tried to respond, but explaining it turned out to be more difficult than he had anticipated. "...and so, Alice followed the rabbit down the rabbit hole. There she met all sorts of strange characters. After getting through a door that at first was too small for her, then too large, she went to a tea party that was hosted by a White Rabbit."

His rambling summary continued and left a totally confused look on Lucy's face. Finally, he tried to wrap it up. "So, Alice watches the Queen of Hearts' servants painting all of the white roses red. Then, Alice gets in trouble with the Queen.... I can't remember why. Oh hell, everything was distorted. But it all was awfully realistic too—in a bizarre sort of way. I haven't read it in many years, Lucy. I'll get it for you—you ought to read it."

"But Alice escape Queen? How story end?"

"Well, I think Alice woke up and was back at home— or maybe that was *The Wizard of Oz*? Anyway, you get the gist of it, don't you?"

"Dah. It like you Alex. You sleep. You dream. You see things. Maybe you like Alice?"

"No, Lucy. I don't think so."

"Why?"

Alex paused, rubbed his chin and considered Lucy's offhand question comparing Alice's adventure to his own dream-visions. "Well maybe."

*****

One evening during their walk in Central Park, Lucy asked Alex about what it was like to grow up as a Jew in America.

"My family belonged to a liberal synagogue in Wichita—Temple Emanuel. That's where I went to religious school. The Temple's Sunday school was a cross between a children's social get-together and memorization of Jewish fairy tales. My family rarely went to Friday evening services. My father said he didn't like to go to Temple because he was an atheist. He told me it was hard for him to believe in a god who had allowed the Holocaust to occur. In that regard, I guess I'm pretty much a chip off the old block. But still, my identity is tied to Judaism. For example, I always wear my mezuzah on a chain around my neck."

Alex pulled on the silver chain hanging around his neck and held out a one-inch-long silver pendant adorned by a single Hebrew letter.

"A mezuzah holds a tiny piece of parchment with parts of an important Jewish prayer written on it. I received this as a bar mitzvah gift and have worn it ever since. I'm not sure exactly why. Being Jewish in America is really different—I mean compared to being Christian. Everybody will tell you this isn't a Christian country. But you could've fooled me. Being Jewish separated me from a lot of people at school. I don't know how many times someone told me they'd never met a Jew before—like it meant I came from another planet. But still, I have always been proud of the difference."

"My mamachik Jew."

Alex's head snapped toward Lucy and he looked intently at her. "What?"

"Dah. I tell you before—my mamachik Jew."

"No, you didn't. You've said almost nothing about your parents' background—nothing at all. You've told me how you guys left Russia, came here—how your father surprised you and your mother by telling you the family wasn't returning to the Soviet Union—but not much more than that. And you said you're Russian Orthodox. Once, you started to say something about your mom—when I was speaking about Papi losing his family. But when you stopped speaking and refused to say more, I just dropped it."

"No. I speak you this before."

"Well tell me now."

"Mamachik born in Belarus. Her mom and pop meet in synagogue. Rabbi marry them before revolution. Grandmom and grandpop have baby. Baby is my mamachik. After revolution, not good thing be any religion in Soviet Union. But especially not good be Jewish. Grandmom and grandpop decide have no religion. Mamachik grow up, no religion."

"I remember you telling me that. You said your mom wasn't religious."

"You not listen good, Alex. I say she not have religion. This because her mama and papa know Soviets not allow synagogue—dislike Hebrews."

Alex recalled a little of this, but realized he had missed much of what Lucy meant to convey.

"When Nazis come Belarus, village people tell soldiers my grandmom and grandpop is Jewish. Soldiers come to grandmom and grandpop home—arrest them. Mom not home when soldiers come. Nazis take grandparents and many Jews they arrest to field by village. Jews told: *Dig deep ditch.* Then, German soldiers shoot Jews. Bodies fall into ditch. Soldiers throw dirt on top of bodies; walk away. No more Jews in village."

Lucy was quiet. Alex watched her. After a little while, she looked up at him and continued. "My mamachik—she leave village quick—hide in forest with others who fight Nazis. She meet my pop. They live at forest one year. Then escape Belarus—go far east—Vladivostok. Pop is Russian Orthodox. Mom and Pop marry in his church. So mamachik become Russian Orthodox too. Baptize me Russian Orthodox. Soviet not like church, but ignore. Russian Orthodox not go away."

"Now I see why you understand my father's experience—your family saw the horrors too. I feel bad that I was so absorbed by my own family's tragedy. I'm humbled. What your mother went through was horrible. Did she ever talk about it much? I mean about losing her parents— about hiding in the forest—fighting the Nazis?"

"Mamachik not talk about Belarus. She never speak about people from village—ones who tell Germans, *This family Jews*. Sometime I see Mom quiet. She look out window. I think she remember parents. I know she have sadness. I think she remember—good things too of Belarus. But after war, all Russian have reason for sadness. What talk do? It not help. Life go on."

"Did she ever speak about her parent's religion?"

"In Russia, not wise say about being Jew. Better forget about it. Mamachik find her peace. She go church— even though she say she not have religion. I see. She pray. Who she pray to? I not know. It matter? I think not."

Nothing was said for fifteen minutes.

"Lucy—I'd like to go with you to a Russian Orthodox church service someday. Would you take me? I'd like to learn more about your faith."

"Agah. That be nice."

*****

It was mid-September. Lucy and Alex were drinking tea at their red kitchen table.

"Yom Kippur is coming up in a couple of weeks. I won't go to services. But I will observe the holiday."

"What Yom Kippur?"

"It's the Jewish Day of Atonement—the most important day in the Jewish year. On Yom Kippur, Jews ask forgiveness from God for sins they've committed in the past year. Traditionally, we don't eat anything on that day. We pray—and like I say—we ask for forgiveness."

"What forgiveness you ask for?"

"Oh—I have plenty to choose from. I let Papi down by quitting school—I didn't communicate very well with him— in fact I haven't communicated with either of my parents all year. I gotta deal with that. Also, believe it or not, I feel guilty about the dream-visions. First off, I feel guilty just for having them—I don't know why—probably some sort of puritan's remorse. It's like I did something shameful by getting high. But—and this is what's really weird—I also feel guilty for *not* continuing to have them—sorta like God gave me this incredible capability—*Do something special with this Alex*— and I haven't used it for any worthwhile purpose. That's Judaism in a nutshell—damned if you do and damned if you don't. Guilt is so often such a double-edged sword."

"Russian Orthodox priests always kind, gentle. Agah—if sin, feel guilt. But mostly not. I mostly not feel guilty."

They sat in the kitchen, drinking their Constant Comment tea.

"I curious Alex."

"About what."

"You say, God give incredible ability—do something special. What special you talk about?"

"Damn. I knew the moment I opened my big mouth on that one that I was going to regret it. You don't miss much Lucy."

"No, it true—I not miss much. But what *special* you talk about here? Say to me."

"Well, as I said, I feel guilty for not considering my dad's past, for not trying to understand what all he went through—why he is afraid for me. And as far as the dream-visions go, I have been given a tool that could allow me to learn about my father's experience—learn about it in a way that is pretty unique. I didn't want to say anything to you about it because—well—because I was afraid it would intrigue you."

"What you mean—intrigue?"

"It would get your attention. We are going to Europe—right?"

"Dah."

"When we are there, I could go back and—I know I am going to kick myself later for admitting this—but I could go back and observe some of the horror that existed there—I could witness the Nazis. I could see Hitler."

Alex got up from the table and filled the two tea cups. He sat down, added a spoonful of honey to his cup and stirred. Then he tasted the tea, took a couple of deep breaths and continued. "You haven't brought up dream-visions for months. I liked that. We've been doing really well together. I didn't want to ruin it. But now that I just said it out loud, I know I have to consider doing a dream-vision in Europe."

"Agah. I be honest with you. I want dream-vision in Europe too. I not say anything—afraid you become upset. But I think of dream-vision too. You feel pain your family. You want see Nazis. You want understand. I feel pain too—my family—my mamachik parents. But I embarrass say you. That not what I want dream-vision about. I want you see something else."

By now, Alex was intrigued. He had a slightly smile on his face when he said, "Go ahead."

"We go Florence and Paris—right?"

"Uh-huh."

"I love great artists—Florence and Paris."

"Uh-huh."

"Well, I see art books. I see paintings—Metropolitan Museum."

Alex put down his cup of tea and looked at Lucy. Her face turned red. She began to stammer. In combination with her rich accent and limited vocabulary, the stammer made it particularly difficult for Alex to understand what she was saying.

"I not say nothing if no more dream-vision. But if dream-vision, I wish you see renaissance artists in Florence—."

She paused, took a deep breath, and blurted out the remainder of her thought. "And impressionist in Paris."

Alex started laughing so hard he almost fell off of his chair—so hard he couldn't speak.

"Please Alex. I never ask like this before. But now I ask this. Please?"

His body was shaking with laughter so hard he spilled his tea. He could not stop laughing.

Lucy looked embarrassed, humbled, angry and wishful—all at the same time. Alex realized he wasn't being very nice. He needed to give her a response—to say something. "We'll see."

*****

The following Saturday evening, Alex and Lucy went to a service at a Russian Orthodox Church in Brooklyn. They rode the subway to Brooklyn's Liberty Avenue stop and walked to the church from there.

During the subway ride, Alex had asked what to expect.

"You see church. You will like. Paintings and icons brought from Russia—time of revolution. Very old. Very beautiful. When revolution happen, religions deep afraid. Bolsheviks not like religion—especially, it true, not like Jews. But they not like all religion. Many priests decide leave Russia, go Europe, or America. Take icons. At service, you see many people pray. I pray. I light candles for Papa and Mama. I light candle for you and me. You see church beautiful. You hear priest and choir sing. You smell incense. You discover church is holy place. You will like."

*****

Half an hour later, they walked into the church. Alex felt as if he had been transported into a European cathedral during the Middle Ages. The large sanctuary was as tall and wide as it was deep. Across the front of the room was a large carved oak altarpiece that incorporated icons of saints. Each saint had a golden halo painted around his head. The icons and paintings that hung on the room's textured plaster walls reminded Alex of European religious paintings he had seen at the Metropolitan. The room had no chairs and only a couple of benches. Those benches were being used by aged worshippers. The sanctuary's coved ceilings added to its mystical aura. Golden oak floors worn with age were complemented by matching oak trim.

The church's worshippers were a mixture of simply dressed working people, businessmen in suits, children and older folk. Some wore plain clothes and others were quite elegantly garbed. Alex wondered if a portion of the older worshippers might have come to New York decades ago—to escape the revolution that had so changed Russia.

An unseen choir—Alex figured it must be in the balcony above the congregants—sang in a language that Alex didn't recognize. The songs sounded like a combination of Gregorian chants, Bach chorales and the Hebrew chanting he remembered from synagogue. The entire sanctuary vibrated with the harmonies created by the choir.

A priest wearing a large, elaborately embroidered robe walked among the worshippers. He slowly swung a silver incense burner hanging from a silver chain. Back and forth the incense burner went, and the deep woody scent of the incense permeated the church. It seemed to Alex that the mood created by the slow even pace of the priest, the scent of the incense, the chanting of the choir and the peaceful intensity of the worshippers, was almost magical.

Congregants stepped forward placing slender candles on ornate silver candelabras. After lighting a candle, each worshipper would close his or her eyes and bend their head forward in prayer.

Alex reflected on how different this church seemed from the modern Jewish temples in which he had worshipped. He thought about the couple of Christian ceremonies he had attended at friends' churches. The ritual he now observed was unlike any of them. It was different from anything he had ever seen. Alex realized that part of the reason he liked Lucy so much was that she came from such a different world than the one in which he had been raised. In some regards, she was like Papi—a stranger in a strange land.

*****

A couple of days later, Alex had a big smile on his face when he got him home from work. "A tenant at the apartment where I work gave me his tickets for the Yom Kippur Service at Temple Emanuel on 65th Street. Will you go with me?"

"I no choice Alex. I feel guilty forever if I not go."

*****

A week later, on a sunny Saturday afternoon, Alex and Lucy walked the sixty blocks to Temple Emanuel. Alex wore the dark grey tweed sport coat and deep blue tie he had worn to his high school graduation. Lucy was dressed in a white blouse and a navy-blue pleated skirt with matching navy-blue jacket.

They entered the sanctuary through massive oak doors highlighted by gleaming brass hardware. The Temple was packed with well-dressed men and women of every age. Alex and Lucy were shown seats near the back of the sanctuary. As Alex sat down, he thought about the two different Temple Emanuel buildings. One in New York City—the other in Wichita Kansas. They may have had the same name, but they had little else in common. Compared to Wichita's Temple Emanuel, this Temple Emanuel seemed like a great cathedral. This version had high ceilings covered with colorful modern mosque-like mosaics bordered with golden trim. It had grand marble walls and arches with large and elaborate stained glass windows that illustrated stories from the Old Testament.

Alex and Lucy sat in awe of the Temple's spectacular features as the service began. A stream of men of all ages wearing dark suits, ornate or simple prayer shawls and black yarmulkes proceeded to the front of the Temple. Each man read a solemn prayer in English from a prayer book or chanted in Hebrew in a monotone voice as they recited from rolled up parchment scrolls. These prayers and chants were interspersed with moments where the entire congregation read a prayer in unison or the cantor sang a solemn Hebrew song to a haunting melody.

About an hour into the service, Alex whispered to Lucy that he wanted to leave. After quietly exiting through the synagogue's elegant oak doors, Alex told Lucy he felt like a kid who had just sneaked out of the service. "The difference is that I always wanted to skip out of Temple when I was young. But I couldn't. Now I can and it felt good."

They walked in silence toward their apartment. It was a beautiful September afternoon—just cool enough to be refreshing.

"Service beautiful, Alex. Thank you for bring me. But why leave early?"

"There are some things about Judaism that make me try to become a better person. Yom Kippur is one of those. When I was a kid, I hated Yom Kippur. The service went on and on—I didn't see the point. Today, it turned out to be meaningful. But I couldn't focus on the prayers. I kept thinking about my parents—about the fact that I left college without adequately telling them why. My father never became Americanized. He is European—Deutsch throughout. He is responsible, formal and punctual. But what distinguishes him more than anything else is that he lives his life in mourning for the people he loved—those who were murdered."

They walked for about a block before Alex continued his response. "Papi wants what is best for me. But his perception of *what is best* is driven by his experience as a youth in Nazi Germany. The advanced science degrees he earned as a young man turned out to be his salvation. He wouldn't have gotten a visa to enter the USA if he hadn't had that PhD. He wants me to have that same security. He wants it for me because he loves me. Both of my parents lost loved ones in the Holocaust. With very few exceptions, those who know my parents in Wichita don't understand that—or how it affects them. They are so isolated. The City of Wichita is such a cultural abyss. Their neighbors and friends have no idea of the terrible sadness that is the foundation of their lives. And now, their only child—their only living relative—me—has disappeared from their lives. That makes me feel horrible."

As Alex spoke, his gaze was on the sidewalk in front of him. He slowed the pace at which he was walking. Lucy, who was intently listening to his words, also focused on the pavement ahead of her.

"I look forward to going to Europe with you, Lucy. But before we leave, I have to visit my parents. I need to speak with my father. I must give some love to my mother. They are so lonely. And Lucy—I want you to come to Wichita with me—I want my parents to meet you. They will like you."

*****

The following morning, Alex called his parents.

His father answered the phone and said very little except that he and Alex's mother were in good health. Then he put Alex's mother on the line. Mutti was more encouraging. She asked Alex how he was doing—how his girlfriend was doing.

Alex took a deep breath.

"Mutti, Lucy and I will be going to Europe this winter. I would like to visit you and Papi before we leave the United States. Lucy will be with me."

Alex heard a moment's silence she responded. "Why sure, honey. That would be very nice."

*****

Over the next three months, Alex and Lucy were frugal. They wanted to build up their savings as much as possible before their big trip. They would give notice to their employers in the first week of January of 1964.

Airfare tickets from New York to Athens were purchased for early February and the first stop on their trip would be a month of relaxation on the Island of Crete. Then they would venture on to Italy, France and Germany.

Lucy called Ruby in early December to tell her they would be leaving the apartment at the end of January. Ruby told her not to worry—she had half a dozen friends who had inquired about taking the apartment if it became available. Ruby wanted to find out more about Alex's weird dreams. Were they still happening? Were there any other embarrassing things that Alex had found out about that Ruby needed to apologize for?

Lucy lied. "Alex forget he speak with Sadie in apartment 104. Sadie say she know about your argument with people. She tell Alex. He repeat. I sorry Ruby. It awful, I know.

Ruby seemed relieved with that explanation. "Listen Lucy. Not my business, but this Alex sounds like really bad news. I think you should lose the bum."

*****

Lucy and Alex went back and forth regarding European dream-visions.

"Florence wonderful city—great history. Possible you see the de Medicis—Borgias! Paris exciting. Early twenty-century Paris artists sit, drink coffee at sidewalk cafe. Imagine: you see Cezanne, Matisse, Braque—together!"

"Lucy—I'm not sure I want to have dream-visions of artists. We'll see. But if I decide to have a dream-vision in Germany, I want to see firsthand the horrid Germany that shaped my parents' life—that really shaped mine."

In preparation for possible dream-visions, Alex purchased a chunk of hashish in Central Park. After he brought it back to the apartment, Lucy wrapped it in aluminum foil and buried it in a jar of face cream she was taking with them on the trip.

"Sadie tell me—this how sneak stuff into Europe. Scare me. But she say it total safe."

*****

Preparations were complete. On a cold, snowy January 31st, Alex and Lucy boarded a Greyhound Bus for Wichita, Kansas.

Chapter 9: Visiting Papi and Mutti

Alex and Lucy's Greyhound emerged from the Lincoln Tunnel going west, towards the snowy New Jersey Turnpike. Lucy rested with eyes closed while Alex stared out the window, considering the past year and all of its assorted adventures. It had been more than a year since Alex had arrived in New York City. Now, he tried to anticipate how his parents—particularly his father—would respond to their visit—how would Papi react to Lucy?

The Greyhound was well into New Jersey before Alex broke the silence. "My parents did a lot for me—I was their only kid. It was sometimes frustrating growing up in a home with parents who were so European. Whatever they did, they did in a German manner. We never owned a TV. I had to always treat adults with super respect. Meals meant sitting down on time at the table with a level of formality that never existed in my friends' homes."

"You think they nice for me? They like me?"

"They're more afraid of you than you are of them. They know I left college and went east to be with you. They are probably afraid you will take me away from them forever. They won't be judging you as much as they'll be watching to see how you judge them."

Alex paused, visualizing the visit—trying to anticipate his parents' reaction to his girlfriend. "They'll like you a lot. What's not to like? They will be relieved when they see you aren't going to treat them harshly. After all, we're probably going to get married—aren't we? They'll be your father-in-law and mother-in-law."

Lucy said nothing for a while and just stared out the window at the nothingness of New Jersey's commercial sprawl. She wiped a tear from her cheek. It was a while before she spoke. "Not ever talk marriage. You want marry?" "If you are asking me to marry you, I accept". She rolled her eyes, bent her head down, shook it and laughed quietly. "Americans."

*****

The bus pulled into St. Louis for an hour layover. It was cold and windy when Alex and Lucy hurried into the bus station for a quick breakfast of bacon, eggs and hash browns. After they got back on the bus, they fell asleep. It seemed like only a few minutes before the bus pulled into Kansas City. They grabbed a couple of sandwiches in the station and boarded another blue, grey and white bus for the final leg of their trip. Four hours later, their Greyhound pulled into a diagonal parking stall behind Wichita's new bus station. Alex and Lucy were waiting for their bags to be pulled out from the cargo area under the bus when Alex's father tapped Alex on the shoulder.

"Welcome home son. Lucy—it's wonderful to meet you. You can call me Klaus. I am pleased you are visiting us."

Then, wonders of wonders, Klaus Schwarz gave Lucy a hug. She seemed taken aback—but obviously pleased. Alex's father led them to his two-tone blue '58 Ford Fairlane and put their bags in the trunk. Alex's father insisted Lucy ride in the front seat. A few minutes later, they arrived at the Schwarz family's small red brick bungalow.

Alex's mother, Anna, greeted them and briefly embraced each of the travelers. "Lucy, you'll stay in Alex's room. Alex, you sleep on the couch in your father's study. Let's have some coffee. I baked poppy seed rugelach this morning. Lucy— rugelach it is one of Alex's favorite treats."

As they drank their coffee and ate on their poppy seed cookies, Lucy said, "Mrs. Schwarz. The poppy seed rugelach so good. Remind me of treats with my mom and pop."

Anna smiled and told her, "I will share the recipe with you. I learned it from my mother and I know Alex will be more than happy to have you bake these rugelach for him."

After coffee, Alex and Lucy went for a quick walk around the block. "I had no idea my parents would treat us so nicely. Of course, I haven't yet had a one-on-one with Papi."

"Agah."

*****

At dinner that night, Alex's mother prodded him.

"Well Alex. Do you and Lucy have plans for the future?"

"We plan on marrying after we return from Europe. Then I'd like to finish my degree. We're not sure where we'll settle down."

Alex's mother seemed pleased with that response. His father said nothing.

After dinner, Lucy and Alex went into his room.

"You make other plans for us I not know? How many children I birth?"

"I'm sorry Lucy. What could I say? I panicked. But that is what I want—though I know we need to talk before I announce stuff like that. I promise not to create any more surprises for you."

"That be nice."

*****

Klaus began to open up to Lucy—and speak to his son. One day while they were having tea, he shared memories of Frankfurt in the early 1930s.

"Lucy—My father, mother, brother and I lived in a flat in a pleasant neighborhood in Frankfurt. The apartment building, an attractive four-story russet colored stone building, was located on a corner lot near the Palmengarten. Lucy—the Palmengarten is Frankfurt's large and beautiful botanical park. It has a modest lake, many beautiful walkways and large—how do you say *Gewächshaus* in English—ah yah—greenhouses with tropical plants. As a young child, I loved the Palmengarten. I played there with my Jewish and Christian friends. My brother and I would often go there for an afternoon. We would rent a rowboat for an hour or play foosball in an open field. Those are some of the happiest memories of my life. However, after 1932, my brother and I had to become much more cautious. We were Jews—and people knew it."

"Papi—after Hitler came to power, how were you treated by Christian friends who you had known in the past?"

"That is a painful question, Alex—the sort of thing I did not tell you about with you when you were small. I tried to avoid speaking about the more difficult things I witnessed. Now that you are an adult and ask about those memories—it is time to give you a direct answer."

Klaus took a sip of tea and looked away from the table, while not appearing to focus on anything. Then he took a deep breath, sighed and continued. "As a small child, I was unaware of any differences between myself and my Christian friends. But as the decade of the 1920s advanced, anti-Semitism increased as a factor in German society. My Christian friends stopped playing with me. I am not sure if it was because their parents had told them to avoid me or if they just didn't want to be accused of being a Jew-lover by others. In any case, my Christian friends were not so much unkind to me. I just didn't invite me over and when I saw them, they didn't greet me. We had Christian neighbors who had been close to our family when I was younger. Maybe they were anti-semitic—maybe not. Maybe they were just afraid of what others might think. Hitler and his friends were bullies—they treated anyone who they suspected of being friendly to Jews as untrustworthy. In any case, those Christian neighbors disappeared from our lives. One family I remember—the Schmidts—lived in our apartment building. They had always been polite and respectful to my mother and father prior to 1932. But after Hitler was appointed Chancellor of Germany, they stopped speaking to us."

Papi, took a sip of coffee and a deep breath. He closed his eyes for a moment, then continued. "By 1930, it was impossible to ignore what was happening. I often overheard my parents speaking about Adolf Hitler. Once, I said to my father, *If Hitler is so terrible, is it still safe for us to live in Germany?* My father slammed his hand on the table and exclaimed: *Any idiot can see that Hitler is verrückt!* Lucy, that means Hitler was nuts. My father believed Hitler and the Nazis would go away. But oh, he was so mistaken."

Klaus looked down and his hands which were folded in front him. He slowly shook his head from side to side, then looked up and said. "After Hitler was appointed chancellor of Germany in 1933, some of my father former friends and business associates joined the brownshirts. They refused to greet him when they saw him on the street and worse yet, some of them participated in beatings of Jews. When I was a youngster, the lady in the flat below us often took care of me. Her name was—let me see—Frau Baumgarten. Ah, yah— that's it. Even she—someone who had been like an aunt to me—would turn away when she saw me walking toward her on my way home from school."

Lucy interrupted. "What allow this happen? Why German people give power for Hitler—why they follow him? "

Papi looked at her and said, "Good question Lucy. Why was Hitler able to do all of this? The end of World War I was hard on Germany and on Germans. Many Germans were poor, ignorant and afraid. They watched as their country—once a world power—became a poor nation—a land of economic chaos. Hitler promised a better life for loyal Germans. By blaming the hard times on others, Hitler offered a scapegoat to those for whom life had become uncertain. He promised the German people that the villains who had destroyed their security—the Jews, the Communists, and the countries that had insisted on harsh terms in the treaty of Versailles—would all be punished. Germans did not care who was blamed as much as they wanted to end the uncertainty in their lives. It was an ugly time."

Lucy said, "Thank you for explain."

"Thank you, Lucy, for asking. You see, my father had been correct—Hitler was *verrückt*. But he was also a skillful orator who effectively enlisted ambitious bullies into a personal political army. Those bullies had been villains in search of a leader—and boy, did they find their leader. "

Klaus stopped speaking and took a deep breath. Then he finished his statement. "And so Lucy, I lost my mother, my father, my brother, my aunts, uncles and cousins, my friends...."

There was silence at the table. Anna Schwarz finally said, "Well, I am going to clear off the table and why don't you, Alex and Lucy, take a nice walk?"

*****

A couple of days later, Klaus asked Alex out for lunch. Alex knew this meant Papi was ready to speak with him about the issues that had divided them. They drove to a nearby diner where each ordered a club sandwich and cup of coffee. While they waited for their lunches, Klaus asked Alex if they could converse in German for old times' sake. Alex was pleased. Alex had spoken German more than English as a small boy; not surprising since both of his parents were German immigrants. But the fact that his father wished to speak in German beckoned back to other times in his life when his dad and he had been very close.

"Your mother has made it very clear that she believes I behaved poorly to you on multiple occasions over the past two years—that I must respect your right to live your life in the way you choose. I have given it much thought and have decided she is correct. Even though I disagree with your decisions, I apologize to you."

Alex had hoped his father would welcome him back to Wichita. But an apology? Alex had never heard his father apologize to anyone on anything.

"We are delighted you decided to visit us before going to Europe. And you have done well in selecting a partner. Lucy is thoughtful, intelligent and obviously very loyal to you."

"Thank you Papi. I understand how much you and Mutti love me. Lucy means a lot to me. Challenging your expectation that I continue at the University of Oklahoma was not easy. But it felt like a necessary decision. Still, an apology from you is neither expected nor necessary."

"Your mother and I have discussed this. I made a decision to apologize. And you—mister—have no right to question my decision! But I must digress. I am so impressed—no, I am proud—that you speak Deutsche as well as you do. Your grammar is excellent. You have the accent of a true *Frankfurter*. Lucy has told us how excited she is to visit Greece, Italy and France. The two of you will have a wonderful time in those countries. But I am especially curious about your decision to go to Germany, to visit Frankfurt. What is your objective in visiting the city of my youth? What do you hope to accomplish?"

Alex decided he must be straightforward. His father had always been able to read his face—to know when Alex was not telling the truth. "Papi—it would be impossible for me to visit Europe and not go to Frankfurt. I have always tried to imagine the Palmengarten—the opera house—the neighborhood in which you lived. Once Lucy and I decided to travel to Europe, Frankfurt became the most certain destination of the trip."

"I hope you will not be disappointed with your visit. Frankfurt was heavily bombed in the war. I am not sure of how much of my Frankfurt remains. And there will be very few people who remember my family. That is one of the reasons I never returned."

While his father spoke, Alex tried to figure out how much he should share. He wanted to be honest. But he did not want to awaken fears that could easily destroy the rest of his visit with his parents.

Alex took a deep breath and plunged ahead. "Papi—I understand Frankfurt will have changed. I will learn how much. But I owe it to you to explain a unique purpose for my visit to Germany. When I moved to New York City, I hoped it would be the beginning of a special adventure. However, what has occurred has been more—much more—than anything I could have anticipated. Papi—I am going to tell you about something extraordinary. And you are not going to like it. But I feel I need to share it with you. And then Papi, I need advice."

Klaus Schwarz leaned forward, put his elbows on the table and his two palms flat against one another with his pointer fingers held together touched his lips. Alex began to describe his unusual experiences over the last year. He began by telling his father the story of Tusko the elephant—and how Tusko had died. At that point, his father shook his head in disbelief and muttered, *"Dummkopfs"*. Alex then described how he and the lab assistants had gone swimming on that hot August day—how one of the lab assistants had stolen some of the laboratory's LSD and ingested it before going swimming—and how Alex had taken LSD as well.

His father interrupted him. "Why would you do something so dangerous, Alex? Taking a drug as potent as LSD? I have read about it—it is powerful—and not well understood. Why would you even consider taking such a foolish risk?"

"Papi—you need to let me finish. I want your input. But you need to let me tell you all that has occurred."

Alex went on to describe his dream-visions during the prior year. Several times while Alex spoke, his father's head leaned forward and his jaw dropped as he looked at his son with wide open eyes. "Who knows of this, Alex?"

"Papi, I know any university would want to research these phenomena. And I am well aware that the military would be informed of my dream-visions if a university was involved. And at that point, the military would not hesitate to find a way to take control of the research. I do not want to be turned into a human guinea pig—or worse yet —a weapon of war."

Alex paused for a moment, watching his father absorb all that he had just shared. When Klaus looked up, Alex continued. "So Papi, I wish to use this special capability as a means to gain insight into what happened in Deutschland during your youth. I know Lucy and I have been playing with fire. But once I discovered what an extraordinary power the dream-vision is, how could I not explore it?"

Alex took looked at his father, sighed and said, "Now I am willing to hear your judgements, your criticisms and your warnings. But what I would really want—what I really need—is for you to give me your blessing—then give me some advice."

Klaus Schwarz sat silently, rubbing his chin with his thumb and forefinger while looking down at the table. Alex recognized the mannerism. It had always meant his dad was in deep thought and required quiet time to finish processing whatever was on his mind.

After several minutes, Klaus Schwarz spoke. "Alex— you constantly teach me that when I am certain I know what to will come next from you, I find I am wrong. What you shared with me is hard to believe."

Papi paused as he looked into his son's eyes. "But I know you, Alex. You are honest. You wouldn't make this up. It may seem crazy. But I have learned that the world is often crazy. One must accept it—then go from there. I think it may be naive to consider this an opportunity. It may be more appropriate to say that you have been saddled with a horrible destiny. But regardless of which of those it is, it is not my role to tell you what you must, or must not, do. I have different responses from differing perspectives."

Papi gave a soft smile, shaking his head slowly from side to side once again. "First of all, as a father, I must begin by chastising you. What you did—ingesting LSD—was irresponsible—foolish! But you did it—and no amount of criticism would now be of value. What is done is done. And, as a father, I share your legitimate concern that if your capability were made known, others would most certainly turn you into a human guinea pig. What a nightmare that would be! My other response as a father is one of fear. You are my only child. Your mother and I were blessed to have such a sweet son. What will this do to you? Will it destroy your life—take you away from us? I am full of fear. And Mutti would not react this calmly. She would be livid with anger that you have thrown your fate to the wind. She would be overcome with fear. You are her only child. For this reason, I suggest you never share this with her."

Klaus stopped speaking, took a sip of coffee, and appeared to be arranging his thoughts before speaking again. Then he did speak. "My second major perspective is that of a scientist. I would be lying if I didn't tell you I am incredibly intrigued—maybe even a little jealous. As a student, I was forced to choose a single field within the world of science— that of course ending up being chemistry. Then I had to select a specific regimen within chemistry. But all scientists are linked beyond the edges of their chosen field by a grand curiosity regarding the nature—the principles that guide the universe in which we live. The chemist, the physicist, the doctor, the biologist, the psychologist and—I should add—

the theologist—are all driven by their curiosity of how the world works."

Klaus took another sip of coffee. He softly smiled and uttered a *hmph* and shook his head again before continuing to speak. "Son, it appears you have been given a window into reality that is beyond belief—but it beckons to be understood. So as a scientist, I don't blame you for pursuing this capability that you have been given—even though as a father, I sincerely wish you would abandon it. Because you were able to corroborate your landlady's outbursts from your first dream-visions, I accept this is not a fantasy. My curiosity— again as a scientist—is seriously teased. My questions— which I do not expect you to be able to answer—go on and on. What does your ability to see the past say about the dimensions of time and matter? If someone can really travel through time—even in a dreamlike state—what does that say to those who believe we live in a completely physical universe? If life is all a dream—if it is an illusion—from what state of being is it an illusion? I am without answers to any of these questions because what you have experienced defies any science I know and is well beyond anything I have tried to imagine."

Alex's father went on to discuss a variety of potential explanations for what had occurred to Alex. Then, while speculating about a five-dimensional time and space continuum, Klaus stopped speaking abruptly in mid-sentence. He simply said, "Alex, I just don't know. This is so far beyond anything—anything I can pretend to understand. Well, I just don't know."

After staring out the window for several minutes, Klaus turned back to Alex, gave him a loving smile and said, "In addition to my response as a father and as a scientist, my most heartfelt response to all of this is that of a Jewish Holocaust survivor. There is so much that occurred in Germany that I would give anything to view one more time—to try to understand the nuances of those involved. I realize that the gift you have does not allow you to change things. But if I had this gift, I would want to see my family. And probably more than that, I would want to see Hitler—to observe anything that would give me some insight into his delirium. In my life, I have accepted many things. But I have not—since leaving Germany—been able to establish equilibrium with my god—with my life—or with the human race—because I cannot understand how what happened..."

Grief overcame Klaus Schwarz. His entire body shook as he buried his face in his hands and wept. It had been almost a decade since Alex had seen his father weep. Watching it gave him a feeling of helplessness he hadn't felt in years. Sometimes, in the late 1940s and early 1950s, when his father had spoken about one of his loved ones or friends who had perished in the Holocaust—often times in the most positive of contexts—his father would remember that that loved one or friend had been murdered—and would weep inconsolably. Alex had learned over the years that when this happened, his dad needed time to collect himself and set aside his sadness.

Alex and his father finished their meal in silence.

Eventually, in English, his father concluded the conversation. "Well, that was probably a whole lot more interesting lunch than either of us had anticipated."

Then, arm in arm, father and son, left the restaurant.

*****

Two hours later, Alex was sitting in the Schwarz family living room with Lucy when Klaus entered and casually handed his son a book.

"This might give you context related to what you may see in Europe. I found it quite worthwhile. The author was a journalist in Berlin during Hitler's rise to power. The book is probably the best available summary of the birth—and the death—of Nazism."

Klaus Schwarz handed Alex a copy of William Shirer's *The Rise and Fall of the Third Reich*.

Chapter 10: Finishing up in Wichita

"My dad and I had a good talk."

Lucy, who had been reading in Alex's room gave him her attention. Alex started out by saying that his dad approved of her. She responded to that with a big smile. Then Alex told her how his father had apologized—and how touched he was by that gesture.

"Your pop love you much. He show it there."

"But I hadn't planned on what happened next. I told Papi about the dream-visions."

Lucy's eyes opened wide and she leaned forward. "You and Papi walk in house—I see closeness, warmth. It make me happy. But now I shocked—not expect you speak dream-visions. I not think this possible. Expect your Papi be furious. But I see him, you happy now. I shocked."

"My dad was shocked too. But I needed to tell him about it even though I felt he wouldn't approve of any portion of what we've done—or what we intend to do. But I was wrong to question doing that. Being open and honest was the right thing—the smart thing to do. Papi approached it analytically and from different perspectives. He looked at it as a father, as a Jew and as a scientist. The fatherly response questioned my lack of caution—he felt I acted like an idiot. He warned me not to tell my mother under any circumstances. His response as a Jew was that of a Holocaust survivor. He was deeply intrigued. But why should that surprise me? My need to understand what happened in Germany—my fixation on understanding Hitler's persona—is something I learned from him. Papi taught me to ask the question: *What creates such a monster?* We spoke for some time about the opportunities that going to Germany represents. But what was most intriguing, and what we discussed more than anything else, was my dad's scientific response. He shared angles of insight into what dream-visions are that are really intriguing because..."

Alex's comments were interrupted by Mutti calling them to dinner. Alex had already been very clear with Lucy that, in his parents' home, punctuality at dinner was a fundamental rule. The conversation ended. They went to the table.

*****

After dinner, Lucy and Alex cleared the dishes. They were about to start washing them when Alex's mom suggested the young couple take the car and go out on a date. During the week since they'd arrived in Wichita, Alex and Lucy had spent almost all of their time with his parents. They were thrilled to get out of the house—on their own.

"Lucy, let's go see *Lawrence of Arabia*. It's playing at the Orpheum. You'll love the Orpheum—it was built in the early 1920s and its ornate art deco decor hasn't been tinkered with. In the twenties and thirties, some of vaudeville's greatest entertainers performed there—including Eddie Cantor. And this might be our last chance to see *Lawrence of Arabia* before we take off for Europe."

Lucy glared at her boyfriend. "No! Tell me Papi conversation—what he think about dream-vision. You say it *so interesting* but not tell me nothing. We not have five minutes alone—two of us—since bus arrive. Now you want cinema? I cannot believe. We find café—we talk! Free evening in Wichita not be in cinema."

"I was teasing. I don't want to go see a long movie about an Englishman on a camel in a desert—not tonight anyway. I know we need to talk. I figured we would go to the

Broadview Hotel Coffee Shop. It's the nicest place for a cup of coffee in this town—and they have excellent peach pie—or at least they used to."

*****

Alex parked the car. Minutes later, he and Lucy entered the Broadview Hotel through its somewhat outdated lobby. From there, they went into the coffee shop. Lucy, who by now was impatient for the conversation to start, said she would have tea, but didn't want piece of pie. She would just have a bite or two off of Alex's plate. Alex, a smile on his face, turned to Lucy. "Now what were we going to talk about?"

Lucy gave him a sneer. Alex knew she did not like being teased.

"OK. I was relieved Papi didn't question whether I was telling the truth about the dream-visions. As you might expect from a scientist, he focused on factors that might have caused the dream-visions—how they happened—what they are. He started out by discussing the possibility that what I experienced was actually a subconscious illusion—that the dreams were an unintended fabrication of my imagination. But the thing that caused him to reject that approach was Ruby's validation of what occurred and our confirmation of historical events.

"He wanted to theorize about the scientific basis for what he called *diese Wahrnehmung durch die Zeit* literally *this perception through time.* He talked about the characteristics of physical matter—about time being its own dimension. He shared a regret that as a chemist, he wasn't prepared to properly analyze what had occurred—that putting together a plausible explanation for what had transpired required a physicist or a psychologist—probably both."

The waitress brought the peach pie. Alex looked at the pie. It looked as good as he remembered. As soon as the waitress walked away, Alex went back to his narrative. Lucy began to take small nibbles of the pie.

"My dad has a colleague—actually a former colleague—who has a PhD in psychology. This woman—Lillian Maier—is also a German-Jewish Holocaust survivor. Since they both worked at Wichita's Municipal University, they saw a lot of one another and became close friends. Lillian was forced leave the University about ten years ago—during Joe McCarthy's red-baiting witch hunt. Since then, she has stayed in Wichita and written and published several psychology papers as well as a couple of books about her experiences in Europe before the war. My father and Lillian stayed in touch after she left the University. When I was a kid, my mother and father had a couple of horrid arguments about how often he *consulted* with her and the nature of those consultations. So, I don't ever bring up Lillian's name in front of Mutti."

Lucy appeared nervous and took small bites of the pie while Alex described the conversation with his father. "Anyway, my dad told me Lillian studied with Carl Jung—the Swiss psychologist. Jung was thirty years older than Lillian. Apparently, Jung got along very well with attractive young women. In any case, Lillian's understanding of human consciousness was deeply affected by the time she spent studying under Jung—so to speak—in particular by Jung's theories about dreams."

Alex stopped and looked at Lucy. "Lucy—I know you're worried. I told Papi how risky we thought it would be to share my experiences with a researcher—they might try to hijack my life. He agrees—our fears are totally valid. But on our way home, he asked if he could consult Lillian about my experiences. Papi said she is not only highly skilled; she is someone to whom we can entrust our lives. Then he warned me, once again, not to mention Lillian to my mom. About five or six years ago, he promised Mutti he would never see her again. You don't need to be a rocket scientist to figure that one out."

"Alex. We agree not speak about this to anyone. But I see you decide different. I not say it wrong that you want speak with dad. I not say it wrong he want share with Lillian. But if we couple, you need speak me first. You like if I decide ignore what we decide together? That be fair? No—I think not. When you decide without speak me first, it not respect me."

"I'm sorry Lucy. I was wrong. It's going to take some adjusting for me—I need to run stuff by you first. I promise to work on that. Anyway, Papi's offer to speak with her would put us in touch with someone who could give us insight into what the hell happens when I smoke dope. I apologize. But I told him to go ahead and speak with her."

Alex watched Lucy's reactions closely while he continued to speak. "After supper this evening, Papi took me aside for a moment and told me he had called Lillian. Lillian asked if we wanted to come by her home tomorrow morning for coffee. I told Papi to tell her we would. And that is what I know at this point. My dad has assured me that Lillian is totally trustworthy. Tomorrow we will find out if she can give us any insight into what I have experienced."

Lucy looked away, across the restaurant, while Alex waited for a reaction to what he had just shared. She was quiet and did not return his gaze. He waited. Finally, she turned her gaze back to him and said, "It bother me that you not check. A lot. But also, I know we need help. Maybe good we visit her. We find what come from it."

Alex looked down at what was now an empty pie plate. Lucy, while listening to him with great intensity, had nervously continued taking small tastes of peach pie and vanilla ice-cream. By the time he had finished telling her about Lillian, the pie was gone.

"Was it good?"

"I not know. I focus what you speak. I forget taste— not realize I eat pie. Sorry me."

They ordered a second piece of peach pie à la mode. This time Lucy let Alex eat most of it. They agreed the pie was incredibly good.

*****

The following morning was brisk and sunny. The walk to Lillian Maier's one-story craftsman bungalow was refreshing. When Alex pushed the doorbell button and they heard the Westminster chimes, a trim woman with graying dark hair dressed in black slacks and sweater opened the door for them. When Lillian spoke, she pronounced each word in a precise manner—something Alex recognized as a similarity to his father's diction. He knew it as a reflection of her native German tongue.

"Alex and Lucy—welcome to my home. It is a pleasure to meet you. Alex—I have often heard about you from your father. Klaus informed me that the two of you are about to initiate a European adventure. I look forward to hearing about it."

Lillian offered coffee to her guests and left the room. While they waited, Alex and Lucy had a chance to look around the living room in awe of its deeply colored, finely woven oriental carpets; elegant pair of French provincial chairs, and settee. On the living room walls were brightly colored paintings. In the attached dining room, a ceramic statue and several small pieces of art glass rested on a mahogany buffet.

Lucy pointed to one of the glass pieces. "That cameo lilac vase is Emile Galle'. It art nouveau. Frost glass kneeling naked woman—that from René Lalique."

She touched the centerpiece on the buffet—a brightly colored ceramic statue of a horned creature. "This Miro—or maybe Picasso,"

When Lillian returned, Lucy had walked into the living room and was looking at a dream-like oil painting hanging over the fireplace. It was a portrayal of a young man and woman.

"This beautiful. They float through air. Original Chagall?"

"Thank you, Lucy, for noticing. Yes. It is an original Marc Chagall. During the 1920s, I had a special friendship with Marc—in both Paris and Nice."

Lillian placed a white tray holding a white porcelain coffee pot, a matching cream and sugar set and three delicate coffee cups with saucers on the dining room table. She invited Alex and Lucy to sit down at the dining table as she poured coffee into the cups.

*****

"Lillian—this is good coffee. The only other person I know who makes coffee this good is my mother."

The moment after he said this, Alex regretted it and felt his face flush. But Lillian merely responded, "Americans do not know how to grind coffee beans—or make a good cup of coffee. I am pleased you are enjoying it."

There was silence at the table. Alex wasn't sure how to move the conversation forward. But Lillian broke the ice by returning the conversation to the painting. "I loved Chagall. His paintings—indeed his imagination—changed the conventions of abstract and realist art forms. In this painting, you see a young couple in love. The colors, the flowing, soaring movement of the lovers' bodies, and the simply sketched birds and trees surrounding them—they are all airy. The entire work attests to a mood of happiness. His work was so much about the human spirit—much more than it was about the physical attributes of his characters. This painting gives the viewer insight into the lovers' souls. I treasured that quality in him."

As Lillian spoke, her voice quavered. Alex saw a shimmer in her eyes. Now it was Lillian's turn to blush. Then she laughed and said, "But I have young friends who are about to travel to Europe in the 1960s. Why do I speak about the 1920s?" She paused, then added, "Pure vanity I suppose."

"I thrilled, Lillian, see original Chagall. I especial like Chagall for he remind me of Palekh Artists of Russia. They paint in magical style with whimsey details for many centuries. See Chagall painting remind me that beauty of Russia."

"Chagall would be flattered by your comparison of his art to the Palekh Artists. You'll have to come back another time when I can get to know you better. I look forward to sharing stories about my dear pieces of art as well as the delightful artists who created them."

Then, Lillian looked directly at Alex. "But this morning, my priority is to hear about your adventures in wonderland—your endeavors through time. Alex—your father has shared his version of the special things you experienced. I wish to hear you describe them. Tell me about each of your—how shall I describe them—unusual episodes, guess. Klaus tells me you call them *dream-visions*. I want to hear about them, including what preceded and followed each one. But, go back further. Start with the bizarre tale of a dead elephant."

*****

Alex spent the next hour recounting his experiences beginning with that day he had gone swimming with the lab assistants; how one of them had stolen the LSD after an elephant died in a failed experiment; how Alex had quit the University and gone to live with Lucy in New York. He retold each dream-vision, trying as best he could, not to skip critical details. Occasionally, Lucy would interrupt to remind him of something he had forgotten to share or had not sufficiently explained. Alex's descriptions were at least as detailed as those he had given Lucy immediately after each dream-vision. While he spoke, Lillian wrote notes at a furious pace into a small leather notebook.

After Alex finished, he commented, "I am surprised how tired I feel after telling you about my dream-visions. It was exhausting to share them with you."

"Alex, the energy expended on visualizing an emotional memory is often immense. Since I am deeply interested in what you are sharing with me, it makes sense for me to be thorough in my note taking. But I also know that if you see me taking notes—paying close attention to what you are saying—you will be motivated to remember your experiences as completely as you are able."

Lillian paused to take a sip of coffee before added to her statement. "An intense focus on taking notes while a patient shares his or her dream is a tactic most psychoanalysts utilize. When a narrator is pushed to recall an event by an avid listener, that narrator recollects more details and explains what happened more fully—almost re-experiencing the event. Thus—your fatigue."

At that point, Lucy informed Lillian that they had each documented every dream-vision immediately after it occurred. Lillian perked up when she heard that telling Lucy that it would be fascinating for her if she were able to review those journals.

The conversation transitioned into a series of Lillian's questions regarding what she referred to as Alex's *conscious-visions*—not the *dream-visions* title used by Alex and Lucy. Her questions focused upon how much Alex might have known about Ruby, Dylan Thomas, the Nazi attempt to sabotage the Grand Central Trains and about Beatrice and Jimmy—before each related conscious-vision. After Alex and Lucy had responded fully to each question, Lillian asked Alex about the clarity—the *realism* as she put it—of his conscious-visions. Did he have a history with illegal drugs including LSD and marijuana? What about the emotion he experienced during his *marijuana-induced conscious-visions?* There were a dozen other similar questions. After each response, Lillian wrote intensely into her notebook.

When all the questions had been asked and answered, Lillian simply said, "I need to absorb what you have shared for several minutes."

Quiet ensued. Lillian gazed across the room. Then she picked up her fountain pen and began to write once again into her notebook. The intense silence of the room was interrupted only by the scratching sound from her fountain pen. Lucy filled Alex and her porcelain cups with coffee, then got up from the table and walked around the living and dining rooms—looking at the elegant furniture, paintings and glass sculptures.

When Lillian cleared her throat, Lucy returned to the table.

*****

"First, thank you for sharing your extraordinary experiences with such clarity. Let me start by putting any concerns you might have about my discretion to rest. I understand these experiences were shared on an absolutely confidential basis. If you were to tell me you wanted to make this all public, I would be concerned. Alex—your fears of misuse of your capabilities are well founded. You would most certainly be used—no, abused by others in ways that would totally dehumanize you."

Alex looked at Lucy who gave a positive closed-eye nod in response to Lillian's statement.

"I have a doctorate in psychology and was able to study with some very great thinkers among them, Carl Jung. What you have described to me is outside of the knowledge or experience base of Jung—or for that matter of any psychologist I have studied. In fact, it goes beyond any literature or analysis to which I have been exposed."

She paused for a second, looked down at the table, took a deep breath, then looked up at Alex, then at Lucy. Jung's studies focused on the unconscious—not the conscious. He compared the conscious mind to that of a parrot—allowing itself to be trained. Dr. Jung emphasized one distinct characteristic of the unconscious mind—as compared to the conscious mind. It does not allow itself to be trained. Jung referred to the unconscious as an *autonomous psychic entity where we can listen but not meddle.*"

Lillian started to pour herself another cup of coffee. Seeing that the coffee pot was empty, she excused herself to replenish it. After she returned, she refilled cups for each of them and returned to her comments. "Unfortunately, what I learned from my studies—with Jung and others—has little value in explaining what you have experienced. You appear to have seen actual events occur in specific places during prior time periods—while in a state of mind that cannot be described as either conscious or unconscious. To put it simply, the experiences you have shared with me break all the rules of any time-consciousness model of which I am aware. I don't mean that what Jung and others have put forward isn't valid; just that what you have experienced goes beyond the structures and conventions they have devised. What you shared with me is truly extraordinary. I am stunned."

Lillian stopped speaking and looked at her two young visitors. She took a deep breath, then nodded as if she had decided how she would approach understanding what had been shared with her. "When Klaus told me about your experiences, I was intrigued. But I must admit, I was quite suspicious. I had not met you. I feared, for Klaus' sake, that you were being dishonest with him. I expected to not trust either of you—to not believe much of what you would say. I had no idea why you would want to create such a labyrinth of lies—but I was pretty certain that that is what I would discover had occurred. Thus, I welcomed you into my home with a high degree of skepticism. But after listening to you— watching you—well, there is no question in my mind you believe what you say to be the truth. I apologize for how much time it has taken me to digest what you shared. But big things are never digested quickly. And let me assure you—this is a big thing."

Her face took on a serious look as she said, "While I agree with your need for confidentiality, you have a responsibility to find a way to share this information—your experiences—with humanity. Your trip to Europe may be deeply meaningful for you personally. But it also can turn out to be of great value to the understanding of the human mind—of the human experience. I would like to be of some assistance in terms of facilitating a safe sharing of this information in the future."

Lillian stopped speaking. Lucy spoke. "We consider your words. Today, we listen what you propose. Decide later."

"Fair enough," Lillian said. "These phenomena are too important to ignore, deny, forget about or not document for scientific purposes. Put simply, it will be difficult to validate that you haven't merely researched these events and created these stories as part of an elaborate scheme. That validation must occur if what you have shared is ever be treated as something more than a potential hoax. With your permission and assistance, I wish to create a record of these conscious-visions. With the exception of your friend Ruby; her friends who were a part of the fits of anger in your apartment; of Dylan Thomas' friend Liz; and Beatrice—if she still is alive—no one exists with whom I can meet to verify the accuracy of your dream-visions."

"Go on," said Alex.

"Since you have already spoken to Ruby and allayed any suspicion on her part, I don't want to contact her again— at least not at this time. If I were to contact her now in order to confirm the events, she would become suspicious that your conscious-visions were not the results of Alex's hearing gossip as Lucy told her. If Ruby shared Alex's dream-visions with other people, your cat might be out of the bag. But at some point, I will want to speak with Ruby. However, at this point, it would be a mistake."

Lillian turned her head at a slight angle as she continued to speak, "Liz on the other hand—the woman who visited Dylan Thomas during your conscious-vision at Hotel Chelsea—is someone who I can approach. I recently read an excellent biography of Thomas. From it, I know Liz is alive. I can get in touch with her. If, under the pretense of writing an analysis of Thomas' psychological make-up, Liz was able to tell me about that evening—and if what she tells me jives with what you described—I will have confirmed your statements with a second source. I promise not to discuss anything that you have said with anyone—except I would like to be able to speak about these phenomena with Klaus. When you return from Europe, we can talk about your experience—on multiple levels—and can discuss how I might be able to document this unique set of experiences without threatening your lives."

"Lillian—Alex speak me in private for moment?"

Lillian indicated agreement and left the room. Alex and Lucy went in front of the fireplace to speak while gazing at the Chagall.

"While she speak, I recall article from her I read at university. Alex—she much respected. We have need for her. After watch her—I think she honest. Give strong analysis to us. We not know what we face for future. It good we have someone like her—connections, knowledge, friendship—we can count on. It offer large value. One more thing. If we lose journals—something happen to us—then everything lost—

your experiences disappear. If Lillian have journals—they safe. I think we bring, leave journals with Lillian before we go Europe. She begin analyze what we write in journals. Maybe she figure out something we overlook—give insight into dream-visions. I know this different than plan we make. But she right. We need accept responsibility come with opportunity. "

Alex was silent as he considered Lucy's comments. "Yah Lucy." He chuckled softly. "We are like that couple in the painting—floating towards God knows what. Anyway, you're right. Your suggestion makes sense. Let's ask her to come back in. We'll offer her the journals."

*****

Several minutes later, a cordial Lillian was thanking Alex and Lucy for their trust.

"I have one more thing we need to discuss. Klaus told me you are hoping to initiate a conscious-vision of Adolph Hitler. Is that true?"

Alex nodded.

"I know your father gave you his copy of *Rise and Fall of the Third Reich*. It is an excellent book. You both should take the time to read it before you arrive in Germany. I have some other things to share with you. A colleague of mine did an excellent analysis of Hitler's psychological profile. It is entitled "Adolph Hitler's Shadow". I want to give you a copy of it before you leave. It will give you insight into Hitler's personality which would prove useful should you initiate a conscious-vision of the man. I also will write a letter of introduction to a colleague of mine at Berlin's Humboldt University. It may prove useful to have an ally in East Berlin to whom you can go for assistance. I will write to inform him that you are doing research for a paper about Hitler and the

Third Reich. I will tell him you are the son of a Holocaust survivor who wishes to return to Germany to better understand the Nazi phenomena. The man is full of himself. But he is also highly influential in East Germany and may be able to open doors for you that normally would be closed to Americans. I am not saying that I like the man—that would be a lie. But should you end up in a situation where you need a contact in East Berlin, Professor Beckman may be useful."

Lillian paused for a moment. Then she directed her look at Lucy. "Lucy—I need to ask you. Are you a U.S. citizen? Do you have your citizenship papers and an American passport?"

"Dah."

"Good. Because if you didn't have those papers and a valid passport, I would never encourage you to cross into East Germany. With the citizenship papers and the passport, you should be safe. But be careful—both of you."

Alex looked at his watch and jumped. It was after two. His mother would have had soup ready for lunch promptly at 12:30. He quickly called home—and lied.

"I am sorry Mutti. Lucy has a girlfriend from New York who is attending college in Wichita. We tracked her down and the two of them had so much fun talking, we lost track of time. We'll be home in twenty minutes. Yes—if you could warm up the soup it would be great. And yah, we would love some of your homemade *Schwarzbrot*."

When Alex got off of the phone, Lucy said to him: "So, my fault—eh?"

Lillian joined in their laughter and added: "Men—we can't trust them and we can't live without them."

They thanked Lillian profusely and said their goodbyes.

*****

The next day, when Alex and Lucy walked over to Lillian's home to deliver the journals, Lillian was as warm as she had been the day before. Alex explained they needed to be brief. They would soon be leaving Wichita and Alex had promised his mother he and Lucy would be back promptly from their walk. Lillian went into her office for a moment and returned with the booklet *Adolph Hitler's Shadow* as well as a letter of introduction to Professor Beckman at Berlin's Humboldt University. She also gave Alex Professor Beckman's home and work addresses and phone numbers.

Lillian wished them well and told them to take care of themselves on the trip and definitely not to hesitate to contact her if help was needed.

They each gave Lillian a warm hug and were on their way.

*****

Alex's mother hadn't told him what she was fixing for dinner that evening. Alex hoped it would be a special meal. His hopes were realized when he heard the loud pounding coming from the kitchen. Mutti was preparing wiener schnitzel.

Alex had told Lucy that wiener schnitzel was his favorite meal—and that his mother served it with home-made spaetzle egg noodles, brown gravy and sweet and sour red cabbage. Lucy went into the kitchen and watched as Mutti pounded each piece of veal until it was as thin as possible before coating it with beaten eggs and bread crumbs, and then putting it on a sizzling hot pan.

As they sat down at the table, Lucy gave a big smile. "My mamachik fix meal similar. She pound chicken, not veal. But it similar—use egg and bread crumb. We eat with mash potato, not noodle, but with gravy. We call it *Otbivnaya*. Bring me warm memory from being child. Thank you Mutti."

Alex's mother stood up, walked over to Lucy and hugged her.

The meal, accompanied with a dry Riesling, turned out to be every bit as good as Alex remembered. The dinner's grand conclusion was *apfelkuchen*—a German apple cake Mutti had served over the years for almost every special family celebration.

*****

Alex was about to travel to the land of his ancestors— and was bringing his fiancé. A feeling of trust pervaded the table. Even though Alex's mom and dad wouldn't see their son or his girlfriend for many months, the mood at the table wasn't sad. The visit had been positive. Hard feelings between father and son had disappeared and a connection had been formed between Alex's parents and their soon-to-be daughter-in-law.

Chapter 11: Greece and Italy

A week and a half after leaving Wichita, Alex and Lucy arrived in the seaside village of Agia Marina on the island of Crete. Lucy later described the month in Agia Marina as "vacation time—play—no work—no worry—much good, fresh food".

They began their days with crusty country bread, yogurt and robust sweetened coffee. Lunch was bread, local goat cheese and fresh fruit. Evening meals were a fresh salad made of onion, olives, bell peppers, tomatoes and cucumber accompanied by either dolmathes, spanakopita, moussaka or souvlaki washed down with chilled domestica, the local white wine.

During the days, they read, walked and swam in the clear cobalt blue waters of the Aegean. Lucy drew still-life charcoal sketches of the village. Evenings were on bare feet along the beach, watching sunsets change the colors of the sky.

*****

Neither Alex nor Lucy had ever been in such a warm place. Regardless of whether they were sitting in a café or walking on the beach, the sun was strong—a new experience for each of them. They enjoyed all of it—or at least, most of it. One minor misfortune occurred.

On their second full day in the village, Alex swam all morning, then spent the afternoon exploring the beach despite Lucy's warning: "Alex—Back look red."

"My skin always burns a little, Lucy. Then, a day later, it turns into a dark tan. Relax. I can handle the sun."

He realized too late that the sunlight on Agia Marina's beach was more intense than he had experienced in Wichita,

Kansas. At four in the afternoon, Lucy described the color of his back as "red like Soviet flag".

"I should have listened to you, Lucy. Lesson learned—swim in the morning or evening; but be cautious in the midday sun; and always listen to Lucy."

After a couple days of torturous blisters and muscle pain, the sunburn peeled and Alex was as good as new.

*****

Alex's focus in Agia Marina was *The Rise and Fall of the Third Reich*. It was a slow read, but provided context to his pursuit.

"You should read it Lucy. *The Rise and Fall of the Third Reich* helps explain the horror of the Nazis. It was painful to read because it's so objective in dealing with the people and events I always reacted to on an emotional plane. But it sets the stage for my dream-visions."

Lucy focused on her book: *Florence, the Renaissance, and the Medici Family*. "Book exciting. So much great art happen in Florence. Medici family create Renaissance. It all so special."

*****

After Lucy finished reading her book, she read the booklet Lillian had given them, *Adolph Hitler's Shadow*. Lillian had written a note inside the front cover of the booklet.

> *Good luck Alex and Lucy,*
>
> *In dealing with someone you have reason to mistrust, always remember it is in your best interests to understand that person—to have a grasp of what motivates them. Most people can be explained by a combination of what they desire and what they fear. Hitler is no exception. Once you*

understand his inner motivation and anxieties, you will have much insight into his behavior.

Lillian

After finishing the booklet, Lucy urged Alex to read it.

"You be fascinated. Explain psychology of Adolf Hitler—behavior. I summarize major points from booklet in journal. Here—you read."

Alex took the journal and reviewed Lucy's notes.

- *Hitler mom live for him. He love her much.*
- *Mom cause Hitler believe he become something special. She die when Hitler 18.*
- *Then Hitler always alone. Distrust almost everyone.*
- *Hitler not close to father—big problem there.*
- *Hitler move to Vienna after mother die. There he fail as student and artist.*
- *Blame failure on others. Never change that. Always blame others.*

- *Hitler love Vienna opera. It teach importance of drama—affect speeches.*
- *Hitler respect composer Richard Wagner. Wagner forced leave Germany for twelve years because he racist, anti-Semite. After Wagner return Germany, he become famous.*
- *Hitler think he like Wagner. He someday become great, famous like Wagner.*

- *Hitler view world like Wagner opera. Hitler think he save Germany same way Siegfried save beautiful Brunhilda by kill evil dragon Fafner.*
- *Hitler think Jews and Communists like evil dragon Fafner—villains that cause Germany lose World War I.*

- *Hitler join German Army. Fight four years World War I at trenches with gas warfare.*
- *He and other Nazi leaders see much agony from gas. It desensitize them to human suffering.*
- *Hitler bitter at Britain, France, Russia and United States. They punish Germany with Treaty of Versailles. Hitler get revenge.*
- *Hard times after WWI create need for blame. Jews easy target.*

- *Hitler anger grow. Driver—sexual frustration. He have no sex with anyone until after he become Fuhrer.*
- *Hitler always like young women—unfilled fantasy from when he young.*

- *Hitler always worry about health.*
- *After become Fuhrer, Doctor Morell regular inject Hitler with strong mixture of cocaine, testosterone, heroine, morphine, belladonna, strychnine and other substances. All dangerous stuff.*

- *Dr. Morell tell Hitler injection is vitamins. But big behavior and health problems come from injections.*
- *In 1940s, Hitler also have Parkinson disease.*
- *Interesting fact—German people with Parkinson killed in Nazi gas chamber.*

Once Alex finished reviewing her notes, he thanked her. "The booklet sounds really relevant. I'll read it.

"You know, Lucy. It surprises me how much you hate Hitler. I mean I know your grandparents were killed by the Nazis—but you didn't even know them. When you talk about Hitler, it seems like you dislike him as much as I do. But all of my father's family and friends and most of my mother's relatives, were killed by Hitler."

"Alex. Sometime you like child. You think your family only one hurt by Hitler. You think Nazis only kill Jews? True. Nazis kill many Jewish. Yes. They kill my grandpop and grandmom. But, Alex—many has Russia people die by Nazis—not just Jews. Hitler hate all Soviets. He kill so many. You know how many people from Russia he kill? You any idea?"

Alex was surprised with Lucy's passion Alex. "In *Rise and Fall*, Shirer said the Nazis killed many Soviet soldiers and citizens. I don't know how many he killed—but I am sure there were a lot."

"Alex you ignorant. Hitler kill twenty-five million Soviet people. Twenty-five million! America say it won war. But no. America not win war. America fight on winning side, true. But Russia destroy Nazis. And cost—oh Alex, cost to my people—cost to my people. Russia defeat Hitler same way it defeat Napoleon. With blood sacrifice. Six of ten people who die in Europe during war are Soviets. Visit Russia today. You not find old men. Reason? They all die in war. Soviet people suffer so much, Alex. You just not know. You want me understand pain of Holocaust for your family. I do. I know Hitler hurt your family. You have plenty reason hate. I accept. But Alex. My people suffer so much. You need learn about Soviet pain. You right. I care. You should know why. You should understand pain—my country—my people. You not know Russia today if you not understand how Hitler punish Russia."

Alex was taken aback. He was shocked at the twenty-five million deaths. He was taken aback by Lucy's intensity.

"Thank you, Lucy. I'm sorry. You are right. I was ignorant."

*****

The vacation in Crete had been a wonderful change of pace, but both Alex and Lucy were anxious to move on. Alex was focused on the visit to Germany. Lucy was fixated on the art and cultural history of Italy and France.

One evening, as they sat at their table finishing a carafe of retsina, their newly acquired wine taste, Alex brought up the subject each had been thinking about, but they had not discussed since arriving in Greece. "We haven't spoken for a while about dream-visions—I mean when they're going to happen—where—and what we want to achieve. I've been thinking about this a lot."

Lucy smiled. "I have ideas too."

"Lucy. I'm looking forward to visiting Italy and France. You've taught me a lot about art and history. I'm excited to learn more. But even though it would be interesting to go back in time and see the Medicis in Florence or to view Claude Monet in Paris, having so many dream-visions is intimidating. Even though seeing my father as a child—walking with his parents in the Palmengarten would be fascinating, I'm not going to do that either. I don't want to take on too much. In the dream-visions, I think I—we need to focus on the Nazis—not take on too much else. It isn't about the limited amount of hashish we have. You remember how burned out I got last year after the dream-visions at Grand Central Terminal? I don't want to get so emotionally burned out before we get to Berlin that I won't have the energy to have one more dream-vision. I want to see Hitler— to get insight into that son of a bitch—the beast who cast such a shadow over my life—over the lives of every Jewish person who has lived since he became Fuhrer. What I am saying is I just don't think I have the emotional energy to dream-vision art in Italy and France—and also dream-vision Hitler in Germany. I'm sorry."

Alex watched Lucy's face and waited to hear what she would say. Lucy did not look at Alex. Instead, she gazed in the direction of several swallows circling the dome of a nearby Greek Orthodox Cathedral. The sunset had given the building golden tones. It was a peaceful sight. But the look around Lucy's eyes was not peaceful. Alex worried about what she was thinking.

Finally, she spoke. "I know Alex. You probably right. Person stretched across time—not me. I respect that. I want you see Hitler—discover why he so cruel. But honest—I deep disappointed. And you know what most painful? Not miss art or artists. We see art. We imagine artists. What disappoint me—make me so sad—I not hear you describe magnificent Lorenzo. They powerful family—not just rule Florence—not only control city-states—not just make art or philosophy—or have political power. It the specialness of all these—come together at one time—one place—one family. It change history—all time. You not speak Italian. You be stranger in dream-vision. Understand you need pick best purpose. I respect—no, I accept. This your decision—your life. You right. I know you need see Hitler."

A silent Lucy continued to look in the direction of the swallows as they circled in the twilight. Alex was now gazing in that direction as well. The two of them did not speak for a while.

Then Lucy continued. "Maybe—after Berlin—we return Florence? You dream-vision Palazzo Medici? Mean so much to me, Alex. Cosimo built palace fifteenth century. It home of Lorenzo Magnificent, Lord of Florence—sponsor for Botticelli, Leonardo de Vinci, Michelangelo. He—Michelangelo—artist there when teenager!"

Lucy stopped speaking and continued to watch the swallows in the evening's fading light. Alex looked at her face again. He could see her eyes were glassy. But she was not going to allow him to see a single tear slide down her cheek.

Alex slowly finished his glass of retsina. He stopped looking at Lucy, not wanting to embarrass her. Instead, he looked again at the sunlight on the dome of the Cathedral. But he was thinking that he hadn't appreciated how much she wanted this. "Lucy, now that I think about it, I think you're right. I do need to see Lorenzo. Yes. I will dream-vision in Florence."

*****

Traveling from the Island of Crete to the City of Florence was a long, tiring trip that began with a ten-hour ferry ride to a port just south of Athens where they spent a night in a cheap flop-house by the ferry terminal. Their next ferry ride took them on a twenty-hour ride on the Ionian Sea past picturesque Greek Islands. The final leg of the trip to Florence was a seven-hundred-kilometer train ride.

Late on a sunny afternoon, the train pulled into Florence's Santa Maria Novella station. Alex and Lucy threw on their backpacks and walked into the grandeur of *Firenze*— the city Americans and British have always known as *Florence*. They found a room at a small hotel in a centuries-old building. An hour later, they went out for dinner. Their meal of chestnut ravioli with pesto sauce refreshed them.

An animated Lucy spoke to Alex about each of the sites she looked forward to visiting in this, the birthplace of the Renaissance. "Before dream-vision, we see cathedral—Duomo. Then we visit Uffizi Museum and Botticelli's *Birth of Venus*. Next is Accademia; see David—famous statue by Michelangelo. And after we go seven-hundred-year-old Palazzo Vecchio—Florence city hall. There Leonardo da Vinci and Michelangelo make wonderful murals. But I save Palazzo de Medici for final day. There, Alex, you dream-vision at the palace where much politics and special art happen. Alex, I so excited, I do love Renaissance. I love Firenze."

*****

Alex enjoyed going through the galleries as much as Lucy promised and far more than he had anticipated. The art and architecture of New York City which he had appreciated so much now seemed mundane when compared to the grandeur of Florence. Alex realized that going back to view the de Medicis during the Renaissance would be really cool.

The day before the planned dream-vision, Lucy scouted out the Palazzo Medici Riccardi to identify the best location for Alex's dream-vision. She selected the Gallery Room, a large richly decorated hall, about one hundred-fifty feet long and thirty feet wide. The hall had an ornate fresco that stretched across the entire ceiling.

"Alex, Gallery Room place with many de Medici feasts. Tourists move slow there. We able stay long time."

Lucy spent the evening before the dream-vision prepping Alex on the de Medicis during the second half of the fifteenth century and on some of the important artists who he might see during the dream-vision. "Be sure think Renaissance people before dream-vision; try identify which de Medici you see—which artist."

After Lucy finished preparing Alex, he admitted to himself he was excited to see—first hand via dream-vision— the extraordinary Medici family and their talented friends.

*****

Alex and Lucy needed a wheelchair for the dream-vision. Lucy approached the hotel's matron who spoke English.

"Alex feel bad—has heart condition. You know where we borrow wheelchair? It make last day in Florence so much better."

Soon, Alex and Lucy were in possession of a dusty old wooden wheelchair that had been sitting in the hotel cellar for years. The chair looked like a museum piece with its slatted oak seats and oak wheel spokes. Alex and Lucy were relieved after they tried it out and found it fully functional.

*****

The morning was sunny. Alex and Lucy made their way through crowds of tourists to the Palazzo Medici Riccardi. While they walked, Lucy had difficulty holding back her smile.

"I so excited—you see Renaissance—describe for me. Be like I there!"

A block from the palace, they turned into a small dark alley. Lucy handed Alex half of a cigarette into which a small amount of hashish had been implanted. Alex lit the cigarette with a wooden match, inhaled deeply and held the harsh smoke in his lungs. Then he sat down in the wheelchair. Lucy pushed him through throngs of tourists to the Palazzo. Having purchased entrance tickets the day before, she was able to wheel Alex directly to the palace's entrance. Then, she pushed the wheelchair with an already sleepy Alex onto an elevator.

By the time the elevator doors opened, Alex had fallen asleep.

*****

Alex awoke. The walls of the hall were a series of mirrors separated by elaborate columns covered with gold leaf. Looking up, he saw a massive ceiling fresco of partially naked men and women—probably illustrations of Greek gods on earth and in the clouds. The fresco, which covered the entire ceiling was the largest work of art Alex had ever seen.

The room held a hundred or more men. The thing that jumped out to Alex was the occupants' dress. Their clothing was not from the fifteenth or sixteenth century—it was modern! Some wore dark formal military uniforms. Others wore white dinner jackets with black ties. Alex was confused. He had anticipated a scene from the Renaissance. And while he recognized the musical sound of the Italian language being spoken in the room, he also overheard the staccato enunciation of German conversations. And there, hanging from the room's columns, were red banners with black Nazi swastikas as well as other banners featuring a perched golden eagle—the Italian Fascist symbol.

Two men in dress military outfits entered the room. Alex recognized them—as did everyone else in the room. The crowd stood in unison, raising their right arms and shouting "Sieg Heil! Sieg Heil! Sieg Heil!" Then the chants were transformed to "Duce! Duce! Duce! Duce!"

Here were Germany and Italy's fascist leaders— Adolph Hitler and Benito Mussolini. Neither man was large. Hitler was of short to average height with a slight build. Mussolini was several inches shorter with a heavier build. In spite of the serious circumstance, Alex couldn't help but see humor in the situation—the two men looked a little like Moe and Curly from the *Three Stooges* comic team.

The two fascist dictators walked to the head table— just in front of Alex. Each of them was dressed in a well-tailored military outfit with black knee-high riding boots. Hitler's uniform was light tan. He wore a white shirt and tan tie. There was a black swastika on his red and white arm band. Mussolini was wearing a light green uniform with an ascot instead of a tie. Across the left breast of his jacket were multiple military ribbons and medals. Hitler took off his black billed officer's hat and placed it on the dining table. Then he sat down. Mussolini removed his brimless fur hat adorned with a large golden eagle. He also took a chair. Then, continuing to emulate the Fuhrer, Il Duce placed his hat on the table.

Adolph Hitler and Benito Mussolini were laughing. They appeared to be having a great time. Alex was about six feet behind them and could hear their conversation clearly. They lavished compliments on one another's leadership skills. Mussolini spoke a passable level of German, albeit with a heavy Italian accent. Hitler either had chosen not to speak Italian or was unable to speak the language.

Alex was amazed. He had seen films and heard recordings during which Hitler had shouted intense, angry, forceful speeches to thousands of ecstatic supporters. But instead of the passionate building rhythmic meter and guttural intensity Alex remembered from those recorded speeches, Hitler was dishing up flattery to his host with ingratiating warmth. Mussolini could not hide his pleasure. He was eating it up!

"Il Duce, the magnificence of the City of Firenze, the precision of the military exercises we viewed earlier and the way your supporters lavish their obvious love for you—these all attest to the excellent reasons the Third Reich has for being in an alliance with Italy."

Not to be outdone, Il Duce rose from his seat and raised his crystal goblet in the direction of Hitler. A hush came over the crowd. Then, in mediocre German, the Italian dictator proposed a toast.

"Reich Fuhrer, the British and French are modeling clay in your skillful hands. As I have often said, a liberal state is a mask behind which there is no face—it is scaffolding behind which there is no building. The travesties of Versailles shall be vanquished and repaid in kind to those who initiated those crimes against Germany. The German people, under your brilliant leadership, shall be returned to their rightful place in history—just as the Italian people are returning to their own prominent world position."

Hitler responded to this toast in a modest— almost humble manner as the crowd applauded wildly. Then several dozen waiters streamed into the hall. Some were serving a first course of soup. Others were pouring white wine. Alex watched the feast proceed. The meal had multiple courses— several of which included meat. But as Hitler ate, he carefully avoided the meat in each course. He did not touch his glass of wine but continued to show interest in the words spewed by the increasingly talkative Italian dictator—who had chosen to enjoy several glasses of wine.

Toward the end of the meal, a Nazi officer approached Hitler. Hitler's demeanor changed. His look became quite thoughtful as the officer whispered into the Fuhrer's ear. The officer then clicked his heals and saluted Hitler with his raised right arm. Hitler responded with a modest raised arm salute and turned back to his meal. The officer quickly walked out of the room. Based on what he had read in *The Rise and Fall of the Third Reich,* Alex realized that he had just seen Germany's Deputy Fuhrer Rudolph Hess speaking with his trusted leader.

The two dictators continued their conversation throughout the meal. Hitler spoke about his love of opera. "When I took an apartment in Vienna as a youth, I discovered the joy of opera. While my personal favorite, of course, are the four operas within Wagner's *Ring of the Nibelung,* I also enjoy Italian composers—particularly Verdi. I recently saw a version of Verdi's *Joan of Arc* that was thoughtfully updated to modern times. It portrayed the Third Reich as the setting for a German Joan of Arc. In this performance, the British were appropriately cast as the villains. They were defeated by the pure hearted St. Joan of Arc and her legions who had utmost faith in her."

Il Duce responded to the Fuhrer: "I would have enjoyed seeing such a brilliant adaptation of so grand an opera."

After a fresh strawberry dessert served in a translucent sauce accompanied by a sparkling white wine, Hitler stood up. Mussolini quickly followed suit, pushing back his chair and standing next to the Fuhrer. Other diners in the hall quickly jumped to their feet, raised their right arms in fascist salutes and shouted choruses of *Sieg Heil* and *Duce.*

Hitler and Mussolini began to take their exit. As they walked past Alex, it seemed as if Hitler looked directly into Alex's eyes—almost as if he saw Alex! Hitler's focused gaze was intense and his face suddenly became quite serious. Then he turned back to Mussolini and made a small comment. The two laughed and left the room followed by their loyal minions.

*****

Alex shook his head as he awoke. Lucy stood over his wheelchair with a look full of anticipation. As they had planned before Alex reported on the dream-vision, they left the Palazzo. Ten minutes later, in front of the Cathedral of Santa Maria del Fiore, Alex stepped out of the wheelchair and sat down on a cement park bench next to Lucy.

"What you see?" she asked with excitement. "Long time—you sleep ninety minutes. See Lorenzo? Michelangelo? What happen? Botticelli there? It incredible like I hope?"

Alex took a deep breath, then exhaled slowly. He was silent for a moment, trying to deal with being in awe of what he had just seen—but also nervous about how to explain it all to Lucy. What concerned him the most was the look that Adolph Hitler had appeared to give him.

Alex turned to Lucy to debrief. "Lucy, you are going to be really disappointed."

He watched her smile of anticipation melt. "I dream-visioned. But my subconscious and your prepping—well, somehow, they weren't in sync. Bottom line—I didn't see

Lorenzo the Magnificent—or Michelangelo—or Botticelli—or anyone from the Renaissance."

Alex saw that Lucy was looking down at the cobblestone courtyard in front of her, shaking her head sadly.

"I'm sorry Lucy. I saw Adolph Hitler and Benito Mussolini dining together with a bunch of their legions. It was the most surreal thing I've ever seen. Mussolini spoke German—more or less. I was able to listen to the two of them kiss one another's asses in front of about a hundred men— there wasn't a single woman in the room. Wait—there was a woman directing a film crew. Other than that, it was all men in military uniforms or white dinner jackets."

Alex went on to describe all he had seen. Lucy listened. But she continued to look down and shake her head from side to side.

"And the most surreal thing that happened—today or in any dream-vision I've had—it occurred after Hitler and Mussolini got up from the table and began to walk out of the hall. As Hitler passed me—he was probably only two feet away from me—he gave me a look in the eyes unlike any I ever have had from anyone—ever. The guy's glare was a dagger. If he wasn't nuts, he must have been stoned. The look lasted only an instant—probably less than a full second. But I don't think I imagined it, Lucy. There was an intensity with which he looked into my eyes—as if he could see me sitting there in my wheelchair. The look was one of anger and hate. It was frightening."

Lucy just sat on the bench, shaking her head from side to side and staring at the cobblestone courtyard. Neither of them said a word on their way back to the hotel room. Alex pushed the empty wheelchair. Lucy, her shoulders slumping, followed him. All the way back to the hotel, she continued shaking her head from side to side in disbelief.

Chapter 12: In and out of Paris

Alex and Lucy decided to make their final evening in Florence special. Dinner was at a bistro on Via Pellicceria. An hour after returning from the Palazzo, Alex and Lucy were seated at a table at La Petite Ristorante enjoying an excellent bottle of Trebbiano d'Abruzzo. They had ordered the specialties of the house—a Tuscan bean soup followed by spaghetti ala Viareggina—pasta with fresh clams, tomatoes and small delicate mushrooms served in a white wine sauce.

As they savored the wine, Alex apologized to Lucy once again for not having focused sufficiently on the images of the Medicis prior to the dream-vision. "It never occurred to me Hitler would have visited that hall—with Mussolini to boot. I'm so sorry. I know how much this meant to you."

Lucy looked up and surprised Alex by laughing softly. "Oh—you should apologize. I only ask you slide back four, five hundred years, visit greatest artists in history. You mess up! In place, you visit worst villains this century. How you confuse these? We go for Paris now—but I not request dream-vision for Paris. I not stupid. I know Hitler visit Paris. I not let Hitler disappoint me at two world best cities."

Then Lucy winked at Alex. "Son-bitch Hitler—always ruin everything! But I serious on this. No more dream-vision until Germany. Maybe no more dream-vision for Europe? You decide. Look Hitler give you, it give me much fear."

They were quiet for several minutes. Then she spoke again.

"I sorry. But this so scary."

*****

Their guidebook described an ancient perfume store located near Florence's train station. *Santa Maria Novella*

Farmaceutica was established in the 13th Century after Dominican Friars converted the Church of Santa Maria Novella into an infirmary. At that point, the friars were using the structure to cultivate medicinal herbs. Over the centuries, the product evolved into perfumes. The following day before they caught their train, Lucy and Alex went there. Its frescoed rooms and alcoves seemed more like a part of the church it had once been than a perfume shop where fragrances were mixed in front of customers. Lucy bought a bottle of their oldest fragrance—Acqua di Santa Maria Novella. The perfume had a fragrant musty orange scent and had been originally created for Catherine de Medici in 1533.

"Maybe you not dream-vision de Medici. But today, you able smell de Medici."

After Lucy placed a dab of the perfume on her neck, Alex kissed her.

"That nice," she said. "Now I concern whether you able stay off me on train-ride."

"Listen Lucy—you smell so good. Stop wondering. There is no way I will be held back."

*****

Before arriving at the Florence train station, they purchased a picnic dinner for the train ride—a bottle of Barbera wine, a flat crusty loaf of Tuscan bread, a thick slice of smoked provolone cheese, slices of prosciutto and a small bag of pears. On the train they met a young couple—Armelle, a French woman, and Daniel, an American. The four of them spent the evening drinking Barbera and eating the picnic meal. They dined, laughed and exchanged stories which highlighted the differences between Americans, French and Russians.

Daniel and Armelle were returning from a weekend trip to Florence. They had lived together in Paris for almost two years. While they didn't earn much as clerks at a Paris branch of an American bank, they traveled cheaply and often took weekend trips across Europe.

Armelle and Lucy spoke about the great art of Europe while Daniel told Alex why he left the United States and would never return. "I'm worried about being drafted. Aren't you? That war in Vietnam is awful— and I'm afraid that if Barry Goldwater gets elected president, the war's gonna heat up. Goldwater is nuts—all this talk about bombing North Vietnam! But don't get me wrong—I don't trust Johnson either. I don't know what it is about politicians. Power seems to be some sort of drug for them—and American politicians are seriously addicted. Once Armelle and I get married, I'm gonna apply for my French citizenship. Eventually I'll probably give up my American citizenship."

Alex listened to Daniel's complaints about abuse of power in his own country. He reflected on Hitler and Mussolini, on Huey Long and Joe McCarthy—and even on the Medici. The misuse of power wasn't limited to the Fascist countries of Europe—nor was it a new phenomenon. Alex sighed as he realized it had existed across the globe, throughout history.

*****

Daniel and Armelle invited Alex and Lucy to stay with them at their apartment in Paris. The invitation was enthusiastically accepted. The train pulled into Paris' Gare de Lyon station early the next morning. The two couples walked to Daniel and Armelle's apartment crossing the Seine on the Pont d'Austerlitz. From the bridge, they stopped to marvel at Notre Dame Cathedral.

On their way to the apartment, they walked through the *Jardin des Plantes*. Lucy bubbled in response to the beauty of the city. "Always wish be in Paris. First, see majesty, Notre Dame. Now, enjoy wonder of park in bloom. Cherry blossom bring wonderful memories of when I small child, visit beautiful park near Leningrad."

Armelle responded in English enriched by a thick French accent. "Lucy—welcome to April in Paris. Spring is the time for lovers—and the city shines. The *Jardin des Plantes* has always been my favorite place for Paris. It has been here during more than three hundred years. It has dazzled its visitors throughout that time. I try to visit the *Jardin* on Sundays. I like to watch families dressed for church—children running ahead of parents—down gravel walkways lined with century old oaks and maples—past aged greenhouses and ivy-covered museums. *C'est magnifique! Non?* I have always loved the garden's classic statues, its extraordinary shrubs and brilliant flower beds landscaped in patterns from the Renaissance. For me, to visit these gardens at any time of the year, is to step into an enchanted dream."

A few minutes after leaving the park, they stopped at a small sidewalk café. Daniel ordered four cafés au lait and croissants with butter and strawberry jam. As they sat at their table, enjoying their small feast, a soft rain began to fall. Daniel spoke about how much he enjoyed nursing a *café au lait* in the rain, under the protection of a bakery's canvas portico.

"This area around the park is special to me. Such wonderful cafés—so many unusual shops—such meaningful historical monuments. During your stay, you will discover the pleasure of watching Parisians stroll past you as you drink your *express*."

They finished their coffees and continued their walk down streets lined with eighteenth and nineteenth century apartment buildings, past weathered wooden doors and the faded colors of old and worn window shutters. They passed more small cafés and saw older French men in berets sipping their express while inhaling Gauloises cigarettes as they read *Le Figaro*. Near a wine cellar and meat market was Daniel and Armelle's centuries-old apartment building. They walked up the stairs to Daniel and Armelle's third floor one-bedroom apartment.

A breathless Lucy responded to Armelle's question about whether she had enjoyed the walk from the train station. "Is truly magic."

*****

The apartment was quite simple. Its small kitchen was crowded with four well-used ladder-back chairs and a battered, thick legged wooden dining table. Its living room was only big enough for a sofa, a coffee table and two more ladder-back chairs. The living room window's view was of the rue Mouffetarde Market.

Daniel told Alex and Lucy to put their bags in the apartment's modest bedroom—he and Armelle would sleep on the sofa-bed. Alex protested with no success.

"Armelle and I will not consider a no. You are our guests."

A moment later, resting on a bouncy bed, Alex said to Lucy, "I now understand why you were so excited to get here. This city has more charm than any place I've ever been to. We're going to have fun here—we're in love—it's springtime in Paris."

"Well," Lucy responded, giving him a kiss and adding, "That true."

*****

Daniel and Armelle had to return to work the following morning. During the week, Alex and Lucy explored the city. They strolled the streets, enjoying lunches on the Left Bank, walks along the Seine and book searches at the *Shakespeare and Company* bookstore. Based on Daniel and Armelle's recommendation, they visited the Louvre, Rodin's studio and Napoleon's tomb. Twice, after dinner, the two couples took in a classic film from the early fifties at the *Cinematheque*—Paris' film museum. On the other evenings, they explored cafes in various arrondissements.

Each day, Lucy selected a museum and the couple took their time going through it. As they went through the museum, Lucy explained the background of the art and the artists they were seeing. "You see Matisse influence Picasso in big way. Matisse whimsey. Picasso bold. They change one other. But they also change art—for whole world. As old man, Matisse not able stand while paint. He sit in wheelchair—cut shapes of colored paper. Assistants put cut-outs on large sheet paper on wall. Matisse give directions. Assistants listen—move color cut-outs on sheet paper—until Matisse find balance he seek."

Lucy looked at Alex and smiled before saying, "Matisse maybe like you, Alex. Sit in wheelchair, make dream-visions—but Matisse make for all to see—for all history."

In Montmartre, Lucy was especially excited. "Alex—we walk on same cobblestone as Toulouse-Lautrec, Degas, Modigliani, Picasso, Pissarro, Renoir, Matisse, Van Gogh, Utrillo. Our footsteps follow history of modern art."

"Lucy, my respect for your knowledge of art and art history grows every time we go to a museum; each time you speak to me about an artist; every time you interpret a work of art. I'm having a ball learning every damned bit of it."

*****

Alex and Lucy joined their friends for dinner at a hole-in-the-wall Moroccan restaurant on a narrow street in an Algerian neighborhood. Daniel explained the local history. "This restaurant was the scene of several assassination attempts just a few years ago, during France's war with Algeria. It was a dangerous place to visit back then. The danger is gone now. But the cuisine—forgive me for putting it like this—is to die for."

At the Moroccan restaurant, the foursome drank three pitchers of chilled Algerian rosé while devouring delicate couscous served with spicy broth, colorful vegetables and tender lamb. After two hours of eating and drinking, Alex was shocked to see that the cost of the dinner for all four of them amounted to the equivalent of less than fifteen American dollars.

As they began their third pitcher of rosé, Daniel asked Alex, "You have not really explained to us why you want to visit the country that persecuted your family. Why are you going to visit a city that arrested your grandparents and allowed them to be sent off to a concentration camp?"

All attention at the table turned to Alex. "Fair question, Daniel. But not necessarily an easy one to answer. Like any kid, I want to see the place where my father grew up. That's the easy part. But the cloud that hangs over me, over my life, is what the Nazis did—what the German people allowed the Nazis to do. I struggle to understand something so horrid. Somehow, I hope to gain some understanding of why the German people allowed Adolph Hitler to murder so many people. The French people fought the Nazis. Why didn't the Germans?

Daniel drained his glass, then refilled it. He took a deep breath, looked at Armelle who was watching him intently, exhaled and responded. "I wish it were that simple, Alex. I wish the French people had been more willing to resist the Nazis. You see the truth is that many French people liked Hitler's approach. They were not so overt about it, perhaps, but...."

Armelle gave Daniel an angry look, kicked him under the table and said, "*Daniel, nos visiteurs n'ont pas besoin de vous entendre réciter ces histoires.*"

But Daniel didn't drop it. "Armelle does not like it when I speak about this subject of French history. Unfortunately, Armelle's father was not only descended from nobility, he had been a Nazi collaborator. After the war, he tried to explain his actions to his family and friends by saying that the best approach to dealing with the Germans was to try to make the period of their occupation as painless for the French people as possible. Tell that to the seventy-five thousand Jews and other Frenchmen who were arrested and eventually exported out of their beloved country to concentration camps in Eastern Europe. Tell that to the twenty-five thousand patriots who died resisting the fascists. It's true that the German occupation forces were horrid. But there were a lot of French elites who cooperated with them thinking that France would be a better place if the Jews, socialists and communists were gone. And when the true patriot, De Gaulle, led the resistance against the Nazis, many of these French patriots supported the Nazis in their fight against the Allies. I think...."

At this point, a red-faced Armelle got up from the table, tears in her eyes but head held high, and angrily left the restaurant.

Daniel grimaced and said, "I should have known better...but it appears, I never learn. Sorry."

Daniel hurried out of the restaurant and raced ahead to catch Armelle as she headed back to the apartment.
*****

The week in Paris passed too quickly. Daniel and Armelle encouraged their guests to stay longer. But Alex and Lucy felt they had already taken advantage of their host and hostess. They needed to move on. Alex purchased tickets to leave Paris on the Sunday morning train to Munich. Alex had decided he wanted to see the Capitol of Bavaria—the first German City Hitler called home, after he read about Munich in *The Rise and Fall of the Third Reich*.

"I think Munich would be a good place for a dream-vision."

"Alex, I think maybe it not good idea have any more dream-visions. It frighten me. What happen in Florence make me think, bad idea dream-vision again."

"Lucy. Relax. It'll be ok. You're over-reacting."

"No Alex. I not. You not listen. Dream-vision there not good."

*****

Saturday evening, the two couples had an early dinner at a café on Boulevard Saint-Michel—the main thoroughfare in the Latin Quarter. After they arrived at the café, Daniel informed Alex and Lucy that he and Armelle had planned a surprise for that evening. Lucy asked what it was. Armelle told her she would just have to be patient.

Alex and Lucy loved the escargot. Using slices of fresh baguette, they carefully soaked up every bit of garlic butter and parsley from the escargot shells. The second course was even better. The café's beef Bourguignon was a fragrant stew of beef roast, small potatoes, carrots, mushrooms and braised onions cooked in red wine and served in its juices.

When their individual carafes of Côtes du Rhône were empty, Daniel ordered a bottle of Chateauneuf du Pape to celebrate Alex and Lucy's farewell to Paris. He announced, "It takes a great bottle of wine to adequately celebrate the City of Light."

They finished their meals and were enjoying the last of wine. Armelle looked at her watch. "Daniel, we must hurry. Otherwise, we be late for the opera."

That was how Alex and Lucy learned about the special plan for the evening. As they walked across the Seine towards the Opera House, Daniel filled in the details. "A friend at work gave me four tickets to tonight's performance. But it is not just any opera. Brace yourself—plan to be totally amazed and thrilled. Tonight, my dear friends, we will see the opera *La Norma* by Vincenzo Bellini."

Alex laughed and said, "I have no idea who Norma is or why you are taking us to see her."

No one else even cracked a smile.

Daniel tried to explain. "*La Norma* is a nineteenth century opera about love and tragedy. It is a good opera, but not extraordinary. But what's special about tonight's performance is that the lead role will be performed by Maria Callas—her first performance in Paris since 1958! This is the role Callas loves above all others. And she is regarded as the finest soprano to take on that role in the one hundred and thirty years since the opera was written."

Daniel was glowing. Alex tried to give a more positive response. "Neither Lucy nor I have ever seen an opera. It should be interesting."

What Alex didn't have the heart to say but was thinking was that he had no desire to see any opera. The train to Munich was leaving early the next morning—he was already exhausted—but what could he say? Daniel and Armelle had been so gracious. Now, they were excited to take Alex and Lucy to what they considered to be a once-in-a-lifetime performance at the Paris Opera.

Alex and Lucy would just have to suck it up and pretend to be happy.

*****

Once they arrived at the opera house, Daniel gave a tour of the building. Lucy and Alex looked around. Men were wearing dark suits or tuxedos. Women were dressed in elegant floor length silk, lace or sequined gowns. Lucy had already commented on the paintings, the architectural details and the grand extravagance of the lobby's chandeliers. She added, "We lucky. I never able visit opera in Moscow. And Paris Opera so famous—it special. But I embarrass. We not dress for opera. Look we dress like tourists."

Alex cracked a grin. "But sweetheart—we are tourists."

Lucy scowled.

*****

When they reached their seats at the back of the opera's main orchestra section, Alex was relieved to sit down. He was exhausted and secretly hoped they would find a way to leave the performance early. But try as he might, he couldn't come up with an adequate excuse. All the while,

Daniel continued to bubble about what an extraordinary event this was—how excited he was to hear the greatest soprano of the century—Maria Callas—The Divine One.

Lucy began to point out features of the grand opera hall. "Golden column and banister set off against red seats and velvet curtains. Opera hall light come from huge fantastic crystal chandelier."

Alex looked up. The chandelier was big. It had to be twenty-five feet across and hung thirty feet below a massive ceiling mural.

Daniel saw what he was looking at and said, "That magnificent mural of angels and troubadours across the ceiling is one of my favorite elements in this hall. Unfortunately, the French government is about to finalize a bureaucratic blunder. It is going to replace that beautiful neo-baroque ceiling fresco. French Minister of Culture Andre' Malraux decided—in his arrogant glory—that great art of the past is no longer relevant to modern France. A Russian painter—not French mind you—Russian—is being paid to replace this extraordinary classical mural with modern crap. It just pisses me off so much. Opera is about tradition! What the hell does Malraux know about opera? What does he think he's doing—allowing a modernist—a Russian from the South of France—some guy named Chagall—to paint a monstrosity over what was once great art! Unless someone can talk some sense into the French government, this wonderful ceiling fresco will be replaced next fall. So tonight, you guys are not only seeing a great diva sing, you may be seeing a great and beautiful piece of art that will not be around in six months. It's a tragedy in the making."

Lucy didn't comment or react.

Daniel's face flushed a bright red. "I'm sorry Lucy. I didn't mean to criticize Russian art—I mean, there's nothing wrong with Russian art. I just meant to criticize modern art—I mean modern art put into a traditional building."

"It ok Daniel. It ok say it not good have Russian painter—modern art—in place with large tradition. I understand. But you wrong. Art is constant change. And change good. Marc Chagall brilliant painter. You very wrong. But you not offend me. Just I laugh a little inside at comment."

Alex remembered the painting by Chagall that hung above Lillian's fireplace. He didn't want to offend their host any more than Lucy already had. But he realized that Lucy knew a whole lot more about art than did Daniel. They were all relieved a moment later when the orchestra began the overture.

Lucy whispered into Alex's ear, "I think Chagall paint something special—but I not say to Daniel. Maybe better if I say less? You think?"

Alex put his arm around her shoulder, gave her a peck on the cheek, and turned his attention to the performance.

*****

Alex had dreaded having to stay awake through an opera—particularly after a full day, a delicious meal and several glasses of wine. But he was surprised at how much he enjoyed the opera's intense melodies. Even though he knew he was anything but an expert, he could appreciate why Daniel had been so excited to hear Maria Callas. It wasn't just Callas' voice—it was the way in which she brought emotion into her role. He surprised himself. He was actually enjoying the opera. The chorus set off Callas' solos in a way that Alex had never imagined possible.

At the first intermission, Alex and Lucy stayed in their seats while Daniel and Armelle went to the rest rooms. "Daniel right about woman singer. We lucky. Tonight, most special night in trip—for me—maybe most special performance I see ever."

They enjoyed the second act as much as the first. At the intermission, Daniel and Armelle raved about the performance. While Alex and Lucy agreed, Alex was beginning to have difficulty keeping his eyes open. During the last ten minutes of the second act, he had stayed awake by pushing his left-hand fingernails into his right-hand palm.

Daniel and Armelle went to the lobby during the intermission. Alex shared his problem with Lucy. "Do you think we can leave?"

"You crazy?"

Alex took a deep breath and prepared for the third act. He drove his fingernails into his hand even more intensely and told himself, "Staying awake is just going to take discipline."

Exactly three minutes into that third act, Alex fell asleep.

*****

When Alex awoke, he was still in his seat. But the opera house was dark. Lucy, Daniel and Armelle were nowhere to be seen and Alex was now alone in the opera house. He was about to rise, to find out where Lucy and his friends had gone, when he heard the sound of a door opening behind him. Suddenly light from the overhead chandelier flooded the opera house. A half dozen men in overcoats entered the hall through a lobby door. Alex suddenly understood what had occurred. The men entering the hall were conversing in German.

Alex looked over his shoulder. He immediately recognized the second man entering the opera house. It was Adolf Hitler. Hitler was speaking about opera performances and about this opera house in an expressive manner.

"How I regret I am unable to stay to enjoy an opera—perhaps something by Verdi or better yet, a wonderful rendition of Wagner's *Siegfried* or *Götterdämmerung.*"

Hitler and his entourage walked down an opera hall aisle that was about fifty feet away from Alex. Hitler was gazing around, looking up at the chandelier and ceiling fresco, then at the various seating levels and private balcony boxes. His eyes glittered as he spoke to someone in his group. "Do you know how deeply I enjoyed the opera as a young man in Vienna? Were you aware that I was close friends with Wagner's widow? Opera is the highest level of art and the Paris Opera House appears to be near the pinnacle of opera houses—outside of German opera houses, of course. By the way, you really must see *Staatsoper Berlin*—and Vienna's opera house, of course."

Thoughts raced through Alex's mind. "Yes. This is a dream-vision. I accept that. But how could it have happened without smoking dope? I knew Hitler came to Paris for a quick tour after France surrendered. I read that in *Rise and Fall of the Third Reich*. But this is too damned bizarre. It's surreal to see him acting like—like a kid getting a tour of Yankee Stadium. It's just too strange—too intense—too grotesque."

Hitler and the others had reached the orchestra pit. They turned back towards the door—this time moving along the aisle adjacent to Alex's seat. They would pass within inches of Alex. Alex felt naked—sitting there—observing the devil about to walk right past him in an empty opera hall.

A moment later—as had happened in Florence—Hitler's gaze fell upon Alex. The dictator's excited, dazzled, happy look turned into an angry stare of cold hate. Alex was certain Hitler had seen him—that he recognized him from the Florence dream-vision. Hitler turned his body towards Alex. He was about to say something. From the look on the Fuhrer's face, those words would express rage.

*****

Suddenly everything went topsy-turvy. Alex realized he was back in the present. Lucy was shaking him. "Alex. You fall asleep. Opera finish. We go."

Alex shook his head—confused by the transition between eras. Once again, men in tuxedos—women in long gowns—streamed past him. Daniel and Armelle were standing—waiting to leave the opera house. But Alex sat in between them and the aisle, blocking their departure. Alex stood up, shook his head, trying to clear out the cobwebs.

"Alex—we need go. What wrong? Something happen? What happen?"

Lucy took Alex's hand and led him. Alex shuffled into the flow of well-dressed opera patrons heading out double doors—onto a grand stairway—and out of the monumental building. Armelle and Daniel were enthusiastically praising the performance while Lucy bit her bottom lip and watched Alex's face.

Daniel didn't notice Alex's confusion in his excitement over the evening's performance. "Callas' interpretation of *Casta Diva* was the most wonderful—the most moving moment of my life." He looked at Armelle, paused when he saw the disapproving look of his girlfriend, and added, "as far as opera goes, that is."

Alex nodded agreement to the rave reviews, but said nothing.

It took half an hour to walk back to the apartment. They arrived there after midnight. During the walk, Alex found his bearings. He apologized to Daniel and Armelle for falling asleep. "I absolutely loved the opera. It was an experience that was, well, unlike anything I have ever had."

*****

Fifteen minutes later, lying in bed, Lucy spoke to Alex. "What happen? You frighten me. What I fear happen—happen? You dream-vision?"

"I'm tired, Lucy. Can we talk about it in the morning—maybe on the train? I am so tired."

And without waiting for a response, he rolled over—and was in a deep sleep.

Chapter 13: The Train to Munich

Daylight! Daniel had opened the drapes and was shaking Alex. "You guys have one hour before your train pulls out of Paris. You gotta hustle. It's too late to take the Metro. You're gonna have to catch a taxi if you want to be on that train."

Alex had a small panic attack. He jumped out of bed and joined Lucy in cramming clothing into their backpacks. Ten minutes later, a haggard looking Alex and a not yet fully awake Lucy gave hugs, kisses and goodbyes to Daniel and Armelle as they slid into the backseat of a sleek black Citroen taxi. After a herky-jerky taxi ride through some of the busiest streets in Paris, Alex and Lucy stood in front of the statuesque, century-old Gare de l'Est. Entering the terminal, they were dazzled by the station's size and grandeur. For an upsetting moment, Lucy believed she had lost her passport. Once Alex found it in his backpack, they both relaxed and turned their attention to finding the correct concourse for their Munich Train.

There was time to purchase croissants and *café au lait* at a stand on the concourse before climbing onto the train and settling into their seats. As the train pulled out of Paris, they each let out a huge sigh. This was a moment to slow down, enjoy the coffee, eat croissants and catch breaths.

Nothing was said for ten minutes. Lucy broke the silence. "Taste buds happy. Coffee good. Croissants better. Flaky on outside; rich, buttery on inside. Strawberry jam make each bite croissant taste like moment of paradise."

As the train traveled beyond the suburbs of Paris, the pace of its rhythmic clickety-clack increased. Their coach was gliding past forests and open fields. Alex and Lucy looked at one another and shook their heads. What a morning!

Alex gazed dreamily at the countryside until Lucy broke the silence. "What happen last night? It seem terrible. You upset. Dream-vision happen? What you see?"

Alex took a deep breath, drained his café au lait, but said nothing. He turned to look out the window at small farms disappearing from their view. Lucy waited—drumming her fingers on the passenger car's window ledge—an intent expression on her face. Alex knew that look. Lucy expected a response.

"I was awfully tired when we arrived at the opera house. The wine had hit me hard. I was dreading the performance. But I really was surprised. I actually liked the opera and understood why Daniel was so excited about Callas. I was totally taken aback that listening to such intense classical music could be so satisfying. But I felt like I needed a couple of toothpicks to keep my eyes open. I was just so tired. When the third act began, I decided to close my eyes for a moment. I was going to try to focus myself—you know—build up the energy to stay awake for the rest of the performance. I guess I fell asleep."

Alex checked Lucy's response to what he had already said. If anything, she looked more resolved to get a complete response from him. Alex continued. "I woke up. I was all alone. The opera house was totally dark. I was confused. For a moment, I figured the performance had ended and somehow you guys had left me behind. Then that huge chandelier began to glow. The room lit up. Some men entered the opera hall from the lobby."

Alex looked at Lucy, took a deep breath, and said, "They were speaking German."

"What! I know what that mean. How can be? You not smoke marijuana! I ask you—why go Germany now? Too much crazy stuff happen. We not avoid Hitler in Italy. Not avoid him in France. Why go Germany? Why play in fire, Alex?"

Alex didn't know what to say. He had only begun to describe what he had seen.

Lucy paused, biting her lip, and looking away from Alex. For a while she said nothing. She just looked out the window at the countryside as the train raced forward. Alex softly caressed her back and neck. He smoothed her hair. She refused to look at him. He saw her brush away a few tears that came down her cheeks. Alex had never seen Lucy cry. It was clear she didn't want him to see it now.

A year and a half ago, Alex thought to himself, *Lucy's biggest concern was that we document everything carefully—that we behave logically while we analyzed what occurred—that we carefully research alternative approaches before moving forward. This is such a different reaction from the completely scientific Lucy I knew in New York.*

Alex reflected for a moment on the dream-visions that occurred in Florence and Paris. He had to admit to himself that this whole thing had gotten pretty much out of control. Alex continued to rub Lucy's back. Finally, her shoulders relaxed. She looked around them—at other passengers on the train. She seemed to be checking to see if anyone had seen her during a weak moment.

Finally, she spoke. "So—you not finish your explain."

Alex described the rest of the dream-vision. He did not attempt to respond to the crucial question Lucy had asked about how this dream-vision had happened without him smoking marijuana. But while he described each moment of the dream-vision in detail—each detail about Hitler and his entourage as they walked around the opera hall—Alex couldn't help but continue to ask himself how it all could have happened. When Alex finished speaking, an emotionally spent Lucy once again looked out the window. Nothing was said for half an hour.

Then Lucy asked the question. "How this happen?"

"I don't know Lucy. You ask me to explain a single aspect of something so much larger—something that we don't understand at all. I can't fathom any of it. Sure—we named it: *Dream-Vision*. That's great. But are we going to pretend we understand any of what has happened to me? I wish I knew how dream-visions happen when I am stoned let alone how I was able to see Adolph Hitler without smoking dope. Maybe the fresh memory in my conscious thoughts of what was in *Rise and Fall of the Third Reich* increased the odds I'd encounter Hitler in a dream-vision. But to the extent that I ended up seeing him when I hadn't smoked dope—I just haven't a clue. I assume Hitler really was at the Paris Opera during his 1940 tour of Paris after the German invasion of France. I assume I saw something that really did happen a quarter of a century ago—that I didn't imagine it. But I can't be certain about that. I just don't know. Sure, it's scary. Hitler did a lot of bad things to a lot of good people. And he hurt my family—and yours. He punished the Jewish people—and the Russian people. So, it's personal. But why the dream-vision when I didn't smoke dope? I don't know. And more bizarre—more frightening, how can Hitler appear to see me—to recognize me? I don't know. That hateful look— the bitter hate it expressed—so much venom coming from one man's eyes. But how? Why? I have no idea. And I can anticipate your next question. I can predict it because I've been asking myself the same goddamned thing: If all this is happening—why am I going to Germany? Why am I not racing out of Europe—like a bat out of hell?"

Alex stopped for a while and intently looked out the window. Lucy watched him closely as he thought about the questions he had just asked. Then he continued. "But I know why I want to go to Germany, Lucy. You need to imagine that you grew up watching your father weep for the loss of his loved ones. From your youngest age, you remember your father's most cherished hope being that his family had not been murdered. My dad didn't know for certain what happened to his family. There were years that while common sense told him his father, mother and brother were probably dead, he continued to hold onto a hope that perhaps they had been taken to the Soviet Union—that they were still alive— that he would get a call one day—or a letter. That they were about to join us in the United States. My dad never stopped hoping. That was my childhood. Then, in 1954, he received a letter from some official organization telling him that his parents and his brother had perished in the camp. It shook his world. I remember that day so clearly. He just was silent. No more tears. Just profound silence."

Alex inhaled, then sighed deeply. He looked down at the floor of the passenger car and shook his head slowly. Then he looked directly at Lucy. "Now that I have been given the opportunity to see the evil person responsible for all of his anguish—to try to get some understanding of what sort of person that villain was—why he did this? Will I walk away? Am I going to let my fear for my own safety steal from me this chance to gain insight into the pain that has overshadowed my life? No. I am not! It may not be rational, but this is how I feel."

Alex paused again for a couple of minutes, thinking through his thoughts before sharing them with Lucy. "And as far as the look he gave me—the fact that he can see me—and that apparently I irritate him. Well, if I can touch Hitler's life with a teeny bit of hell—I will do whatever I can to make that happen. What's my plan? I don't know, Lucy. But I'm driven. I also know that the woman I am in love with is one pretty smart cookie. You are upset today, Lucy. I know that you are trying to protect me. I appreciate that. But today I need something else. You are also capable of analyzing a lot—and I trust you. You are my partner. Today—today you need to help me do whatever the hell I need to do...."

This time it was Alex who fought back tears—raw emotion had emerged with an intensity he hadn't anticipated.

*****

The train continued eastward—across France—toward a Deutschland that was no longer under the control of a conscienceless tyrant. Alex and Lucy did not speak. They were both emotionally exhausted. They looked out the window. Soon they fell asleep—holding hands—Lucy's head resting on Alex's shoulder. When Alex awoke hours later, they were near the German border. Lucy was wide awake, gazing out the window, with a focused expression. The look told him she was putting pieces of the puzzle together and that the analyst was back.

Alex went to the men's room. When he returned, Lucy was writing furiously in her notebook. He chuckled to himself. He liked this in her so much. He knew he needed her skill and determination to put things into context. He had lost his objective grasp on what was happening—but his partner had not.

When Lucy stopped writing, Alex asked her if he could read her notes. She smiled and handed him her journal. "Read."

Alex sucked in a breath of air—a nervous response to her smile—and took the notebook. As she had in her previous journal entries, Lucy began with date and location. Her notes summarized Alex's dream-vision at the opera. Alex quickly looked over her description; as concise and straightforward as her speech. As Alex read, he thought to himself that he couldn't have written as complete or precise a summary of his own dream. Lucy had shown him once again that she was a hell of a listener.

Alex moved on to Lucy's conclusion.

How Alex have dream-vision if not smoke marijuana?

- *In New York and Florence, Alex smoke MJ. He fall asleep, have dream-vision.*
- *At Opera House, he not smoke MJ. He still fall asleep, have dream-vision.*
- *Possible explain:*
  - *Alex changing—more inclined dream-visions.*
  - *Combination tired + alcohol=set of chemical phenomena in Alex brain similar to cannabis.*
  - *Maybe Hitler unique—cause Alex dream-vision in Paris?*

  How Hitler see Alex?
- *Hitler at edge of sanity.*

- *"Adolph Hitler's Shadow" author believe Hitler on drugs always—from injections.*
- *If Alex able travel from present to past when smoke MJ, maybe Hitler able see into Alex from future because injection drugs.*
- *They meet in middle?*

Alex face danger?
- *Situation far beyond anything understand—we only guess.*
- *Rule out nothing.*
- *What we try prove now?*
- *Hitler horrible man. But Hitler lose war. He gone. He commit suicide.*
- *Nothing more for winning.*
- *It time we return USA—immediate!*

Alex now sleep. When nap end, I tell him—we get off train in next city, go back Paris, fly back USA. I not want tragedy—I not want lose Alex.

*****

When Alex finished reading her notes, the train was about ten minutes from Strasbourg—the last stop in France. Lucy had watched Alex closely as he read her journal.

When Alex looked up, she said, "It true. Alex. We need return United States. It time start pursue future—not chase past. Please Alex—we near Strasbourg. Take bags, get off train, return home."

Alex rubbed his chin between his thumb and forefinger. As he gazed out the coach's window, he thought about what Lucy had written. He said nothing for several minutes, gently rocking his head from side to side—having a conversation with himself—examining the pros and cons of each alternative next step.

"You might be right, Lucy—about the dream-visions. I'm just not sure. Asking what we're trying to prove is a more than appropriate question. If I choose to have another dream-vision, I'll owe you a good explanation of why. But my dad was raised in Germany. I have never been there. And if I do not go to Germany now, I don't think I ever will. Maybe we are just going to be tourists. I don't know. I have to give your questions more thought. But we could just go to Munich—we already have paid for the tickets. Let's spend a couple of days there and see the city. After that, I want to go to Frankfurt. I want to see my father's childhood home. I want to meet some people from Frankfurt—some of those we'll see were around when my dad was here. They aren't Hitler—but they allowed his diabolical schemes. Maybe there is something I can learn from meeting them. And I always wanted to go to West Berlin. But maybe, we should just forget about having any more dream-visions. Let's spend a couple days in Munich—then head to Frankfurt for a couple days. After that, we can start back to the USA if that seems right. But before we decide to leave Europe, we need to think more about it, talk more about it. I shouldn't make a decision without giving it a lot of thought."

Alex figured he had just offered a reasonable compromise. Not so from Lucy's perspective. "Alex. It make no sense. I understand why you speak this. But in Munich, maybe you drink beer. You tired—fall to sleep. What I do then? We not able control when you dream-vision any more. What if you dream-vision in beer hall—Hitler recognize you—cause you unable return to present time? You play with open Pandora box—you take on more we can control. In New

York, you tell me about Alice. Now, I fear you fall into Alice rabbit hole—and not be able climb out. I not want lose you, Alex. Hitler been every place in Germany. We cannot escape where he visit. Dream-vision constant threat. Time for us become much afraid—is now!"

*****

The train was pulling into Strasbourg. Its gothic cathedral stood majestically over the rest of the ancient city. But Lucy wasn't looking out the window. She was intently watching Alex.

"Look Lucy. I realize I'm being sort of inflexible."

"Sort of inflexible? Sort of? What part of you act rigid, stubborn, not willing consider any idea, not listen me ever? What part of that—only *sort of* inflexible?"

Alex was stunned with the strength of Lucy's response, but also thrown off guard with how she had expressed it. He tried to repress a giggle, but couldn't hold it back. He giggled for only a moment. Then his giggle turned into a laugh. Lucy's scowl began to thaw. She rolled her eyes, looked out the window. Soon Lucy was giggling as well. Then both of them were laughing—so hard that tears streamed down their faces.

"Men," Lucy said. "Can't live without. But never, ever, take them visit Adolf Hitler."

*****

Meanwhile, the train pulled out of Strasbourg. Lucy rolled her eyes and shook her head. She turned to look out the window as the beautiful City of Strasbourg disappeared from view.

When she looked back at Alex, he spoke. "Ok, I'll take back *sort of inflexible* and substitute *obstinate and irrational*."

166

"Thank you. That more true."

Alex took both of Lucy's hands and looked her in the eyes. "This is what I propose: Number one, I won't drink alcohol until after we leave Germany. Number two, I will not go anywhere without you. And number three, if—for any reason—I feel like I may fall asleep in any place except our hotel room, I will immediately tell you. In that case, you can pinch me as hard as possible. It will wake me up. This way, unless we sleep in a hotel room that Hitler slept in, we've cut out the possibility that a dream-vision will occur—unless we choose to seek it."

*****

The train was now moving at a good pace. Alex and Lucy decided to go to the dining car to have a late lunch. Lucy ordered in English, "*Weisswurst* sausage, sauerkraut and beer."

Alex told the waiter he would have the same.

Lucy corrected Alex for the waiter's benefit. "No. Sorry. Friend here decide have apple cider instead. Him not have beer."

For a moment, the waiter looked totally confused. Alex's face turned a little red. Then he chuckled and said, "*Ich trinke Apfelsaft, danke.*"

Lucy laughed. The waiter made his way to the kitchen to turn in their orders. And the train continued to rumble toward Munich.

Chapter 14: Munich

A steady rain was falling as Alex and Lucy's train pulled into Munich's modern station. As Alex looked around at the railway terminal's impressive architecture, he considered how much Germany must have changed since the war.

"German cities are going to look different for us than when Papi was here. Buildings destroyed by Allied bombing have been replaced. Case in point—this train station is about the future, not the past."

A little while later, Alex updated Lucy on what he had learned at the visitor's information booth. "The oldest parts of the city came through the war pretty well. There are a bunch of inexpensive hotels in old Munich. If we walk about ten blocks east of here, we'll have our pick."

As they walked, Alex held their one small umbrella to shield both of them from the rain as they took off in search of a room. Fifteen minutes later they had checked into a hotel on the fourth floor of a centuries old building two blocks from Marienplatz—Munich's town hall and central square.

*****

Alex opened a brochure he had picked up at the train station and translated portions of it to Lucy. "*Hitler came from Vienna to Munich before World War I. There, he tried to establish himself as an artist. Years later, after serving in the Great War, Hitler returned to the city. During the next decade, he made many political alliances in Munich which he utilized for the rest of his life.* Tomorrow, let's visit some of the places where he hung out."

They went out for dinner. But since Lucy felt a cold coming on, she wanted to get back to the hotel as soon as possible. On their return, they stopped at a pharmacy where they bought sage honey lozenges for her sore throat.

Back in their room, Lucy went to bed. "I tired Alex. Feel awful. You explore city tomorrow. I stay here—sleep."

*****

The following morning was cold and rainy. Lucy's head cold had set in. She stayed in the room and rested while Alex went out to find breakfast. He returned in minutes with coffee, orange juice and brotchen with butter and jam. Lucy opened her eyes and smiled when she saw the breakfast on the bed. After eating, Lucy rolled over in bed, closed her eyes and was quickly asleep.

Alex left the hotel to explore the city. He walked past a toy shop with a window display of elaborate wooden toys. Down the street, he looked in the window of a clock shop and saw scores of handmade cuckoo clocks and intricate brass and silver antique timepieces. He passed artisan bakeries with elaborate pastries, cheese shops with every imaginable cheese and vender stands with beautifully arranged vegetables.

The different architectural styles, colorful tile roofs, bronze statues, painted coats of arms, detailed mosaics and elegant church spires were fascinating. But Alex had no real understanding of what he was seeing. He regretted Lucy wasn't with him.

Marienplatz was full of American tourists going through Europe on five dollars a day. The elaborate mechanics of the massive antique glockenspiel clock that stood over the square amazed the tourists. Alex wasn't entertained by the life size mechanical sixteenth century knights and royalty that danced above the crowd to the music of ancient bells. He was just too cold, too wet. He felt Lucy's cold coming on.

Alex purchased cheese, bread, olives, tomatoes and a bottle of orange juice at the square's public market. He carried the provisions back to the hotel where he and Lucy shared lunch and treated their colds to a brief nap.

*****

When Alex awoke, he felt a little better and went out again—still by himself. He decided to visit two Hitler historical sites: the Bürgerbräukeller, the beer hall where Hitler and his cohorts had attempted to take control of the Bavarian Government in November of 1923 and Osteria Italiana—formerly named Osteria Bavaria—Hitler's favorite restaurant in Munich.

The rain had stopped. It took twenty minutes to get to the site of the Bürgerbräukeller. Alex discovered the old beer hall had been replaced with a modern commercial tavern. He decided not to waste his time there—particularly since he'd promised not to drink any beer. He turned back toward the Old Town to find Osteria Italiana.

Walking back to the hotel, Alex saw Germans of all ages in their daily lives—going to and from their businesses, schools or markets. He wondered about them—imagining the questions that he would have liked to ask, but of course, couldn't.

Had that old man served in the army during the war? Had he been a Hitler supporter—a Nazi? Had that fat man with the cane laughed as businesses owned by Jews were shut down—their inventories tossed onto the street?

Had that grey-haired woman in the dark blue sweater and thick woolen skirt believed that Jews like his grandparents were disgusting? Had she benefitted financially from the tragedies of Jewish families?

When he was young, did that middle-aged businessman in the suit know that Jewish people—of all ages—were being sent to concentration camps to die? Had he been a soldier—maybe an SS officer? If so, was he ashamed—did he feel guilt? Do his current neighbors, his family know if he supported Hitler?

And that young couple crossing the street—do they know if their fathers were Nazis? Are they ashamed of their parents? Are they relieved that the Third Reich is gone—or do they secretly regret that Germany lost the war as well as all of the power that would have come with winning it?

Alex suddenly was very tired. He decided to go back to the hotel. He and Lucy could take a taxi to the Osteria Italiana later. As he walked, Alex realized that the questions he was asking were not new. He had always wondered about how the German people dealt with what had happened in their country.

Heading back to the hotel, those questions continued to flow. *What was it like to have been part of a Nazi mob—to have beaten up Jews in the streets? Are any of the older people I see heroes who risked their lives by resisting the Nazis? Did they defend, hide or fight for victims? And those kids playing soccer in the street—do they even know what happened? Would they care if they knew?*

Would Hitler's loyal followers—if I asked them—deny they had been Nazis? Would they all claim to be innocent— saying that Hitler had duped them? I would give anything to be able to read their minds—to know their hearts. I would love to stop some respectable looking older person—to ask him or her questions about the history of their actions, their attitudes. Were they complicit in the crimes that resulted in the death of my grandparents—my uncle—the millions of other people—most of whom were not Jews—who the Nazis murdered?

*****

When he arrived in the hotel lobby, Alex saw an animated Lucy conversing with a desk clerk who was speaking to her in English. Lucy and Alex returned to their room.

"You look like you're feeling better."

"Dah. Cold much better. I decide go for walk. On way out, I ask desk clerk for information about area. His name Otto Berger. He speak perfect English. I ask questions on his life. Otto tell me much. He share horror story—real, true, horror story. He tell experience—his nightmare—living during Nazi time."

"Tell me about him, Lucy."

"Otto born Munich. His mom's parents Jewish. Father Catholic. Pop was successful Munich businessman. Otto family not belong any religion. He never go church or synagogue. Because pop's factory produce important machines, family allowed continue live in home until 1940. Then factory sold—but not really sold—more like given—to Nazi officer. Otto family move into two-room apartment. Since pop Catholic and factory help German economy, pop believe family not have risk. But Nazis arrest pop in fall 1941. Two months after, rest of family arrested—sent to concentration camp in Poland. Reason Otto family arrested—since mom's parents Jewish, Nazis believe whole family Jewish. Otto sent to Auschwitz. He show me tattoo Nazis on arm. He speak me horror of Auschwitz. Camp guards kill with gas—old, young, weak, most women—

anyone not be good in labor. Because Otto able work, he not killed.

Alex commented, "This whole country is full of pain or horror. It just doesn't stop."

Lucy continued. "Near end of war, Russian army come near Auschwitz. Nazis force sixty thousand hungry, poor dressed prisoners walk forty miles in freezing weather—most of them Jews—include Otto. Fifteen-thousand die on walk. Fifteen thousand! Die from cold. Die from hunger. Die exhausted. Die from shooting. Die from beating—by Nazi guards. So cruel; so not human. At end of death march, all who survive put on railroad cattle cars. Sent to Germany—to concentration camps. Otto sent to Dachau—near here—become free labor for German factories. Otto assigned work Munich factory—factory once belong to Otto's pop. Otto describe torture at Dachau. Everything always be perfect clean. If not, prisoner made suffer. If prisoner not stand perfect straight in roll call, forced stand naked in freezing weather. If bed not made perfect neat, prisoner forced crawl through snow by barrack. Then SS guards beat. Difficult for me understand cruelty."

Lucy stopped for a moment, looked out at the street, and sighed. Then she continued to tell Otto's story. "Prisoners sometime choose run into electric barbed wire fence. They not try escape—they know they be shot by SS guards—they decide end misery in life. Forty-one thousand Jews, Communists, Gypsies, political opponents die at Dachau. No medical care for sickness. Sick people at Dachau die in pain we not able imagine. Otto speak me about horrible experiments on sick—experiments on healthy. When Otto tell me about this, I think how sorry for self I feel because my cold. I ashamed. I have nothing compare to horror at camps.

Otto twenty-two-year-old when made free from Dachau—April 1945. He weigh less than ninety pound—from one-hundred fifty pound when arrested. Otto not learn until 1947 that mom, pop, sisters die at concentration camps."

Alex and Lucy sat on the side of their bed, looking down at the wooden floors, in shock.

"Alex—I learn how horrible Hitler is when I child. I say you before, twenty-five million Soviet people die from Germany in World War II. Nazis burn, rape, destroy across Soviet Union. They destroy much of Russia. No Russian ever forget this. But, Alex, when I speak with Otto, he teach me close-up Nazi horror. When your father speak to sadness—lose family, I hear. But Otto explain terrible pain—so awful. I understand hate you have to Hitler. I agree—you need chase the devil. It true, he enemy of Jews. I know already, he enemy of Russia. But truth, he enemy all good people."

Then Lucy wept.

*****

They laid down to rest and ended up sleeping for a couple of hours. After waking up, Alex asked Lucy how she was feeling.

"I feel better, but sad. Horror Otto share make my cold seem so nothing. Cold better."

"Yah Lucy, my throat feels better as well. Let's go out for an Italian dinner. We'll catch a taxi. I looked up *Osteria Italiana* in the guidebook. It's the other place I wanted to visit in Munich. It used to be called *Osteria Bavaria*. It was Hitler's favorite place to eat."

*****

Thirty minutes and a taxi ride later, they walked into *Osteria Italiana*. A tuxedoed maître d' seated them at a table in the center of the room.

"Restaurant nice, Alex. White cloths on tables, white jackets on waiters. It make me feel like dine in fine restaurant at Florence. We celebrate with good meal."

Alex suggested a bottle of Chianti.

"You forget Alex. No wine, no beer, no alcohol. Sorry. We agree at this."

From Alex's perspective, the substitute drink—a bottle of sparkling water—wasn't much of a satisfying resolution. They split a spinach salad. Alex ordered veal scaloppini; Lucy mushroom ravioli. The meals were good—not excellent—but good.

During dinner, Alex told Lucy he wanted to return to the restaurant and have a dream-vision there. "I have a strategy for getting us the privacy that'll allow me to dream-vision here."

When the waiter presented them with the check, Alex asked in German if he could speak with whoever was in charge of the restaurant. He wanted to pass on his compliments and make a request. After the waiter saw the amount of the Alex's tip, he promptly went to find the restaurant manager. He turned out to be the maître d'.

"My wife is an artist. She loves your restaurant's ambiance. Would it be possible for us to return—at some point when the dining room is empty—so she could make some sketches? She would need less than an hour to do her drawings."

As Alex spoke, he handed the maître d' a ten-mark note.

The maître d' paused, took the ten marks and said, "Our dining room is empty each day from three until four. Would you and your wife like to return tomorrow at three?"

"Thank you so much, *Herr Ober*. We shall return—with my wife's sketching materials —tomorrow at three."

The maître d' held out his hand. Alex gave him another ten-mark note. Alex and Lucy returned to their hotel.

*****

The next day, Alex and Lucy caught a taxi to *Osteria Italiana*. They got out of the cab a half block from the restaurant and went into an alley where Alex smoked a hash-loaded Lucky Strike. Moments later, the restaurant's maître d' welcomed them. He watched Lucy lay out her drawing pad and pencils on a dining table and begin to draw. Then he excused himself saying as he left the dining room, "Remember it is only until four o'clock. Call me when you are done."

Alex sat down on a comfortable, overstuffed chair near the restaurant's entrance. He watched Lucy's pencil move across the paper for a moment. Then his eyes slowly closed and he was asleep.

*****

Alex opened his eyes, looked across the room and saw linen covered tables in a different configuration from what he had seen moments before and chair backs were wooden instead of upholstered. But other than those differences, the dining room appeared to not have changed much from what he had observed minutes before except there were now guests dining at some of those tables. Then Alex's attention was drawn to a table in the back of the room—on the right. There, in a grey suit, white shirt and dark blue tie sat a relaxed and smiling Adolph Hitler. He looked considerably younger than Alex remembered from the dream-visions in Florence and Paris. He had his trademark moustache; but it was not as carefully trimmed and his hairstyle had less of the cartoonish precision Alex had become familiar with from photographs. And Hitler seemed much more relaxed than Alex remembered him being in the other dream-visions.

The Fuhrer was conversing with two slim, elegantly dressed, attractive women. Each had light brown hair. Neither wore makeup. One of the women wore a white blouse with a navy-blue pleated skirt—the other had a black blouse, grey skirt and pearls. The woman in the white blouse was flirting with Hitler who seemed to bask in her attention. Alex could not hear what they were saying. So, he stood up and walked over to their table. Alex wondered if Hitler would see him. But the Nazi leader showed no indication he was aware of anything out of the ordinary.

Adolph Hitler's almost empty plate had the remains of hard-boiled eggs, fruit and a green salad. He pushed the plate away, apparently finished with his dinner. His attention was riveted on what the woman in the white blouse was saying.

Hitler took a sip from a glass of water while keeping his eyes tightly focused on her. Then he spoke in an easy, rhythmic German cadence. "Unity—you flatter me. I am just the son of a low-level government official who cares deeply about his fatherland and has responded to the needs of the German people. An attractive and sophisticated woman like you should not be wasting her attention on a humble public servant like myself."

The woman called Unity responded in German with a distinct British accent: "Oh my Fuhrer—you so understate your presence. You are leading the German people out of the dark dungeon into which the Jews and communists have placed them. It is I who am overwhelmed with humility in your presence."

The other woman spoke in English with a strong British accent. "Unity—you lay it on so thick—why don't you just offer your body to the man and get it over with."

"Diana," responded Unity in English while continuing to smile at Hitler, "I am trying."

"Tell me my Fuhrer," Unity continued—once again in German, "Is it possible that the Third Reich will be able to achieve a peace with Great Britain and still gain its rightful destiny?"

Hitler responded with a shake of his head and a slight chuckle. "That would be my wish, my young and sweet friend. But this decision rests with the arrogant leaders of your country—not with me—and not with the German people. We only desire peace and progress while ridding our land of its thieves and enemies."

At that point, a tall and muscular officer wearing a dark black Nazi uniform with matching cap entered the restaurant. He walked directly up to Hitler who listened intently as the officer spoke quietly into his ear. Then the officer walked out of the restaurant.

Hitler turned to the two young women. "I regret that I am not able to spend more time with you. But important duty calls. I must respond. As always, it has been a pleasure to see your beauty—to hear your wit. Your presence gives Britain credibility. It gives all of us reason to hope that Germany and Britain will one day be able to build partnerships for the future of our races."

With that, he softly raised his arm in the Nazi salute. Both women rose in response, enthusiastically lifting and straightening their right arms in unison. Hitler strode out of the restaurant. Alex watched him take the backseat in a large black Mercedes Benz with shiny chrome detailing. The officer who had come into the restaurant took the driver's seat and they drove away.

After the Mercedes was gone, the woman named Diana turned to Unity. The two women looked at one another for a moment. Then they both giggled.

*****

Alex woke up a moment later. Lucy was focused on her drawing.

"Boy—that was weird. Let's walk back to the hotel. I'll fill you in on the way. It was totally—completely—absolutely bizarre."

Lucy pulled together her drawing materials while Alex opened the door to the kitchen and called out to inform the maître d' that they were done. When the maître d' entered the dining room, he asked Alex if his wife had been successful in her drawing. Alex translated the question for Lucy who opened her sketch book and showed them both a drawing of a wide-awake Alex sitting in the restaurant—smoking a cigarette.

Alex was impressed. The maître d' asked if she would sell it to the restaurant. Alex relayed his request on to Lucy. But Lucy shook her head and answered the maître d' herself. "*Nein danke.*"

*****

A couple of minutes later, Lucy and Alex were walking down Ludwigstrasse heading towards Old Munich. Alex was giving a detailed description of the short interlude he had witnessed. As Alex completed sharing his observations, he stopped walking for a moment and looked at Lucy.

"One of the weirdest things was how that woman—Unity—kept moving her tongue around on her lips. I mean—it was—uhm—very suggestive. She also moved the tip of her pointer finger across her lower lip a couple of times—just a little. It was almost like she was trying to seduce Hitler. He obviously loved it—but he didn't respond. He just soaked it all in—then left. And the other thing—I was standing right at the table—looking down at the three of them. Hitler gave no sign that he was aware of me in any way. Maybe I just imagined it those other times. I don't know."

Lucy, who had listened closely, paused before responding. "Well—we learn difficult predict what you see for dream-vision. But I make personal comment—on what you see. All men love be flattered. More important man is, more flattery he want and receive. Some women lower self—not have shame—to flatter man. And you, Alex—this I make very clear—you not with one those women."

Chapter 15: Off to Frankfurt

Alex was thrilled to arrive in the city of his father's youth. Utilizing advice from the visitors' desk at the Frankfurt Hauptbahnhof, Alex and Lucy walked to an inexpensive hotel in the old quarter of the city.

It was raining lightly. Alex began to recall things his father had shared with him about Frankfurt. "I remember Papi telling me that in 1930, Frankfurt's thirty thousand Jews were still an important part of the city. Sure, there was a lot of anti-Semitism and the Nazi Party had become popular, mostly among the uneducated. But Jews had lived in this city for more than 800 years. Frankfurt was their city too."

As they walked in the rain, Alex wondered about how the city had looked different when his father was kid. He continued. "When the Nazis came to power in 1933, things deteriorated. Jewish businesses were boycotted—many were closed. As the 1930s progressed, the situation got worse. Nazis blamed Jews for every economic and social problem the city faced."

Alex looked at his map, got his bearings and they turned down a street with many old shops. "I remember the sadness on Papi's face when he first told me about *Kristallnacht*—the Night of Broken Glass—how synagogues were burned—in Frankfurt—all across Germany. Gangs of brownshirts roamed the streets smashing glass windows of Jewish shops. They pillaged those businesses and beat up any Jewish people they came across. That was in November of 1938."

They walked silently for a couple of blocks. The rain let up. Alex continued to share his father's memories. "In the days that followed, well, thousands of Frankfurt Jews were arrested. They were held as prisoners in a large public hall—many of them eventually taken to concentration camps. By 1939, when Papi finally was able to leave Frankfurt, there were less than fourteen thousand Jewish people in the city. Most of them—most of those people, like my grandparents, like my uncle...."

Alex took a deep breath and didn't finish his thought. He and Lucy continued to walk toward their hotel. The day had taken on a somber tone.

*****

After getting a room at the hotel, Alex and Lucy walked down a picturesque old-town street headed toward the *Hofbrau Haus*—a restaurant the hotel's desk clerk had recommended. The clerk had said it served "the finest wiener schnitzel in all of Frankfurt".

The Hofbrau Haus had an elegant old-European atmosphere. A string trio played Strauss waltzes. Waiters were dressed in tuxedos with tails. Tables had fine linen tablecloths and fine porcelain dinnerware. When Alex saw the restaurant's elegance, he worried that the meal might turn out to be expensive. But once he saw the prices on the menu, he not only was relieved that the meal would be affordable, he understood that the German economy, twenty years after the war, was still in a recovery mode.

The dining room environment was a window into the culture of old-time Germany. Their waiter, a tall gaunt man whose black thinning hair was combed directly back, clearly treated his job as a serious profession. Alex and Lucy enjoyed being the beneficiaries of his formal manner.

Before they ordered, Lucy surprised Alex. "We celebrate tonight. Make big exception. You drink beer. I drink too. This good?" Alex responded with a huge grin. After the waiter delivered their beers, Lucy smiled and raised her large grey clay stein. Alex responded in kind. They each said *Prost* before taking a large drink of cold refreshing beer. Alex added, "Lucy. This beer is the perfect means of washing down the ideal German meal. Thank you so much."

Their orders of wiener schnitzel, red cabbage and spaetzle were soon placed in front of them. Each delicate, but crispy, schnitzel covered an entire plate. The red cabbage and spaetzle were served on smaller side dishes. Alex and Lucy agreed that the golden schnitzels were delicate, yet perfectly crisp; the red cabbage had a fine balance between tart and sweet; and the spaetzle—the German egg dumplings—melted in their mouths. What a meal!

*****

The next morning, after a quick hotel breakfast of brotchen with elderberry jam washed down with milchkafee served from large steaming stoneware pitchers, Alex and Lucy caught a streetcar on *Bockenheimer Landstrasse*. The streetcar dropped them off at the Palmengarten—Papi's favorite park.

They explored paths the park—walking past varied groves of trees, through flower gardens and greenhouses. As they walked, Lucy offered a running commentary on the plants they were seeing. "That gymnocalycium cactus. That anthurium. There bougainvillea and this—it red ginger. It beauteous."

"Where did you learn all of that stuff about plants?"

"I curious person, Alex. Take course on plants—easy credits at University in Oklahoma. Sometimes just study something fun. But I good student Alex. I take course; I study; and I learn. You need understand that in me."

Alex could only shake his head and chuckle. Every time he felt he knew Lucy, she surprised him with another new talent or unusual perspective.

Alex and Lucy made their way into the park. They sat down there on a bench, watching children, sometimes accompanied by a parent, rowing wooden boats on a small lake.

"I've been trying to visualize Papi—as a kid—coming to this park with his brother—getting into one of those green wooden boats and rowing around the lake."

*****

The Palmengarten was full of activity. Women pushed infants in baby carriages. Young boys and girls raced ahead of their parents down pebble park paths. Old men smoked pipes as they sat on their park benches. Alex and Lucy enjoyed watching this multi-faceted spectacle. But every child they passed caused Alex to think of his father as a young boy visiting the park. "Lucy—it's haunting—almost like a dream-vision. This is what it must have been like when Papi played here with his brother."

*****

When Alex and Lucy were done exploring the park, they went into the Palmengarten gift shop and bought picture postcards to send back to Alex's folks. After leaving the Palmengarten, they walked back to Bockenheimer Landstrasse. Alex was hoping to find the little pastry shop his father had often visited as a kid with his uncle Alex.

Alex in Deutschland

"My dad used to tell me about how, when he was small, his uncle Alex—I was named after Uncle Alex—would take him to Café Laumer for hot chocolate and a pastry. My grandmother would say: *Alex—you spoil the boy. Klaus eats too much sugar already—you reward him with more.* My grandfather would step in and chastise my grandmother. *A little sugar never hurt anyone. Let the boy go. He will only be young once.* Papi remembers putting his hand into Uncle Alex's large hand and they would walk to Café' Laumer."

They walked for a few minutes before Alex said slowly, "Uncle Alex died in a concentration camp in 1943."

*****

And there it was—Café Laumer. The three-story stucco building was painted an almost whimsically intense shade of yellow. Ten steps led from the street up to a large turret, the entrance to the cafe. Inside the cafe, Alex and Lucy were seated on elegant upholstered chairs at a small, round linen-covered table. Alex honored Papi's adventures with Uncle Alex by ordering his father's childhood favorites—hot chocolate and *apfelkuchen*.

After beginning to walk away from Café Laumer, Alex looked back at the café for a moment and said to Lucy, "I now understand why Papi has such warm memories of this place. It's magical." Then he hesitated and added, "But I can't help wondering what Café Laumer must have been like in the late nineteen-thirties and early forties—when those charming little tables were crowded with soldiers in uniforms marked with swastikas."

They turned onto the nearby *Freiherr vom Steinstrasse*. Three blocks down the street, Alex spotted a white stucco and red stone apartment house—the building in which Papi's family had lived. Alex stopped walking and spent a few quiet minutes looking at the building—imagining its past. He looked for the window from which his father, a quarter century before on Kristallnacht, had watched the nearby synagogue go up in flames.

Outside the building's main door, there was a name and a doorbell button for each apartment. Alex recognized only one name—Baumgarten. He pushed the button next to that name. An elderly woman's voice answered: "*Wer ist da?*"

Alex responded in German. "Are you the Frau Baumgarten who used to take care of Klaus Schwarz?"

There was a pause. Then the voice responded haltingly, "Yes. That is me. Why do you ask?"

*****

A few minutes later, an aged Frau Baumgarten was serving tea and butter cookies to the young American couple. She fawned over Alex. Lucy, who was not able to understand the German conversation, patiently sipped tea and watched the face of her hostess.

"My god—Alex. You look just like your father. He was such a good boy. I enjoyed taking care of him so much. Klaus always had a smile. And he liked butter cookies—as much as you appear to."

They talked about the sunny day, about Alex and Lucy's travel, and about the beauty of the Palmengarten. Then Alex changed the subject. "Frau Baumgarten, do you know what happened to my grandparents and my uncle after my father left Germany?"

Frau Baumgarten absorbed the question, leaned back, took a deep breath and then responded in a slow and deliberate manner. "Alex—you speak of a difficult period. Few Germans understood what was happening. The Nazis kept so many secrets. I didn't know what they were doing—what was happening. Your grandparents were very special to me. They trusted me. And, as you know, I took care of your father and his brother when they were young."

Frau Baumgarten stopped speaking. She picked up the cookie dish and offered her guests another cookie. Alex and Lucy who had just finished their treats at Café' Laumer passed. Frau Baumgarten put the plate back.

There was a moment of silence before she began speaking again. "By 1932, we had suffered through more than a decade of difficult times. We all were hoping Adolph Hitler would help Germans live better lives. Newspapers and radio stations had only praise for Hitler. After all, he was uniting the country."

Frau Baumgarten paused for a moment, took a sip of tea, and seemed to be considering how to continue her response to Alex's question. Alex waited.

"At the time, I believed what I heard. It is true that Nazi hooligans were in the streets. But what country doesn't have problems like that? We heard rumors of brownshirts beating civilians—Jews and the like. But there are always rumors. Which of the things that you hear should you choose to believe? Hitler focused our country on moving forward. He gave us pride to be German."

She paused again, pouring tea for Lucy and Alex, then continued. "Your grandfather and grandmother were always good to me. I didn't see anything they ever did that was unkind. I never would have supported the Fuhrer if I believed he was going to be so hurtful to the Jews. But what was being done to the Jews was kept a secret by the Nazis. I had no idea that Jews were being punished for their beliefs—no idea—none. And if I had known, Alex, what could I have done?

What can one person do? Things happened so quickly. And I was already an old woman. Yes. What could I have done? What could have been done differently?"

"Did you remain friends with my grandparents until the time they moved out of their apartment?"

Frau Baumgarten gazed out the window for a moment—almost as if she was trying to see back across time—to view her life, more than a quarter of a century before. She looked down, smoothed her skirt over her knees with both hands, and then looked up and responded. "Oh yes. Your grandpa and grandma were such kind people. Of course, I remained friends with them. I swear—on the savior's blood—that I was devastated—as shocked as can be when the Gestapo came to our building and took Klaus's father ..."

Frau Baumgarten stopped speaking. It was clear she was not certain of the appropriate description needed to complete her thought. Finally, she just finished her sentence with the word "away".

"When did that happen?"

"Your father's family was arrested in June or July of 1941—more than two years after your papa left for the United States. I was devastated. The Schwarzs were, as I said, such kind good people. What possible thing could they have done that would result in their arrest—their being taken away?"

"Did you ask the officials why my grandparents and uncle were taken away—what was going to happen to them?"

Frau Baumgarten gave a distressed look. "Oh, no—oh no. I knew better than to question the Gestapo. If you questioned the Gestapo, they might end up arresting you. I was distressed that your family was sent away. But there was nothing I could do, Alex. It was a frightening time. I was powerless. None of us knew what was happening."

"Do you know what happened to my grandparents and my uncle after they were arrested? I know eventually they were taken to Majdanek, in Poland—where they were murdered. But do you know if they were sent there immediately—right after they were arrested?"

Frau Baumgarten shook her head slowly, from side to side; then quietly repeated—almost as if she were speaking to herself: "I knew nothing. There was nothing I could do. Asking questions was very dangerous. I was just an old woman—nothing—nothing I could do."

Alex looked at her. It was clear she was uncomfortable. He guessed she was probably ashamed of her inability to say anything she had done in support of his grandparents. But he noted that she didn't admit to any shame. She just continued to mutter to herself how powerless she had been.

"Frau Baumgarten—my father told me about a family that used to live in this building—the Schmidts. Do they still live here?"

"Herr Schmidt was a local Gestapo official. I am not sure what his duties were—just that he wore a black uniform. That was, by itself, frightening. After your grandparents left, Herr Schmidt walked around this apartment building like an important man. I was told he had spoken to local officials and had negotiated the purchase of your grandparents' apartment. However, shortly after the Schmidt family moved into your family's old apartment, Herr Schmidt was sent off to the Eastern front—like so many others—to fight the communists. And like so many others, he never returned.

Frau Schmidt died about ten years ago. Schmidt's daughter and her husband live in the apartment now."

Frau Baumgarten looked up at Alex and said, "I think you should meet her, Alex. Her name is Mary Becker. She is probably home. I don't know if she will be able to tell you much about your grandparents. She was so young when the Schwarz family lived here."

The three of them sat in Frau Baumgarten's living room, quietly looking out the window. "We have taken too much of your time. Thank you so much for the tea and cookies. We will try to visit Mary Becker later today. It was a pleasure meeting you."

*****

It was one o'clock. It had been an emotional morning and Alex told Lucy, "I need a break. Let's go to Cafe Laumer."

Since the conversation with Frau Baumgarten had been in German, Alex quickly updated Lucy. Afterwards, Lucy asked, "How honest you think, Frau Baumgarten to you?"

"Well—probably a lot of what she said was the truth—as she prefers to remember it. The thing that stands out to me is that Papi told us that after 1935, she cold-shouldered the family. I doubt the Frau was a Nazi. I'm sure she didn't want my father's family to be hurt. But she was a good German—and probably afraid. Bottom line—when my grandparents were officially undesirable, her friendship with them ceased. I have no idea whether it was out of fear of being labeled a friend to Jews or because she actually believed Germany's problems were caused by Jews. But Frau Baumgarten survived. My grandparents and my uncle didn't. What was she going to say to me—*I was their friend until they needed my friendship*? I don't think so. The reality is that once Hitler came to power, Jews didn't have a lot of friends."

Lucy pondered Alex's description before commenting. "Body language speak loud. Old lady uncomfortable—more than uncomfortable—she shamed. What tragedy! I wonder—person like this ever honest with self? Ever say to self, *I was maybe wrong. Maybe should have express sympathy, love, support?* I think not. Rest of life they try forget. Try justify behavior. Say to self—*nothing I could do. Not understand what happen.* If ever in this circumstance, I hope have courage—stand for principle—not throw away integrity."

*****

As they entered Café Laumer, Lucy stopped for a moment, turned to Alex and said, "Forget promise not drink alcohol during Germany. It better, you enjoy, relax. It intense here." Alex gave her a quick kiss and they were shown to a small table in a corner of the restaurant. In addition to sharing a plate of bockwurst, brötchen and sauerkraut, they lingered as each savored their glass of Henninger beer.

After leaving Café Laumer, they walked back up *Freiherr vom Steinstrasse*, a block beyond Papi's old home, to the Synagogue. The massive granite synagogue was topped with a red tile roof. Its most prominent feature, a large dome, was above the main sanctuary. A quarter century before, on Kristallnacht, Westend had been the Frankfurt's least severely damaged Jewish house of worship. The fire department had extinguished the fire to avoid damage to nearby apartment buildings. As a consequence, the Westend Synagogue was the only Frankfurt synagogue rebuilt after the war.

Lucy was impressed with the building. "Dome make synagogue look like mosque. Not look Jewish Temple—except for gable has large Star David."

A locked wrought iron gate blocked the front of the building's entrance. As Alex looked through that gate, he imagined his father, uncle and grandparents going into what was then a liberal synagogue for Friday evening Shabbat services. His next thought was that his father's family—in fact most of the people who worshipped there twenty-five years before—were eventually killed by their own government.

"You know Lucy, Papi often spoke about the pain of losing his parents. But I never really tried to fathom how he must feel about losing his brother. The two of them had been very close. Papi must feel an enormous amount of guilt for having survived...." Alex paused, looked down and sighed, then finished his thought. "For having survived while his brother perished."

*****

Fifteen minutes later, they were back at his father's former home. Alex rang the doorbell of the third-floor apartment which had once belonged to his grandparents. Speaking over the intercom in German, Alex introduced himself. "Good day Frau Becker. My name is Alex Schwarz. I am here with my fiancé Lucy. We are visiting Frankfurt for the first time. My father's family lived in your apartment in the 1920s and 1930s. I was hoping that you would allow us to view the apartment."

There was silence for a moment, then the voice said, "Please come up." And the doorknob buzzed. After they entered the building and climbed the flights of stairs to the third-floor apartment, Alex knocked. A young woman dressed in a light blue housecoat came to the door. She had pale skin and wore her dark hair loosely clipped in a bun.

The woman took a deep breath, her face flushed, and then surprised her visitors by greeting them in excellent English. "Welcome to Frankfurt, Mr. Schwarz, Lucy. Please call me Mary."

Mary Becker led them into a sunny room, offered them seats on a brightly upholstered sofa. Alex and Lucy sat down. Their hostess offered them tea. After they accepted, she left them briefly. A moment later, she returned from the kitchen and sat down across from them.

"Mr. Schwarz, I may save you some time because I can guess why you are here. I was too young to have gotten to know your father, your uncle or your grandparents. But I have often wondered what became of them. I hoped that one day, one of the children or their grandchildren would visit. There is so much I wish to hear—so much I need to say."

"Mary, please call me Alex. My father came to the United States in early 1939. He was the only member of his family who survived the war. My grandparents and uncle were sent to a concentration camp where they perished."

Mary Becker took a deep breath, looked down for a moment, then looked directly at Alex and responded to him in a deliberate manner, "I am devastated to hear of their deaths."

She was quiet for several moments. Alex said nothing. Then Mary Becker spoke again. "I have never heard anything but good things about your family. What Germany did—what Hitler did—what the German people allowed the Nazis to do—to innocent people—to good people—is a crime that our nation will never be able to step away from—never be able to forget. My father, whom I hardly remember, was complicit in all of this. I was only two years old when our family moved into this apartment. I remember the last time I saw my father—he was wearing a black uniform—leaving us to go to the Russian Front. My mother was weeping."

Mary took a deep breath and slowly exhaled. She looked at Alex, then at Lucy, leaned forward, and continued. "Of course, I had no idea what war was—let alone any understanding of that war. I still cannot put together all of the pieces of the crazy history that led Germany into the war. But I am part of a different generation of Germans. We recognize that atrocities were committed by our parents' and grandparents' generations. We accept they should never be forgiven."

Mary Becker looked down for a moment. When she looked up, she added, "My mother passed away several years ago. Before she died, she told me about your family. I asked her straight out about my father's involvement in the war. I asked if he had been a Nazi—if there was disgrace on our family name."

The tea kettle whistled. Mary Becker excused herself to fix a pot of tea.

*****

While Mary was in the kitchen, Alex looked around the apartment. He imagined his father, as a small child, playing in the living room. When he looked into the dining room, he was able to imagine Sabbath dinners that had occurred there, decades before. He tried to visualize what it must have been like when his grandparents and uncle were arrested. He wasn't able to picture the terror that the family members must have experienced.

Mary interrupted his reveries carrying a wooden tray that held a floral design porcelain tea pot, sugar bowl, creamer and three cups with saucers. Mary was silent as she poured tea. She asked Alex and Lucy if they wanted sugar or cream. Both gladly accepted. The three sipped tea for several minutes before more was said.

As Alex drank tea from his cup, he wondered if maybe that cup, that set, had belonged to his father's family, if he could possibly be drinking from a cup from which his grandparents had sipped tea. If this and many other things in the apartment had once been the belongings of his family.

Mary continued where she had left off minutes before. "My mother initially refused to discuss my father's war record or anything about what he had—or had not done. All she would say was that my father had died in Russia during the retreat from Stalingrad—that he was a hero. I was young and self-righteous—angry that my mother would not share what she knew about my father. After a few days— during which time I refused to speak a word with her—she relented. one rainy day, in this room, sitting on this davenport, my mother spoke the truth to me. She told me of my father's sins. She explained that the 1920s had been hard for her and for my father. He had taken work wherever and whenever he could find it. But there was rarely enough food—never anything left over for simple luxuries like cookies or coffee or meat for a special meal. It was a hard time for Germans."

Mary took a deep breath and let it out, shook her head sadly, then continued. "My father joined a workers' party in the 1920s. Mother explained that he came home from a meeting in Munich at which he had heard Adolf Hitler speak about the crimes of the British and the French against the German people. He told her that Hitler had spoken clearly about why and how the economy had been destroyed by those we had fought against in the Great War and—yes—by the Jews. My father told my mother that Hitler had explained how, if the German people stood together, they would be able to return the nation to its rightful place—that German families would no longer need to suffer the hardships that had become commonplace.

Mary was silent for a minute. She looked out the window, eyes unfocused, shaking her head from side to side. Then she looked back to Alex. "Mother defended my father. She told me she believed he had no idea how hateful the Nazis would become—that he was just overjoyed to find a leader had finally arisen who would return the Fatherland to prosperity. During that conversation, I asked mother about your father's family—since they were Jewish and both my parents knew your grandparents. Mother told me that when she asked my father about them, he had responded: There are some good Jews; it is true. But you will notice the Schwarz family does not go hungry as we often do."

Mary stopped speaking to take a sip of tea. She looked around the room as if she was remembering that conversation there years before. "I am ashamed to tell you my father became active in his support of the Nazi party. Mother told me she didn't know what his role was but he often went to meetings. In 1933, after Hitler became Chancellor, my father was appointed to some sort of lower-level position within the government. Mother told me she did not know what the position was; only that he received an income and life became easier for them. A few years later, I was born. My father was by then a respected member of the community. My mother refused to tell me about the circumstances under which this apartment was vacated or how my father arranged that we live in it. She avoided my questions—in different ways at different times. She didn't know—or she couldn't remember—or she just wouldn't discuss things."

Mary stood up, went to the window, and looked down at the street. From there, she continued speaking. "Mother told me she had heard rumors about Jewish people pushing for communist revolution or cheating others in business. She had seen Jewish people beaten and thrown out of their homes onto the street. But she figured it was probably because they were communists or dishonest people. Mother said she was helpless. Anyone who challenged the forces that were creating change would themselves be punished."

Mary came back to the living room and refilled the cups of tea for her guests. Alex could see her hands shake as she poured the tea. "And so, my mother—she went about her life—she ran our home—this home—and she raised me. When father died in the war, Mother began to receive a small pension. But she had to go to work to support us. Mother said she did not learn until after the war—not until after Hitler had died—about all the terrible things—about how the Jews and all of the others had been treated.

Mary looked directly at Alex as she said, "Alex—I just don't know if my father had a role in driving your grandparents from this building. I don't know how much we benefitted from your family's tragedy. I just don't know. But I am ashamed—my generation is ashamed—of what my parents—our parents allowed—by what they did. The horrors of what occurred are overwhelming. What occurred was...."

At this point Mary Becker stopped speaking. A moment later, she began to sob. It was strange for Alex to watch the pain of this German woman, a person who had been a beneficiary of his family's tragedy. He was surprised.

He felt sorry for her. Lucy moved next to Mary and embraced her. Mary's whole body shook as she wept. A moment later, Mary collected herself and wiped away her tears. "I am so embarrassed, so ashamed, so confused. Your arrival here today—you coming to my flat—this was something I always hoped would happen—and always feared. I am sorry for the tragedy that befell your family. I am ashamed for my father—and yes, for my mother as well. I am so ashamed. So many Germans were inhumane."

"Mary—we not choose parents bring us to world. We not pick nationality—not decide economic class—or religion. We given these at birth. My heart reaches to you. It also reaches to Alex father Klaus. Different reasons. So much sadness for each. You both carry heavy weight you not create. Weight you not want or ask for. Please not feel shame. It make me humble meet you. It honor meet you. You touch me—you speak from heart of integrity, sincerity, courage."

*****

Silence gripped the room for what seemed like minutes. During that time, Mary regained her poise and Lucy, who Alex had rarely heard speak so openly, seemed suddenly embarrassed by that openness. The conversation transitioned uncomfortably into small talk. Alex and Lucy told Mary about their trip to Greece. Mary explained that she had learned to speak English because her gymnasium had required English fluency before high school graduation. Then, after graduating, Mary had worked for three years as a secretary in the Frankfurt office of an American company.

"Mary—I envy you learn English so good. Hear you speak, make me jealous."

Almost as a relief for all three of them, a baby's cry came from another room. Mary started to excuse herself so that she could get her daughter up from a nap.

"Mary—Lucy and I need to leave. You have been a gracious hostess. It has been a meaningful visit. *Vielen Dank* from the bottom of my heart."

There were promises made to stay in touch. Alex gave Mary his father's address and wrote down the name of the hotel where he and Lucy were staying. As Alex and Lucy walked down the stairs and out of the building, Alex was lost in confusion—and sadness. It would have been such a comfort to dislike Mary—to be able to hate her for having taken the home of his father's family—to have found someone to focus his anger upon.

But that was not the case.

Chapter 16: A Day Trip

The next morning, Alex and Lucy were once again sitting on a Palmengarten park bench looking at the picturesque lake.

"I need to digest yesterday. It's gonna take time. I'm sort of numb—a combination of emotional exhaustion and intellectual bewilderment."

"Maybe—go back apartment? Find way—dream-vision? See grandparents?"

"No Lucy. This is too hard—too painful. Seeing the apartment—hearing about what occurred. It was a lot. I need time to process it all. Dream-visioning is amazing. But it's emotionally exhausting. I am not sure I could stand the sadness—going back in time—seeing Papi's parents and brother before they were...."

They sat quietly while Alex collected himself.

"Given how tough it was just to hear about the past, why would I ever want to return to that apartment?"

Alex stared emptily at the lake. A few tears slid down his cheeks. He wiped them away. Lucy was kind enough not to notice.

"It was tough seeing Mary's pain. It caught me off guard. When I was young, Papi would weep sometimes. In the late forties and early fifties, in the middle of a simple conversation in which he had been sharing a happy memory from his childhood, he would suddenly begin to weep with an intensity I've rarely seen from anyone else. But Mary showed that sort of anguish today."

"Alex. We sometimes not see pain in others. They not share feelings. But that not mean pain not there. I grew up in world of pain. Grief all around me, I grow up. Many millions die in Russian famine of 1932, 1933. Then Stalin send millions to gulag to suffer. Final, Hitler murder so many Russians—burn cities—destroy farms, steal crops and kill livestock. I grow up in country in shock. Russians not talk much about pain but they hurt inside. Soviet children grow up in world after so many suffer so much. They see lines on parents and grandparents' faces. They learn sadness from those faces. And you right. Mary have sadness. Perhaps most America not know pain like your father know, like Russia know. But I recognize, Alex. I see Mary know pain."

****

Alex and Lucy returned to their hotel. But they stopped first at a small grocery where they purchased a lunch of a bottle of chilled Mosel wine, Tilsit cheese and a few fresh pumpernickel rolls.

After returning to their room, Alex opened the wine and tasted it. "The Mosel is good—it's a little like you, Lucy— you know, sharp and sweet."

Lucy hurled a pumpernickel roll at Alex who ducked, but too late, catching it in the side of his head. Soon they were both laughing. They tore apart the pumpernickel rolls and cut up the Tilsit with Alex's old boy scout knife totally enjoying their lunch.

After finishing lunch, Alex sat silently, looking out the window. Lucy was watching him and asked, "What you think?"

Alex responded, "Oh, I was just thinking about yesterday. Frau Baumgarten probably admired Hitler. But now, she tells anyone who'll listen that she didn't really know what he stood for until after he died. She kept repeating *I am just an old woman—not responsible for anything I did, or didn't do.* In the 1930s, she quietly supported a comforting solution. Now she takes no ownership of its consequences. But Mary—she's different. It's odd that I felt so much sympathy for the daughter of a Nazi—the daughter of a man who may have been partly responsible for deaths of my father's family. She ended up benefitting from my family's tragedy. But my heart goes out to her. Life is sometimes so strange."

They sat quietly.

Alex broke the silence. "I'm ready to leave Frankfurt, Lucy. There is more sadness here than opportunity to learn—more sorrow than I am willing to try to absorb."

"You make big decisions, Alex. You decide no more dream-visions in Germany. You decide leave Frankfurt. These big decisions."

"I still want to understand the past—I just realize that I can't handle dealing with the pain of my grandparents. But I am here in Germany now and may never come again. This is my opportunity to explore the ghosts that have haunted my family. So, I want to continue on to Berlin as planned. And yes, I think there will be another dream-vision. I need to pursue the ghost of Hitler."

*****

It was still early in the afternoon. They escaped the intense emotion that had dominated their trip to Frankfurt by going to a nearby movie theater and watching a matinee viewing of *The Pink Panther* starring Peter Sellers as the bumbling Inspector Clouseau. The film had German subtitles with the original English soundtrack. The film was funny. They laughed until tears streamed down their faces. They did not stop smiling as they walked back to their hotel—their *rrrhhume* as Inspector Clouseau would have said it.

Lucy summarized the day in this way. "Sometime laughter perfect medicine."

****

When they entered the hotel lobby, the desk clerk informed Alex that he had received a telephone call. He handed Alex a written phone message. The call had been from Mary Becker and the message requested he return her call.

Lucy watch Alex as he called Mary using the hotel lobby phone.

"Alex—I'm glad I was able to contact you before you left Frankfurt. I have a suggestion. Would you and Lucy like to take a drive with me tomorrow? My husband is letting me take our car for the day. My mother-in-law will watch my baby. I want to visit a place that will be uncomfortable for all three of us, but a place you should see. Near Munich is located Dachau—the site of an awful monument to Nazi Germany—a concentration camp. I realize it will be emotionally painful to visit this place. But I want to offer you the opportunity to see it. I think it would be meaningful. If you are interested, I can pick you up at your hotel tomorrow morning at seven."

Alex accepted Mary's invitation and thanked her. He returned to the hotel room and updated Lucy.

"It worthwhile, but it haunt. You dream-vision there? I think it too much pain see firsthand agony—camp prisoners."

"I agree Lucy. A dream-vision there—would be a nightmare."

"I relieved. It be too much pain."

*****

With Germany divided into two countries by a wall, traveling to West Berlin from West Germany was a complex task. Commercial flight was the most expensive means of traveling to West Berlin, but it was also the simplest. The hotel's desk clerk helped Alex and Lucy purchase Air France airplane tickets to West Berlin for the day after their drive with Mary.

That evening they ate dinner at a Polish restaurant. While waiting for their pierogi to be served, Lucy told Alex, "I figure something out. I analyze dates for dream-visions. Try understand Hitler's behavior changes from dreams. First dream-vision at Palace in Florence. Hitler recognize you—just brief—but he recognize you. Second dream-vision at Paris Opera. Hitler react strong. In third dream-vision in Munich restaurant, you say Hitler not see you at all. I try understand pattern. Why he see you sometime, not other time? Now have theory explain."

Lucy had all of Alex's attention.

"First—Hitler slowly go insane."

"It doesn't take a rocket scientist to figure that one out."

"No, Alex. You listen close now. No wisecrack. It time for serious. We not know certain what cause Hitler go insane. Probably drug from doctor, pressure of politic and he neurotic. We only guess, but time pass, it clear—it get much worse. I find date Hitler visit Florence in *Rise and Fall* book. It 1938. We not know certain year he at restaurant in Munich. Certain it before war if Hitler at restaurant without guards. Guess maybe 1935? Book tell date Hitler be in Paris—1940. That right after Germany invade France. Use dates you had dream-visions: first Florence; second—Paris; third—Munich. Hitler change in behavior not make sense. But use dates occur for Hitler: Munich first; Florence second; Paris Opera third. Then it make total sense. Hitler recognize you more—react more—as time pass. This coincide anger increase, behavior more volatile, described by *Rise and Fall.*"

"You're right, Lucy. Of course! There's growth from one event to the next—based on Hitler's experience in time. If I have another dream-vision and it occurs—say—in 1934. He wouldn't see me. But if I have a dream-vision that occurs toward the end of the war—well that might be pretty intense."

Lucy said nothing. She gave a self-satisfied look, nodded agreement and smiled. Alex, not certain what would be a more appropriate response, just stood up, walked around the table, leaned over and gave her a kiss on the lips.

*****

The next morning, Alex and Lucy were waiting in front of their hotel when Mary Becker pulled up to the curb in a banged-up, pale green, early nineteen-fifties Opel. Alex opened the coupe's passenger side door, greeted Mary and folded the front seat forward so Lucy could climb into the back seat. Alex returned the front seat back to its upright position and got into the car. They were on their way.

The Opel was small compared to American automobiles. It reminded Alex of a shrunken early-fifties Chevy that had clearly seen better days. The car wasn't comfortable. Its engine whined and its tailpipe smoked as the Opel accelerated into the traffic flow. Each bump in the road caused the car's suspension to bounce and groan. Each time Mary changed gears, Alex heard the gearbox grind.

"I rarely drive the car. Going as far as Dachau will be a long journey for me."

Alex offered to drive part of the way. Mary gladly accepted his offer.

"But before we get on the highway to Munich, there is something I must show you. Yesterday, after I called you, I spoke with Frau Baumgarten. I told her about our conversation. I let her know I would be going with you to Dachau today. Frau Baumgarten told me she was pleased you visited her. She said you, Alex, remind her of your father. But she added that she was so overwhelmed by the visit—and all of the memories it revived—that she neglected to recall or share some critical information. Frau Baumgarten told me she had known, even before your relatives were taken away, that Frankfurt Jews were being moved from the city—in cattle cars—to Poland. She had heard that the Jewish population was being resettled within Polish communities. And while she didn't know what would happen to your father's family, she felt badly because she knew no good was going to come from anyone being transported to a new home in a cattle car."

Alex noticed that the Opel appeared to be heading toward the Palmengarten. He said nothing and continued to listen to Mary.

"Frau Baumgarten told me about the day your grandfather was taken. It was a Friday morning in the summer of 1941. An SS officer came to your grandparents' home and asked to speak with your grandfather. Your grandfather was told he was to be questioned at the Gestapo headquarters at Lindenstrasse 27—only seven blocks from their apartment. She told me that she saw your grandfather taken out of the apartment building from her window. They took him out front and shoved him into the back of a large black SS van. Moments later, your grandmother came down to Frau Baumgarten's apartment. Your grandmother told her she was terrified—her husband had done nothing wrong—why was the Gestapo taking him? Frau Baumgarten told your grandmother she was sure that the Gestapo just had a few questions. He would certainly return home in a few hours. Obviously, that did not happen. Your grandfather must have spent that weekend in the basement jail cell of the Gestapo headquarters at Lindenstrasse 27. I have since learned of the terror that took place in that building's cellars. It was there that the Gestapo interrogated and tortured Jews and others who were deemed unwelcome by the Nazis. And yes, I understand people sometimes died during those interrogations."

Mary had been driving the car west on Bockenheimer Landstrasse—the route that would have taken them to the Palmengarten. But instead of turning to the right, toward the park, one block past Café Laumer, she turned the small car to the left onto a beautiful tree-lined boulevard full of large elegant buildings. Mary pulled over to the curb in front of the sixth large home on the left side of the street. It was a stately mansion surrounded by gardens.

She continued speaking. "Monday morning, your grandmother was notified by an SS officer that she must come to the SS Headquarters. She should bring her son and pack a suitcase for each family member. She was given a printed pamphlet telling her what she could pack in her bag—and what she couldn't. Everything else was to be left in the apartment. Your grandmother told Frau Baumgarten that she had been directed to walk the seven blocks to the Lindenstrasse 27 SS Headquarters. She would be informed of the new location of the family's home when she arrived at the SS Headquarters. Your grandmother was terrified of what was about to happen. But she was more afraid of what would happen if she did not strictly obey instructions. Frau Baumgarten watched your grandmother and uncle walk up Freiherr vom Steinstrasse towards the Gestapo Headquarters carrying their three suitcases. She told me she has always felt guilt that she did not say goodbye. But then she added, how does one say *goodbye—until we see you again* to someone who may be going—God knows where?"

Mary paused, sighed, and added, "Frau Baumgarten wept when she told me this. She said she had never shared this series of events with anyone. She was relieved she could share it not with me, and have me share it with you—before she died."

There was silence in the car. Mary finished her statement. "This is Lindenstrasse 27."

Alex and Lucy got out of the car and looked at the building. Underneath the imposing four-floor granite-block structure, they saw the windows of a basement—the cellar which Mary Becker had just described. They spent several minutes walking around the building, looking at it, imagining all that might have occurred there—to so many innocent people. Then they returned to the car.

When they were back in the Opel, Mary added, "Frau Baumgarten said she did not know if the family was taken to the trains that day or the next. All she knew was what my father told her later that week—that the Schwarz family had left Frankfurt to resettle in Poland. He said this at the same he informed her he had purchased the apartment. That was everything Frau Baumgarten shared with me."

Alex looked at the building, thinking about the horrors that had happened to his grandparents and uncle had faced there a quarter of a century before.

Alex in Deutschland

*****

The old Opel merged into the southbound lanes of the autobahn. The speed of the cars that passed them amazed Alex. It had been a while since he had travelled by private car and he wasn't sure if he'd ever been in an automobile on a six-lane highway.

Once they had settled into the flow of traffic, Mary spoke again. "The other day, after you left the apartment, I felt empty. I knew you must wonder what sort of beasts we Germans are—to have sponsored—as a society—the attempted annihilation of Jews, Gypsies and others. But I am not the only young German to feel horror at what transpired. Many of my generation are ashamed of what happened. We want to change our country—to force it to learn from the past. But when you left, I realized that I had missed an opportunity to build a bridge to someone who had been hurt by what we Germans had allowed to take place."

Mary moved into the center lane to pass a Kübelwagen—the German's response to the Jeep during World War II. The Kübelwagen was hauling a trailer filled with manure. After she had returned to the right lane, she continued. "When my husband returned home from work that evening, I told him how badly I felt. He suggested today's journey. My husband's friend was incarcerated at Dachau at the end of the war. That friend once told me about the history of the site and we thought I should share a little about it with you."

The traffic on the autobahn suddenly slowed down. Mary's complete attention returned to navigating traffic. Minutes later, they saw the problem. It was an early 1930s Opel Blitz truck laboring up a hill and producing a massive dark stream of exhaust smoke from its tailpipe. After passing the Blitz, Mary took a deep breath, chuckled for a moment, then continued speaking.

"Dachau was Hitler's first concentration camp—built in 1933. By 1940, it was severely overcrowded. It had over ten thousand inmates. Prisoners slept in crowded bunks—two to each small bunk. But by the end of 1944, there were thirty thousand prisoners—three times the number of 1940. They were packed into the same thirty small dormitories. Rations of food had been reduced to a starvation level. Disease was common. A typhoid epidemic broke out."

Mary shook her head sadly, then said, "When the camp was abandoned by the SS just before the Americans arrived in the spring of 1945, the liberating soldiers found thousands of malnourished inmates and two thousand prisoners—crowded into eighteen rail cattle cars—all dead."

She paused and said, "This was the Germany my generation inherited."

*****

There was an ominous silence in the car that lasted an hour. During that time, the only sound was the hum of the tires on the road. Then Mary took a deep breath and spoke again. "There is one other story I must share with you—that of a personal friend. When my friend was still a child, he was among those sent from Frankfurt to a concentration camp in Poland. The year was 1941—the same year your grandparents were forced from their home. My friend—his name is Fritz— was fourteen years old at the time. One morning, an SS official came to his family's apartment. The Nazi official directed his parents to pack the family's belongings. They were not told where they would be going—only that they should pack one bag for each family member. Everything else should be left in their apartment. The family—Fritz, his parents, his brother and sister—were ordered to be at the Frankfurt Market Hall at two that afternoon. Since it was no longer legal for Jews to ride street cars, the parents and three kids had to walk the five kilometers to the Market Hall. The day was hot and the walk long. Carrying the suitcases with their belongings exhausted Fritz's family. Passers-by, seeing the yellow Stars of David sewn onto their jackets, shouted comments like *dirty swine, thieves* or *Christ killers* at the family as they walked toward the Market Hall."

Mary glanced at Alex. "I am not sure it is fair that I burden you with all of these tales. Would you prefer that maybe I should just stop—you know—say no more about it and let the camp speak for itself. I have been droning on about misery. Maybe I am just throwing too much at you. Maybe I should be quiet."

Alex responded. "No Mary. This is painful to hear. But we came to Germany to learn about the horror of the Nazis. I appreciate your willingness to share these uncomfortable memories."

Mary said nothing for several minutes. Then she took a deep breath and continued. "When Fritz and his family arrived at the Market Hall, they were directed by SS officers to stand with several hundred other detainees who had already arrived. A small crowd of people stood near the frightened prisoners and shouted cruel comments. Fritz's mother tried to console his younger brother and sister. Finally, it all was too much for her. She just wept. At about seven that evening, Nazi Officers with machine guns shepherded the detainees onto a loading dock behind the market, about four hundred meters from where the family had spent the afternoon. There, the thousand or so Jews and other captives were forced onto rail boxcars. A couple of men objected to the treatment. They were pummeled with rifle butts by Nazi guards. Fritz was pushed onto a freight car with about a hundred other prisoners. About ten freight cars were packed in that manner. A little after sunset, the loaded train pulled out of Frankfurt."

She paused, then said, "Suffice it to say, Fritz was the only member of his family who survived the camp. Fritz described the horrors of the camp. But I think that is enough for now."

Mary pulled off of the autobahn and into a gas station where she filled the car with fuel. Minutes later, they were back on the road. There was quiet in the car. Alex looked out the window at the fields, forests and towns they passed. Each village was quaint—complete with churches and a train station. But Alex could not get out of his head that each town was a place whose inhabitants had supported the genocide of people like his grandparents. A little while later, Mary turned off the highway and pulled into one of those villages. She parked the Opel near a meadow which had a small creek running through it.

"I brought a lunch for us," she said.

They got out of the car. Mary took a basket out of the trunk and led them toward the creek. "I know this town well. My grandmother lived here."

Mary placed a large woolen blanket on the grass. She opened the wicker basket. In it, in addition to plastic cups and plates, was their lunch. There were cheeses, sliced sausages, a small jar of olives, brotchen and a bottle of sparkling apple cider.

While they sat on the blanket, Lucy told Mary about Otto, the desk clerk from Munich, and all that he had shared with her. After she finished, they ate their lunch without more conversation. They just watched the water in the creek flow past them.

*****

On the way back to the Opel, Alex offered to drive. "Danke, Alex. Driving allows me to let off the anxiety related to thinking about the sad things of which I speak. But on the way home, I would be pleased to let you drive."

A half an hour later, they turned off of the autobahn and began to see signs for the Village of Dachau—from which the neighboring concentration camp had gotten its name. A couple of minutes later, Mary parked in a gravel parking lot.

"Here we are at Dachau. You will see that the administration buildings are still here. The original barracks were torn down. Today you will see two rebuilt barracks and outlines painted on the earth of the twenty-eight other barrack buildings that were not rebuilt. Dachau Memorial is not scheduled to formally open until next year. So, there are no guides, no signs, no brochures or exhibits. But the terror of Dachau is not hidden. Instead of showing you around, trying to explain to you what was once here and clouding Otto's description of the experience of those who endured Dachau, I will let you wander—and picture what once was."

*****

As Alex entered the camp, he noticed there was no longer a wall or barbed wire around the camp. The Nazi gate which had once read *Arbeit macht Frei—Work makes you Free*—had been removed. Mary, Lucy and Alex walked past marked spaces where barracks had once stood and through an area where roll call for all prisoners had taken place in all kinds of weather. At the far end of the camp, Alex saw where the bodies of innocent people had been piled after they had perished from hunger, disease or beatings. Beside that space were the ovens in which corpses had been incinerated. He passed the gas chamber and walked through a room in which people had undressed and surrendered their clothing when they arrived at the camp.

As he wandered over the grounds, Alex silently said a prayer for his grandparents and his uncle whom he had never met. They hadn't died here—not at this camp. But he felt a quiet sadness as though this was where they had perished.

*****

Alex realized it would be unwise to have a dream-vision at Dachau and he did not want one to occur spontaneously as it had at the Paris Opera. He wanted to leave Dachau as soon as he could—and never return. He looked at Lucy. She had been watching him closely.

She asked, "We leave now?"

He nodded. The three of them headed back to the Opel. Mary said she wanted to continue to drive. Alex was relieved. Lucy started to get into the back seat. But Alex said he preferred to be back there—by himself.

They soon were on the road. Nothing was said—even when they stopped a few minutes later at a gas station to get fuel for the drive back to Frankfurt. Alex was tired. He fell asleep. He dreamt uncomfortable dreams—not dream-visions—but night terrors that a person might have after visiting the site of his or her family's murder.

*****

When Mary left them off at their hotel later that evening, Lucy was the one who verbalized how special and loving Mary's treatment of them had been.

"One day, wish you, your family visit Alex and me—in United States."

Mary smiled. "Maybe. That would be nice."

214

As Mary drove off, Alex saw her wipe tears from her face.

Chapter 17: Berlin

A day later, after checking into the Spree Hotel, a small hotel located near the Berlin Wall, Alex and Lucy began to explore West Berlin's unique downtown. Their guidebook described the area as "an urban patchwork of architecture and war."

"See, Alex—guidebook right—it a patchwork. Centuries-old brick building next to modern concrete structure. After that, tall steel construction. Then empty lot—shell of bombed building. See that building there—see bullet holes? Next one—it shiny new glass. Then splendid old brick structure—unharmed. True, I love variety—but Berlin make me sad. Variety driven by violence of war. And now, see barbed wire on top of Berlin wall? Old war may be over. This now a new war."

When they returned to the hotel, they were both exhausted. After a quick dinner, they turned in for the night.

*****

The next morning, a Saturday, was spent looking through their guidebook over coffee and rolls in a small café. Alex was trying to figure out where he should have his final dream-vision.

"Alex, why you want one more dream-vision? You see enough Hitler. Let us visit Berlin Museum. Then we leave Europe."

"I know what you say makes sense, Lucy. But I'm just not satisfied. This is a one-time opportunity. I will kick myself for the rest of my life if I pass this up. I will always be wondering *what if*? I need to do this. Instead of questioning that, couldn't you help? I need to find a place to dream-vision."

"Ok, Alex." Lucy sighed. "I help. Not like it—at all. But I help."

Alex paged through his guidebook for the next few minutes. "Damn. Allied bombs destroyed almost every Third Reich office building. The only ones still standing are in East Berlin."

"Maybe this why Lillian suggest professor? You need call him—I think."

Alex shook his head and laughed at himself realizing how much he benefitted from Lucy's common sense. "Thank you, Lucy."

Alex found Professor Beckman's contact information and walked over to a payphone on the café's back wall. He dialed Beckman's home phone number. A moment later, a he was introducing himself to Beckman in his most formal German.

"Good day, Professor Beckman. My name is Alex Schwarz. I was given your name by a colleague of yours..."

Alex was interrupted—in English. "Good morning, Herr Schwarz. Lillian Maier wrote that you might make contact. She explained you are writing a paper about changes in Germany since the war. Lillian informed me it was possible you would request assistance. It would be an honor to help you in any way I am able. I have tremendous respect for Lillian. Any friend of Lillian's is a friend of mine."

"Thank you, Professor. I am trying to find a location that I will use in my paper—a place where Hitler might have met with other Nazi leaders. If we can get together, I will fill you in. We are staying at the Spree Hotel. It is located..."

"I know exactly where the Spree Hotel is located. The Spree is a somewhat quaint, but still pleasant hotel. I would be pleased to meet with you and your girlfriend—Lucy isn't it—tomorrow. I live in East Berlin. It will take a little while for me to get to West Berlin. But your hotel is not far from Checkpoint Charlie—the crossing point I generally use when I visit West Berlin. Why don't I meet you at the bakery across the street from the Spree at ten tomorrow morning?"

*****

Sunday morning, Alex and Lucy were waiting at the bakery when a short man wearing a brown plaid three-piece suit, a dark red bow-tie and a brown fedora walked into the café and approached their table. The man had a goatee and moustache. He looked to be about fifty years old.

"Good day. I assume you are Alex and Lucy. I am Dr. Werner Beckman. Ah, but you must call me Werner."

Alex and Lucy stood up and shook hands with Beckman.

"Thank you for being available to meet with us on a Sunday."

"It is my pleasure. Any friend of Lillian's is a friend of mine. I thought you might find it interesting if I gave you a little background about myself—it might give you some insight as to how I could be of assistance in your project. I am an academic purist. I study Psychology in order to enlighten those who explore vistas of the future rather than rehash the statuary of the past. I have brought you a recent article I authored that explains my approaches quite well. You might find it interesting. After reading it, I would appreciate it if you would share it with Lillian."

Beckman handed them a printed copy of a recent article in a German psychology publication. The article was entitled *The Psychology of Psychology—New Frontiers.* Beckman then spoke for some time about the article and his academic career.

Later that day, Lucy complained to Alex, "He expert on ego. Not suffer much from humility."

"You are probably wondering how I learned to speak English so well. I was a student in Great Britain during the late thirties and learned to speak English almost perfectly at Kings College in Cambridge. I could have had a successful academic career in Great Britain..."

Professor Beckman continued to review his credentials and experience. Alex did not interrupt. He decided that ten or fifteen minutes of allowing him to expound on himself was sort of a payment in advance for any assistance Beckman might offer in finding a spot for a dream-vision. The conversation finally moved on to chit-chat including discussions of Lillian's art collection, Wichita's location, Berlin's art scene and Werner's hope for world peace.

Finally, Alex found an opening. "In conjunction with my request, Dr. Beckman, I am looking for a location for my fictional piece—a story about an imaginary meeting between Hitler and his associates."

*****

Alex had previously shared with Lucy this strategy for identifying a location for the Hitler dream-vision. Lucy had laughed at his approach.

"Why you say paper fictional? That weak premise."

"Lucy, an academic always will respond more enthusiastically to an inane idea than to one that is mundane. You tell me. What better justification can you suggest for asking for access to space where Hitler had met with his team?"

"I not have better plan."

*****

Beckman didn't question Alex's explanation.

"I am sure I can help. The moment I received Lillian's letter, I decided I would find a way to service you regardless of what you needed—assuming of course, it was legal."

"Thank you, Dr. Beckman. It would be terrific if you could find a place where Goering and Hitler met—one which I could use as the setting for my story. We'd like a place where Lucy and I could spend a couple of hours alone—documenting the details of the location for my story."

Beckman paused before responding.

"Your request is not a simple one. However, there is one place in Berlin that will give you exactly what you want. But it is located in East Berlin. The good news is because Humboldt University is located in East Berlin, I can invite you over as academic emissaries from the United States to see this place. The only remaining major office building used by senior Nazi leaders is the Reich Aviation Ministry Building. It housed Goering's Air Luftwaffe administration. The Ministry Building is of colossal size—the Nazis boasted that it was the largest building in Europe. Through some miracle, the building survived allied bombing during World War II. It is now the home of the German Democratic Republic's ministerial offices."

Beckman looked around the room, almost as if he were expecting an imaginary audience to applaud him for his suggestion. Then he continued. "I go to the building whenever I need to meet with East German officials. While I have personal access, getting you inside—and giving you privacy during your visit—will require finesse. I will prevail upon friends in the East German government to accomplish this. You are fortunate I am so well connected. The room I am thinking of is the Great Hall. Goering utilized it for major meetings and conferences with senior officials. The Fuhrer attended a few of those meetings. The room is large and architecturally fascinating. Does that sound like a space that will work for your purposes?"

Alex responded enthusiastically, "That building will be perfect."

"Then, it is settled. I must work to arrange your use of the site. But I must ask, how is Lillian doing? Might she return to Deutschland—to visit? —to teach? Did you know about her—uh—relationship with Professor Jung?"

Lucy started to respond. But suddenly Beckman took a large golden pocket watch from his vest pocket. He held it out and looked at it with some alarm.

"Oh, I am full of regret, but I am late. Unfortunately, I have another important date. I will contact a governmental colleague tomorrow morning to see if I can get you authorized to visit the Great Hall on Tuesday afternoon. I will telephone you at the Spree Hotel at two tomorrow to let you know if I have been successful."

Beckman shook hands with his two *American visitors* as he referred to them. A moment later, he strutted out of the bakery.

*****

Lucy shared her impressions of Beckman as they left the bakery.

"Beckman have big stick up butt. I hear him speak. Think *pompous fool*. It surprise me—Lillian who so sophisticated—would friend someone so in love with self. Alex, I not like him—not trust him."

Lucy looked quite pensive for a moment, then she continued. "It necessary we be careful. We bring hashish to East Germany. Tough drug laws there. We play with fire.

True—not Hitler—Nazi type fire. But it Khrushchev style, Soviet fire. I know that fire, Alex. It plenty hot."

"I don't disagree with your assessment, Lucy. But I want to have one more dream-vision. And we weren't able to identify a good place for a dream-vision in West Berlin. So, I don't have an option. If I am going to do this, we're going to have to take some risks."

"You decide this, Alex. Not me. I not like."

*****

Monday afternoon, precisely at two, Alex and Lucy's hotel room phone rang. It was Beckman. "I have good news. I worked everything out. My government colleague has agreed that you will have access to the Great Hall between five and seven tomorrow evening.

"I will meet you at Checkpoint Charlie at noon. We shall have lunch at a splendid little Czech restaurant—my treat! I will then give you a brief tour of Humboldt University. You will see my office as well as the beautiful buildings that make up the University's campus. At four-thirty, we will arrive at the East German Ministries Building—formerly the Reich Air Ministry. Then at five, you will have two hours in the Great Hall."

"Thank you, Dr. Beckman. How can we possibly repay you for your thoughtfulness?"

"Your appreciation is everything I could want. As I told you on Sunday, any friend of Lillian's is my own dear friend. We shall see you tomorrow at noon at Checkpoint Charlie."

Alex updated Lucy. "It was a little weird that he used *we* instead of *I* when he talked about meeting at Checkpoint Charlie. For a moment I wondered if we are going to be followed. Then, I realized he was just probably using the *royal we.*"

"Agah. Hail to king."

*****

The following day, Alex and Lucy arrived at Checkpoint Charlie early. There were three armed guards in front of the small West Berlin gate house—one each from the United States, Great Britain and France. Alex told the American guard they were there to meet a professor from Humboldt University. The guard checked their passports and went into the small structure, returning a minute later.

"You can go to the other side. Professor Beckman is waiting. However, as American visitors, you'll first have to answer a few lame questions from the East Germans. Don't worry about the questions—it's just their bureaucratic crap."

They walked past an ominous sign written in capitals in English, Russian, French and German:

"YOU ARE LEAVING THE AMERICAN SECTOR".

Alex and Lucy walked past the East German gatehouse's imposing guard towers. As they entered the gatehouse, they saw Beckman. He smiled and waved at them. After a few meaningless questions from an East German guard, Beckman was guiding them to the nearby Czechoslovakian restaurant which he promised would be excellent.

Half block before they arrived at the Czech restaurant, Lucy suddenly gave a big smile and said, "Look— Russian restaurant. Dr. Beckman, think we maybe eat here? It look good."

Beckman looked through the window into a small café. Then he looked at the white letters painted on the restaurant's window: *Maschinka—Feine Russische Küche.*

"Well Lucy. Ordinarily I prefer to read the reviews of a dining establishment before giving them my business. And I know from reputation and past experience that the Czech restaurant is simply outstanding." He looked at the obvious disappointment on Lucy's face, gave condescending smile, added, "But I think I can afford to be flexible for a friend of Lillian Maier."

They entered the restaurant and were seated. Beckman introduced himself to the waiter. He explained he was giving a tour of East Berlin to American friends who hoped to have a wonderful meal. After saying that, Beckman ordered sausage, potatoes and sauerkraut for himself.

The waiter turned to Lucy. He gave a warm look when she smiled at him and said, "*Zdravstvuyte*". The waiter and Lucy proceeded to have an animated conversation in Russian. Alex didn't understand a single word that they said to one another. But it was clear, based on the mixture of laughter and more solemn interchanges, that the two Russians were comfortable with one another and pleased to meet a fellow countryman.

A few minutes later, when the waiter turned to him, Alex simply said, "I will have whatever Lucy is having."

The waiter responded in German. "You are obviously smarter than many." Then he left their table, walking into the kitchen to turn in their orders.

Almost an hour later, Lucy and Alex were glowing, as they left the restaurant. Alex thanked Beckman for the wonderful lunch of vinegret, Russian beet salad; klotski, clear broth filled with potato dumplings; and piroshkis, small pastries filled with finely chopped meat and vegetables.

Beckman responded, "I am glad the cook knew how to fix something well. My sausage, potatoes and sauerkraut were quite mediocre—if that."

Neither Lucy nor Alex said any more on the subject of lunch.

*****

Beckman led them on a brief tour of East Berlin, walking along Berlin's *Unter den Linden* which Beckman described as Berlin's primary boulevard. After listening to Beckman babble authoritatively about architectural highpoints, it was clear to Alex that Lucy understood a great deal more about architecture than did Beckman.

They arrived at Humboldt University. During a quick tour of the administration building, Beckman showed them the painted portraits of the twenty-nine prior Humboldt University faculty who had won Nobel Prizes. The only portrait Alex recognized was of Albert Einstein.

Lucy paid a lot of attention to the portraits. "I impressed! Twenty-nine Nobel Prize winners. They famous—make important science developments—change history. But twenty-eight men, Werner. Only one woman? This speak to different problem."

Beckman looked at Alex and shrugged. He said nothing to Lucy and continued the tour.

They left the University and Beckman continued his dissertation on the history of Berlin. Beckman's pompous style reminded Alex of the University of Oklahoma lab assistant—John—who had given Alex the extra drop of LSD.

After crossing the Spree again, they walked past the 17th-century Charlottenburg Palace and several cathedrals. Lucy was enthralled. "I thrilled with architecture we see: Bauhaus, Neoclassic, Beaux-Arts, Renaissance, Gothic

Revival, Romanesque, Greek Revival, Modernist, Medieval, Art Deco and Byzantine. However, I be honest—say you Mister Beckman, East Berlin new construction ugly. West Berlin construction attractive."

"It's Dr. Beckman, not Mister."

Then Beckman pulled out his large golden pocket watch and looked at it. "Oh—we're late again. Time has passed so quickly. We must head to the Ministries Building."

*****

A few minutes later, they approached an enormous concrete office structure.

"My friends, this is the famous Ministries Building."

Beckman walked up to a uniformed clerk at the building's reception desk. The clerk made a call. Five minutes later, they were met by a middle-aged man with a comb-over that began at his left ear and ended behind his right. He was wearing a poorly fitted grey suit and his large pot belly stretched his dirty white shirt so much that the shirt buttons looked like they might pop.

Taking a lit cigar out of the side of his mouth, the man spoke to Beckman in German. "How goes it, Werner? So, these are the famous American friends?"

Beckman nodded.

Then the man turned to Alex and Lucy. Still speaking in German, he addressed them. "Welcome to the German Democratic Republic. My name is Dieter Schmidt. I apologize—but I do not speak English. My friend Werner has told me one of you speaks excellent German. Ordinarily, Americans cannot get access to this building. But Werner Beckman is a friend of mine. He tells me you are writing a novel featuring a meeting of Nazis in the Great Hall. Werner and I will leave you to work on your project for two hours while he and I go to my office and converse about old times."

At that, Beckman briefly removed a pint bottle from the inside pocket of his grey tweed sports jacket and showed it to Schmidt. The bottle's label read *Schladerer Kirshwasser*.

Beckman put the bottle back in his pocket as Schmidt grinned and said, "Herr Doctor Beckman has such excellent taste. Please follow me."

Schmidt led the group past the receptionist, through a marble atrium into a large hallway. At the far end of the hallway, was a grand marble staircase. When they reached the top of the steps, Alex saw an impressive carved door. Schmidt walked up to it, pulled a ring of keys from his pocket, selected one, then unlocked and opened the door. Alex and Lucy walked into a huge marble-floored conference room with dark walnut paneling and thirty-foot-tall ceilings. Along its left side were floor-to-ceiling windows separated by columns. In the center of the room was a large U-shaped wooden table surrounded by fifty leather upholstered chairs.

"This is the Great Hall. I hope it meets your needs. Werner and I will return at seven."

Alex heard the door shut and its lock engage.

"Schmidt and Beckman strange couple. Belong in scary film."

They walked to the far end of the room where they sat down at the end of the table. Lucy reached into her purse and pulled out a pack of *Lucky Strikes* and a book of matches. She removed a cigarette. It had a small ink-pen x-mark on its side. Alex took the cigarette, lit a match and inhaled deeply. He felt the sting of the hashish on his lungs, but was able to stifle his desire to cough. Then he exhaled, leaned back in his chair and looked up at the wooden paneled ceiling. After a couple of minutes, Alex's eyes closed. He had fallen asleep.

*****

There was a deafening noise. A startled Alex looked around. He was no longer seated at the wooden table. His chair was in front of a roomful of uniformed Nazi soldiers who were generating a thunderous applause and shouting "Heil Hitler".

The Great Hall had changed. It was no longer paneled. The room's hanging lights had been replaced with indirect lighting coming from deeply coffered squares in the ceiling. Behind Alex, at the near end of the hall, was a twenty-foot-tall wall carving of a golden eagle perched on top of a large swastika. About two hundred men were seated in the room. Most were wearing dark grey uniforms and military caps. They were applauding three men entering into the hall. The three men softly lifted their right arms in response to audience members' strident right arm salutes and shouts of *Sieg Heil*.

One of the three men was Adolph Hitler. He was wearing a light brown uniform with a red Nazi arm band and black knee boots—similar to the outfit he had been wearing when Alex had seen him in Florence.

The second man was wearing a light gray Nazi uniform with knee boots and a dozen large shiny military medals displayed on the front of his jacket. He was taller than Hitler and had slicked back hair. His pink fleshy face had closely shaved cheeks. He was obviously quite pleased with the event and was having difficulty holding back a smile of satisfaction. Alex realized that this must be Goering—the German Reichsmarschall who was second in command to Hitler and commanded the Nazi Air Force.

The third individual made Hitler look tall. He was small, walked with a noticeable limp and wore a dark grey uniform with a single decoration—a black Nazi armband. The man had a thin hawkish face and thick, black, combed back hair. He did not smile. He appeared instead to be deeply engrossed in his own thoughts—or perhaps just impressed with his own self-importance. He had to be Goebbels— Hitler's Minister of Propaganda.

Judging from the fact that there were fewer wrinkles on Hitler's face, Alex figured the timing of the event had to be before Alex had seen him at the Paris Opera.

*****

Goering addressed the crowd first. He spoke at an even pace—without any expression. He thanked those in the audience for being there that day and for all they had done to prepare Germany for its future challenges. Then he raised his cadence and voice. "Your work is so important that our Fuhrer has asked for the opportunity to personally thank you for your Aryan courage—your daring—your willingness to fight for our fatherland."

Alex surmised from his comments that this was a celebration for newly trained Luftwaffe pilots. Those young men were being thanked for bombing missions they had not yet made. Goering ended his speech with a shout of *Heil Hitler*. Then he stepped back as Hitler calmly walked to the podium while the audience chanted *Sieg Heil*. Hitler had a serene but intent look as basked in his audience's enthusiastic welcome.

As the chants of *Sieg Heil* began to subside, the Fuhrer began to speak in a low tone, at a slow and measured pace. "Thank you, comrades, for your appreciation of a simple German who loves his fatherland—an ordinary man who spent four years during the last war in the trenches fighting the criminal British and the cowardly French. But doing this was not a sacrifice—for I was able to fight for the Deutschland I love."

Hitler went on to speak about the Treaty of Versailles—the agreement that had unfairly punished his beloved land. He spoke about the brave young German soldiers who had been sold out by that traitorous agreement. Hitler began to accelerate the tempo of his speech, addressing challenges his government faced when he came to power—from outside of Germany—and from within. The soldiers in the audience were on the edge of their seats. The Fuhrer's tone was not angry. Alex had heard recordings of Hitler in which he appeared to be shouting at his audience while speaking at a ridiculously intense pace. Those recordings had always sounded to Alex like the ranting of a mad man. But the Hitler Alex was watching was a capable speaker with a clear and strong voice. His audience was spellbound.

As Hitler increased the tempo of his remarks, he explained the challenges he faced as their dutiful leader. "I have no disrespect in my heart for those who have struggled to make ends meet. But the jackals who stole from racially pure Germans—the Jews, the communists, the anarchists and all of their allies—those diabolical characters are beyond redemption—for them, there must be no sympathy."

The Fuhrer developed his theme—speaking faster, but retaining his hypnotic meter almost as if he were reciting a poem. As the tempo of his words slowly increased, the pitch of his voice also was raised. His pauses built a tension that added suspense. But those pauses also were an invitation to his enthusiastic audience to shout their admiration for their leader; their support for the way in which the Third Reich was taking on the challenges Germany faced.

Hitler spoke about patriotism with a fervor that reminded Alex of an evangelist preaching in a tent. Alex had seen the movie *Elmer Gantry* with Burt Lancaster. Elmer Gantry's preaching was more like Hitler's oratory than anything else Alex had ever heard.

"You who sit in front of me today will have your opportunity to show patriotism and skill in the same way that your brothers in Spain are showing the world the Luftwaffe's skill and tenacity."

It occurred to Alex that Hitler must be preparing these pilots to bomb Great Britain. The Fuhrer had offered himself as savior for the German People. Now he was delivering his commandments, sweeping the crowd of Luftwaffe pilots forward with calls for patriotism. It was at that point that Hitler significantly increased the pace of his meter and the level and pitch of his voice. He called out the actions Deutschland must take in order to avenge the wrongs that had been done to it. The audience roared in response to those commands, then cheered as Hitler demanded punishment for the nations which had attempted to destroy the fatherland—the criminals who had used the Treaty of Versailles as a weapon.

Hitler was shouting now. It reminded Alex of recordings he had heard in the past. But Alex noted that Hitler had carefully built to that level of intensity employing a discipline and structure that seemed almost like a staged production—like an opera.

Hitler's speech turned into a litany of moral pronouncements. The crowd's intensity peaked as Hitler concluded. "Those who have stolen from the good and innocent people of Germany; who have disregarded the future of our beloved fatherland; who are guilty of conspiring with the devil; they must be given a certain and absolute reckoning. What is bad has no place amongst us!"

His audience exploded in passionate cheers and shouts of *Heil Hitler.*

Hitler surveyed the audience, then resolutely walked back to Goebbels and Goering, shook hands with each of them and politely listened to the compliments they offered to him, their Fuhrer. Hitler's look—a combination of intense seriousness and unbendable confidence—seemed to Alex be the look of a man who was either deeply crazy, or very holy.

Then Hitler, Goebbels and Goering began to walk out of the hall. However, Hitler stopped for a moment—looking straight at Alex. His smug public face changed to surprise-- almost bewilderment. It was as if he could see Alex—as if he recognized him. Hitler silenced Goebbels with an outstretched hand—and started to speak.

But at that point, the dream-vision ended.

*****

Lucy was shaking Alex. "Alex—it almost seven. You need wake up."

Alex shook his head. He was dazed. The room in which he sat was once again almost empty. Its decor had returned to one of sedate paneled walls. Alex was struggling to awaken.

Lucy hadn't woken Alex a moment too soon. They heard the door unlock. It opened. In came a grinning Schmidt with an equally contented Beckman. Both were smoking cigars. Schmidt walked over to Alex and asked if the session had been successful.

Alex, who was now almost fully awake, assured him it had.

Schmidt, whose red face and cheery demeanor communicated how much he had enjoyed the Kirshwasser, offered a cigar to Alex. "These are the finest Cuban cigars, my friend. You should not pass on this opportunity to smoke one."

"Thank you, Herr Schmidt, but I just don't feel like it this evening."

*****

On the way back to Checkpoint Charlie, Beckman told Alex and Lucy that Schmidt had suggested another site in Berlin they might want to visit. "I know of a large apartment in an East Berlin suburb which belonged to a senior Nazi official. The Fuhrer came to that flat several times for dinner. If the two of you are interested, we could arrange for you to visit the flat and have all the privacy you need."

"Dr. Beckman—thank you. Yes. We are very interested. How do we proceed?"

"Why don't the two of you meet me at Checkpoint Charlie tomorrow at four. We will go out for an excellent dinner. After dinner, I'll take you to the apartment."

When they arrived at Checkpoint Charlie, Alex and Lucy profusely thanked Beckman one more time, then said goodnight.

Chapter 18: More Berlin

As they walked toward West Berlin, Lucy commented, "Schmidt seem evil. Think he not have belief system—other than self. Meet him cause me trust Beckman even less than before. They two of kind—both dishonest and selfish. But my big question—how go dream-vision? What you see? It worth effort?"

Alex gave a detailed description of the dream-vision including the intense look he received from Hitler. "You know what's weird? I always thought of Hitler as a raging madman—someone who always ranted, raved and screamed—and that the German people, for some mysterious reason, just lapped it up. But he was actually quite sophisticated—maybe even a brilliant orator. He played his audience like a skilled musician works his instrument."

As they walked, Alex was silent for a couple of minutes, thinking through what he had just seen, trying to understand it. He continued speaking. "Hitler read them as though he understood the level of their fury at each moment and he managed every aspect of his delivery as he cultivated their passion. The result—his audience was closely tuned into him throughout the speech. We've talked about it before—Hitler applies to politics the lessons he learned from opera. This performance demonstrated that. He introduces a theme; improvises on it; and builds intensity while continually coming back to that theme. Then he closes out with a grand finale—again totally tied to his theme."

They walked silently for a while.

"Once, when I was in high school, I saw a documentary about Huey Long—a Louisiana politician. I'm not saying Huey Long was a bad person—I'm making no judgements here at all. I'm just saying he knew how to manipulate people's emotions. Huey Long had a way of blaming other people for all of his constituents' problems. He told them things they wanted to hear. He promised to fix everything that was wrong. Huey Long knew how to read his audience. He anticipated and managed their fears and hopes for their lives. It was similar to what I saw from Hitler."

Alex gave a quizzical look, took a deep breath and then turned to Lucy. "I always figured people succeed in politics because they are willing to lie—they know how to lie. But now I realize that they also have to know their followers well. They must understand how to communicate with them; how to manipulate them. Those politicians get away with blaming all of their followers' problems on other people— another group—another individual. It makes me sick. I realize this because what I saw today was a politician—ok, yes, an *evil* politician, a nuts politician—but a politician none-the-less. Why aren't people smarter? Why don't they recognize it when they meet an evil salesman—when they are about to shake hands with the devil?"

*****

Alex and Lucy were a few blocks from their hotel. Lucy broke her silence.

"Alex—year dream-vision occur—I think it 1938. You say he speak bombing of Spanish Civil War. Guernica bombed 1937. You see Hitler several times now—three times 1930s; once 1940."

"I want to see him one more time, Lucy. Just one more time—hopefully close to his demise."

*****

Alex and Lucy were exhausted. Before returning to their hotel, they had a light meal of borscht and cabbage rolls at a Polish restaurant a block from their hotel. After dinner, as they entered the hotel, they were stunned to hear someone call from a corner of the lobby.

"Alex, Lucy. Thank God! You are here."

They turned in the direction from which the voice had called. Lillian Maier rushed up to them. She hugged Lucy first; then Alex. "I was so worried. I have been sitting here, waiting for you since early this afternoon. I was afraid something bad had happened!"

"It's great to see you Lillian—but it's a really big surprise. Why are you here? What's up?"

"It's a long story, Alex. But I am famished. Can we go somewhere and get a bite to eat? I'll update you over dinner."

They headed back to the Polish restaurant. Lucy recommended the borscht and cabbage rolls. Lillian took her suggestion. She also ordered a bottle of 1957 Dingac—a Yugoslavian wine she told the young couple they would enjoy.

After the waiter poured the wine and they each had tasted it, Lillian lowered her voice. "I know you are wondering about my sudden arrival in Berlin. A very dear friend of mine, Jordan Church, is officially stationed with the U.S. embassy in Bonn. But Jordan lives in Berlin and generally works out of the U.S. Mission here. When your father received your last letter posted from Frankfurt—I think it was sent on the day you toured his old apartment in Frankfurt, I wrote Jordan telling him that the two of you would be coming to Berlin to research a paper on the Holocaust. In the letter, I informed him I had given you Werner Beckman's name as a contact. Yesterday, I received a telegram from Jordan. It stated that Beckman was not a safe contact for you. In the telegram, Jordan used the words *grave concerns.* He suggested I have you immediately contact him at the U.S. Mission in Berlin."

Lucy interrupted, "What U.S. Mission?"

"The U.S.'s diplomatic embassy for West Germany is in Bonn. But the Mission is our official headquarters here in West Berlin. The Mission is much more than a diplomatic office—it provides—how shall I say it—important intelligence information for our government and armed forces. I have known Jordan for many years and trust him. I know him well enough to understand he would not idly give a warning about just any situation. Jordan always understates things. That he chose the phrase *grave concerns* told me this is quite serious. I had no way of contacting you. I telegrammed Jordan telling him I was coming to Berlin immediately. When my flight from New York arrived in Berlin eight hours ago, I called him at the Mission."

A waiter brought Lillian her dinner. She started her soup while continuing the update to Alex and Lucy. "Jordan was waiting for my call. He had alerted Checkpoint Charlie to watch for the two of you and was notified today when you crossed into East Berlin. As part of your border crossing paperwork, you gave your hotel name. Jordan met me at the hotel this afternoon and brought me up to date on everything. He explained the peril you face. I knew you would want me to gain as much information as I could about that danger. In order to do that, I had to give Jordan the truth about what you are doing in Europe. I didn't feel I had a choice."

Lillian looked at the young couple. They were focused on her every word waiting for her to complete the update. "I learned that Werner has severely compromised himself. About five years ago, he was arrested by East German authorities for reselling stolen artworks. He worked his way out of that situation by giving up anything that remained of his integrity. He has been selling out friends and now regularly trades favors with the East Germans. In some situations, he has aligned himself with individuals who are sympathetic to former Nazis."

Lucy muttered, "Prove Beckman evil."

Lillian glanced at Lucy, then continued. "Jordan also gave me background on Schmidt. Schmidt is a senior leader of Stasi—the East German Secret Police. As a young man, he served as a Nazi Stormtrooper. Schmidt's father was quite high up in the Nazi power structure. And while Schmidt was too much of a bit player to be tried as a war criminal, he is known to be sympathetic to several Nazis who were tried by the war tribunals and has alliances with others who were able to escape prosecution. My immediate concern was that I guessed you would be crossing the border with a cannabis cigarette. In East Germany, getting caught with any amount of marijuana is sufficient cause to put you in jail for at least a decade. And, if you were so charged, there would have been nothing that the United States could do to help you. Nothing!"

Lillian stopped eating and looked directly at Alex. "But brace yourself, Alex. Jordan told me of a story—discounted by most, but believed by some—that Hitler was aware of a person—a young German Jew who came—almost like a ghost—to spy on him. The story has it that Hitler was fixated on that belief. He demanded that that the young man be caught—he wanted him to die."

Alex's jaw had dropped. He said, "That's too incredible."

Lillian responded, "But Alex. That isn't all. Some of the Fuhrer's closest associates believed that this was just another paranoid fabrication of an over-medicated man. Others took Hitler's words and his request literally. In the days before the final destruction of the Reich, Hitler recognized the allies would be victorious. He blamed the Third Reich's failure—his failure—upon this young Jewish spy. He made his most trusted allies—including Schmidt's father—promise that they would make sure this young man— who he speculated might well have travelled from the future—would suffer serious consequences. Jordan told me the United States has always discounted the story of the young Jewish spy as the ravings of a lunatic. But Jordan added, if you were caught coming into East Germany with drugs, the United States could do nothing to help you under any circumstances."

Lillian refilled each of their now empty wine glasses with Dingac, emptying the bottle. She took a sip from her glass and said, "Guys—I am so sorry. I feel so guilty. I unknowingly have put your lives at great risk. You—we— need to fly out of Berlin as soon as possible. Jordan will get us on a military flight to Frankfurt leaving early tomorrow morning. From there, we will return to the U.S. on a State Department flight."

*****

Lillian asked the waiter to bring them another bottle of Dingac. After the wine was delivered and their glasses filled, they sat quietly sipping the excellent Yugoslavian wine.

"Alex, Lucy—tell me about more about today. Tell me about the past few months."

Lucy gave a brief rundown of their trip across Europe. She told Lillian about their travels and the moments leading up to each of Alex's dream-visions. Alex briefly recounted those dream-visions. Lucy shared her theory about why Hitler's ability to perceive Alex had changed—that as Hitler's psyche became more deranged, his doors of perception slid open, resulting in a capability to perceive Alex through time. Lillian listened closely as Lucy shared her theory.

"At first, I not understand differences why Hitler see Alex one time—then not see him next. It make no sense. Then I realize I focus on date in Alex life when he see Hitler—not date in Hitler life when Alex dream-vision him. Hitler ability see Alex increase as he take more strong drugs—as stress build—as Parkinson condition get worse. Hitler reaction to Alex increase over time. All dream-visions between 1934 and 1941—Hitler time. Now, if Alex have Hitler dream-vision 1944 or 1945, Hitler probably see Alex more clear—react to him—more intense."

Lillian raised a finger to her lips, took a deep breath and looked down. Alex understood she was processing what Lucy had just shared. Lucy stopped speaking. They waited.

Then Lillian gave a sly smile. She looked up at Lucy.

"My dear young Russian friend, I like the way your mind works. Your conclusions seem quite valid."

Alex gave a worried look.

"Lillian—we have a big problem. Lucy and I agreed to meet Beckman tomorrow evening—to visit one more site Hitler frequented."

Then he described Beckman's proposed plan for the following evening. Lillian listened closely. After Alex stopped speaking, she shook her head and chuckled.

"In all likelihood, when you were in the Great Hall, you were being watched by Schmidt and Beckman with a video camera. The two of them more than likely figured out what Alex was doing. The chances that either of you would return to West Berlin after tomorrow's planned dream-vision are slim to none. It is a setup. You would be arrested and sent to prison for carrying illegal drugs—at best. At worst, you would be tortured until you are dead. The Stasi does not fool around."

Lucy and Alex were shaken. They looked at one another. Each took a deep breath. There was silence.

Alex finally responded. "Damn. I wanted one more chance to see that son-of-a-bitch."

He paused, and added, "I mean Hitler."

Lucy and Lillian laughed in spite of the seriousness of the situation. They agreed later that they had each thought, at first, that Alex was speaking about Beckman, not Hitler.

"One more opportunity. If I had one more chance—I could communicate to Hitler in a way that—well—would royally piss him off. If I had just had one more chance—to meet with him in a dream-vision—getting to him late in the war. I do think he would see me—might even be able to hear me. I could say the things I need to say—for my father—for my father's family—for all of those victims. Beckman is focused on Wednesday evening. Today is Tuesday. We have some time to set something up. Lillian—you know how much this means to me and are familiar with people and places in Berlin. Couldn't we find a place that is safe? Some place Hitler visited—a place I could have one last German dream-vision? Then I will be more than ready to leave—and will never come back to Europe. I just want one more chance to communicate with this beast—this animal responsible for the death of my grandparents, my uncle, my aunt—I just want a chance to...."

And Alex stopped speaking. He fought to hold back his tears.

*****

Nothing was said for several minutes.

Finally, Lillian spoke.

"I am sorry Alex. I understand how personal this is for you—and I understand why. I lost many family members and friends as well."

Once again, there was silence at the table.

"But no matter how strongly you feel—how satisfying you might think it would be, is it worth risking your life? — risking Lucy's? I have taken a room at your hotel. But it is no longer safe for any of us to stay there. I need to call Jordan. After I speak with him, we can discuss next steps."

Alex and Lucy watched Lillian go to the pay phone at the back of the restaurant and make a call. Lillian was animated during the conversation gesturing with her arms and hands as if she was speaking with someone face to face. Based on her body language, Alex surmised that Jordan must not have been agreeing with whatever she was saying. Toward the end of the call, she smiled. Then she nodded her head, indicating an accord had been reached.

Lucy turned to Alex. "Look like Lillian win. Now, find out what that mean to us."

*****

Lillian returned from the phone booth. "Jordan Church has invited us to stay at his home. We will go to our rooms now and pick up our luggage. A car will arrive shortly to transport us to Mr. Church's home. It has excellent security. But even with that, additional safety measures will be initiated to assure your safety."

Alex looked down in disappointment. He was not going to have another opportunity to have a Berlin dream-vision.

"You are going to love Church's home. It was designed by Walter Gropius."

Lucy sat up straight—her interest obviously peaked.

"And I sure you know Gropius, personal friend—right?"

Lillian chuckled before responding. "I've met the man—and while I appreciate how important Bauhaus was to the development of abstract art—I did not consider him a friend. He did not seem to think a whole lot about Jews—and I can assure you, he definitely was not enamored with strong women."

Alex looked confused.

"Who is Walter Gropius?"

Both women broke into laughter. In so doing, much of the day's tensions appeared to disappear. Alex had no clue what they thought was so funny. However, without understanding why, he joined in their laughter. He was soon laughing so intensely he couldn't speak.

Chapter 19: Neveroyatny!

An hour later, Lillian, Lucy and Alex were riding to Jordan Church's home in the back of a large black Mercedes Benz limousine. Lucy asked Lillian, "You think Beckman, Schmidt will figure out plan fall apart because we not at hotel?

"They will certainly have concerns. I left a message at the hotel desk that may help cover our tracks. If Beckman telephones and asks to speak with you, he will be informed you took a room at a less expensive hotel—that you will meet him tomorrow, as planned. Hopefully, Beckman will believe the East Berlin date for Wednesday is a go. I think he's too smug to be cautious. He and his buddy Schmidt are probably confident you will be arrested shortly after you cross into East Berlin. If that occurred and anyone accused Beckman of entrapping you, he would simply plead total innocence—he didn't know you were carrying illegal drugs."

*****

Alex again asked: "Who is Walter Gropius?"

"Gropius is a famous German architect. While he has worked in the United States for decades, he is originally from Berlin. When he became an architect in 1908, he was hired by an architectural firm that also employed Mies van der Rohe and Le Corbusier. You have heard of them—haven't you?"

Alex meekly indicated he was not familiar with them.

"Well anyway, after a couple of years practicing in Berlin, Gropius started his own design firm based on the principle: *Form reflects function.* After World War I, he became the head of an important Berlin arts and crafts school known for having started the Bauhaus movement—

the merger of modern art and industrial design. Paul Klee and Wassily Kandinsky, were on the school's faculty. In the early 1930s, Gropius left Germany to teach at Harvard. Before leaving Berlin, he designed a series of modern factories, commercial buildings, lines of furniture and a few homes including a home on Lake Havel—here in Berlin. That is where we are going to stay. All of the furniture in the house was designed by Gropius.

*****

The Mercedes turned off of the road onto an access road that was blocked by a gate. The gate slowly opened. The limousine proceeded to a circular driveway in front of a white house shaped like a giant sugar cube. Facing the driveway was a row of windows spanning the second floor. On the first floor, only two windows and one door were visible. Alex was not impressed. Sure, it looked expensive. And yes, it was modern. But it was hardly unique. Alex had seen many similar homes in magazines.

Lucy was succinct in her reaction to the house.

"Neveroyatny!"

This was a Russian word Lucy used from time to time. She had explained to Alex that *neveroyatny* meant *fabulous*.

*****

The driver retrieved their luggage from the Mercedes' trunk and led them toward the house. The front door opened. A woman with shoulder length white hair greeted them. She wore grey slacks, a black sweater and pearls. She and Lillian embraced.

"Lillian," the woman began. "It has been entirely too long. It's wonderful to see you."

The woman's dramatic, almost British accent reminded Alex of Katherine Hepburn.

"Alex and Lucy, this is Eileen Church, our hostess for the next few hours."

"Pleased to meet you Lucy, Alex. Jordan will be home shortly. But all of you must be absolutely exhausted."

"Thank you, Eileen. I am sure these two young people would enjoy resting for a few minutes."

"I'll show them to their room. That will give us a chance to chat about old times—and, if you are interested, to have a martini."

Lillian smiled. "I thought you would never ask."

*****

Eileen Church led Alex and Lucy through a living room that was full of brightly colored geometrically shaped furniture. Alex wasn't sure what to make of the furniture. It was unusual—sculptural rather than traditional furniture forms. The chairs and sofa were totally covered with brightly colored fabric—not a single bit of wood was visible on any of the pieces. Across the room, through a large window, Alex could see the moon shining down on a large lake. He looked into the dining room. It too had modern furniture as well as a colorful painting made up of abstract shapes—shapes that almost seemed to be moving.

Eileen looked back and noticed Alex examining the painting. "That, my young friend, is a Kandinsky. It was installed in the dining room when the house was built. Gropius believed that art and architecture should be tightly linked. That painting was created with this house in mind."

Eileen continued to lead them down a hallway. Alex stopped looking at the furnishings and hustled to catch up. Alex and Lucy were shown a small bedroom.

Once they were alone, Alex let Lucy know his opinion of the home. "The house is nice. Sure. But it looks a lot like

other contemporary homes I've seen in magazines. It's just
not that unusual."

"Alex—you need consider, home, furniture designed
forty year ago."

That was when Alex realized the house was really
something special. "Oh hell," he said. "I guess I don't know
anything about art or architecture."

They lay down on the bed to rest—and quickly fell
asleep.

*****

An hour later, there was a knock on the door. It was
Lillian.

"Jordan has arrived. I am sorry, but I needed to give
a complete update to both Eileen and Jordan. I know I
should have asked you first—but we just don't have the time.
We can trust both of them to be absolutely discrete. I have
some bad news. The Stasi has been quite active. As a result,
we must get you out of Berlin as soon as possible. But I also
have something to share that will please you, Alex. I didn't
want to build up your hopes before. But I had made a request
of Jordan. He just informed me that he has agreed to that
request. You see, Hitler has dined at this house and, Alex, you
can do your dream-vision here. But because of the time
constraint, you need to have it soon."

Alex gave a big smile. "That's fantastic, Lillian. I'm
ready right now!"

"I knew Hitler had been here, but that was about all I
knew. Eileen just gave me more of the background. In 1934,
the home's Jewish owner left Germany for the United
States—obviously under duress. The house was quickly
appropriated by a senior Nazi official—Stephan Funk. Funk's
wife had been a movie starlet in the 1920s. Hitler knew of

her, but didn't actually meet her until 1943. Hitler was apparently—how shall I say it—quite charmed by Mrs. Funk. In 1944 and early 1945, he dined here with the Funks several times."

"Since the dining room is apparently where Hitler spent most of his time when he visited the house, that is where you should have your dream-vision. But Jordan asked a favor for himself and his wife—and I want to ask the same favor for myself. Can we—Jordan, Eileen and I—sit with you while you have your dream-vision?"

Alex was still getting his bearings after his nap. This would be different. But he only thought about her request for a moment before responding. "Yes. Of course, you can watch. That'd be fine. Give us a moment and Lucy and I will join you."

*****

Lucy finished placing a chunk of hashish in the end of a cigarette.

"Not much hash left. Put all—in this cigarette."

She finished stuffing the hash into the cigarette. Then they walked down the hall and into the dining room. The dining room table was an oval shaped clear glass surface supported by a black metal frame. The chairs around it had cube shaped bases with rectangular backs. They were upholstered with bright yellow fabric and the backs were supported by a black framework similar to that on the table.

Alex and Lucy entered the dining room. Jordan, Eileen and Lillian were already seated at the table. Church was a tall man with a slim build. He had well combed grey hair and looked quite at ease with a grey cardigan sweater over his white dress shirt and was puffing on a golden-brown meerschaum pipe, the bowl of which was shaped like the head of a bearded man.

"Good to meet you Alex and Lucy," Church said from the side of his mouth without removing his pipe. "I hear the two of you have been having more fun than squirrels in a beehive."

Alex didn't know what that meant. But it sounded funny. He chuckled and agreed. Church continued to speak. "I'm sorry to have to rush everything, but it seems that your East German buddies are upset about your leaving the hotel. My staff tell me the Stasi are now fully involved. Agents are asking all sorts of people about your whereabouts. We need to get you out of Berlin as soon as possible. My driver—whom I trust with my life—is the only person other than the five of us who knows you are staying here. But, it's just a matter of time till someone makes a lucky guess. There is a military flight out of Tegelhof at two this morning. We'll get the three of you onto it. It goes to Frankfurt Rhein-Main Air Base. You'll have a short layover there and then fly on to DC. We can get you back to Wichita in a couple of days. But we are going to have to be careful. We can talk more about that later. Now it's time for Alex to visit the Fuhrer."

They each sat down at the table on one of the bright yellow chairs.

Alex had a glass of water in front of him. He took a long swallow of the cold water. This was intimidating—trying to have a dream-vision in front of four other people. He wondered if that would affect the dream-vision. Maybe there wouldn't even be a dream-vision this time. Maybe he would have a dream-vision and see someone other than Hitler? In any case, Alex felt like he'd been asked to perform.

Lucy handed Alex the infused cigarette and a packet of matches. Alex lit a match, then the cigarette and inhaled deeply. The smoke was harsh. Lucy had put a lot hash in this Lucky Strike. He held the smoke inside his lungs as long as he could. Then he coughed. He took another drink of water. He was tired. He leaned back. The chair was actually surprisingly comfortable. Alex closed his eyes.

*****

Alex woke to the sound of laughter. He was sitting at the same table. The room was almost unchanged—except that the abstract painting had been replaced by a landscape. Alex looked at the four people seated at the table. There was a short, heavy set, balding man in a brown broad lapeled suit. There was a stylish woman wearing a sheer silk blouse—a blouse that did not make any attempt to hide that she was not wearing a bra. She was probably about forty years old—a blonde with crown braids. There was also a wholesome looking woman with long light brown hair. She was probably in her mid-thirties, conservatively dressed in a skirt and cardigan sweater. And there he was: Adolph Hitler in a brown tweed suit with his signature white shirt and tie.

It appeared that the foursome had completed their meal and were just chatting. Alex assumed that the round-faced man must be Funk; the blonde, his wife; and the brown-haired woman was probably Eva Braun. Funk, his wife and Braun were laughing hard. Hitler's facial expression seemed to communicate a sort of modesty—as if he had just told a great joke. But hey—anyone can tell a great joke, can't they?

As the laughter died down, Hitler spoke. "The fat Italian kept nervously repeating: *It's got to be here— somewhere.*"

250

The other three roared with laughter once again. Hitler apparently had repeated the punch line to his joke.

Hitler had aged a lot since the episode at the Paris Opera. His face was rounder. His hair had turned grey on the sides. His moustache was now a salt and pepper grey. The Fuhrer's face had developed deep wrinkles and there were dark shadows below his eyes. His left arm shook visibly and his back appeared to be slightly stooped. He had even developed a bit of a double chin. Alex was taken aback at how much the German despot had changed since the dream-vision at the Opera house in Paris.

Suddenly Hitler's eyes turned toward Alex. His attention became riveted on Alex's face. Hitler turned away and he spoke to Funk. "My friend. You and your beautiful wife have offered to show us the gardens going down to the lake. Could you give that tour to my dear Eva now? I would like to spend a couple of minutes thinking about important strategic issues. Your gracious hosting of Eva would be most deeply appreciated."

Funk jumped up, thanked the Fuhrer for the opportunity to show the garden and the lake to the lovely Eva; raised his right arm in the Nazi salute; said *Heil Hitler;* and accompanied the two women out of the room.

After Alex heard the house's back door close, Hitler turned to him and spoke in an angry but controlled voice. "Who are you? You have haunted me these past six years. What sort of devil are you?"

Now it was Alex's turn to speak to the individual who had murdered his father's family. "Herr Hitler, why have you persecuted innocent, virtuous people who just tried to live their lives? What gain was there in being such an evil tyrant? And you—Herr Hitler—it is you who are the devil. Not me; it is you. If you are an example of the Aryan master race, then that master race is a colossal joke. I am here to inform you that one day all German people will understand your myth of a master race was a big lie—that you were an insecure fraud. I am here to tell you that in the future, you will be hated by all German people for the harm you did to their beloved Fatherland. The German people will be ashamed of everything you ever did. The world will see you as Germany's weakest moment."

Hitler responded—this time more rapidly and with greater intensity. "You lie. If the Jews had not conspired with the Bolsheviks to undermine everything that is good about our land—if they had not chosen to steal from common men—then, I would not be their enemy. However, as it is, because of the Jews' historical desire to destroy what is good, I, together with the patriots of the Third Reich, have been forced to annihilate them."

Alex paused, reached inside the collar of his shirt, and pulled out the necklace from which his mezuzah hung. He held the mezuzah up so Hitler could see it.

"I am Jewish and I am your worst nightmare— because I come to you from the future. You killed my grandparents. You murdered my uncle. You slaughtered six million Jewish human beings—six million human beings who had hopes, fears, dreams and loves. And you killed many millions of other innocent people. You are the great shame of Germany. I am here to tell you that the result of your hate was not a thousand-year Reich. Your evil plan, in a period of only twelve years, destroyed the Germany you say you loved."

As Alex spoke, Hitler's face tightened into an angry scowl. His left arm began to shake even more visibly.

"History has completed its judgement of you—Herr Hitler. You have done more to injure your beloved Deutschland than any person—of any nationality—of any race or of any religion. You have caused more shame for the people of Deutschland than anyone in all of Germany history."

Hitler stood up and reached inside his coat. He pulled out a small pearl handled hand gun. "You are a pig. Jews are swine—they are filth. The destruction I envisioned for your race was too kind. You are lying. My people will regard me as their savior!"

And, with a shaking hand, he pointed the gun at Alex, and pulled the trigger.

Alex was startled. He saw the gun being fired and waited for the pain—but there was no pain. The bullet passed through him. Alex realized he had not been harmed. The Fuhrer was not able to attack a vision from the future.

Then Alex became angry. He began by laughing at Hitler. "Adolph Hitler—your gun is as impotent as your sexual organ! History will laugh at you—you inept, incompetent, impotent old fool. The German people will despise you—you will be remembered as a villain—not a hero—in your own cheap, shabby opera."

Hitler swore and fired the gun five more times. Then, when he saw Alex had not been harmed, he dropped the gun and shrieked, "Jewish vermin!"

Adolph Hitler raised both arms and charged Alex— trying to place his hands around Alex's neck. But Hitler was fighting an apparition. The angry tyrant ended up falling on the floor.

Moments later, Funk came running into the room. His wife and Eva Braun following closely behind. Funk was shouting, "What has happened, my Fuhrer?"

A moment later two SS Officers rushed into the house through the front door—pistols drawn—searching for an assailant. All any of them saw was an angry despot cursing as he lay face down, spread eagled on the floor.

"Get out of here." Hitler said. "All of you—Out of here!"

*****

Alex woke up. He was again sitting at the table with four people. But they were Lillian, Jordan, Eileen and Lucy.

Lillian spoke first.

"What happened? We heard nothing—but your face—its expressions spoke to us—something extraordinary happened. It frightened me. Tell us what happened."

"I woke up. There were four people seated at this same table—in fact most everything was the same in this room except for the painting. This abstract painting wasn't there. There was a landscape of a river and a forest."

Then Alex described all he had seen—what had happened to him—what he had said in his dream-vision—and how Hitler had responded.

There was quiet in the room after Alex finished his tale.

Jordan stood up and slowly walked around the table.

He went behind where Alex was seated and pointed down at a section of the wall. There, on the textured wall, were six small smooth patched-over spots. Repairs had been made. But they had not been patched so thoroughly that they hid the original damage from the six bullets.

Lillian, Jordan, Eileen and Lucy were silent—staring at the six patched-over bullet holes. A grandfather clock in the living room chimed twelve times.

Jordan said, "It is time to take our friends to the airport."

*****

Half an hour later, they were saying goodbye, hugging and shaking hands.

Jordan spoke. "Alex—this evening turned into one of the most unusual events in my life—and that is saying something. Thank you for your courage. Thank you for including Eileen and me in your wonderous adventure. Please take care of yourself."

Alex, Lucy and Lillian got into the Mercedes—on their way to Templehof Airport—on their way to catch a military transport to Frankfurt Rhein-Main Air Base—and then back to the United States.

Chapter 20: A Bat out of Hell

A moment after sinking into his seat on the Boeing 707, Alex was asleep.

Lucy and Lillian were fully engrossed in a conversation about Alex's amazing adventure in the Gropius house dining room.

"Eileen say Kandinsky painting in home since it built. Alex see different picture during dream-vision. But Alex see landscape. You explain why different?"

"Eileen said the painting was installed in the dining room when the house was built. That's different than saying it had been continually displayed in the house since it was built. The Kandinsky was taken down from the dining room wall in 1937. Even though neither Funk nor his wife had met Hitler at that point, it was because of Hitler that the Kandinsky painting was replaced with a nice, but unremarkable, landscape by Caspar Friedrich."

Lucy gave a look of confusion. Lillian continued with her explanation.

"As a young man, Hitler wanted to become an artist. During his late teens and early twenties, he produced many run-of-the-mill traditional landscapes. At that time, abstract artists like Wassily Kandinsky, Paul Klee, Pablo Picasso, Max Beckman and Georges Braque were experimenting with abstract art and receiving great praise from critics and art connoisseurs while Hitler's work was ignored. Adding insult to injury Kandinsky and Hitler were both painting in the same city—Munich—prior to World War I. Kandinsky was the darling of Munich's art world while Hitler's work was ignored."

Lucy closed her eyes and nodded, a facial expression which communicated she was following Lillian's point. Lillian continued. "That lack of public respect during Hitler's formative years never was forgotten. Kandinsky and the other abstract painters became targets for Hitler's actions— actions driven by unconscious feelings rather than by a conscious plan. In other words, Hitler's attack on abstract and modern art was really a failed artist's jealous rage against other artists who had succeeded."

Lillian shook her head sadly for a moment. Then she continued. "In 1935, Hitler made a public pronouncement to the German people damning modern art. He proclaimed that it was not the mission of art to show human beings in a state of decay. That pronouncement was a sort of directive to all art lovers to get rid of their modern art. In 1937, the Nazis went further to illustrate how bad modern art was. They sponsored two art exhibits in Munich—at the same time. One exhibit was called *The Great German Art Exhibition*. It displayed traditional romantic paintings by German artists of women, men and landscapes. The other was called *The Degenerate Art Exhibition*. It displayed abstract and other modern art that had been confiscated from German museums and artists. *The Degenerate Art Exhibition* pictures were poorly displayed—paintings were hung at angles and placed next to graffiti which criticized the paintings and all abstract art. One of the abstract artists targeted by *The Degenerate Art Exhibition* was Wassily Kandinsky."

Lillian took a deep breath and sighed, then spoke while gazing out her window. "As a result of Hitler's personal failures, museums throughout Germany were ordered to remove all Kandinsky paintings from their collections. And the Funks also did what was required. They took down their Kandinsky. But—and this is what I find so very fascinating—instead of burning the painting, the Funks hid it in the back of a closet. Imagine that! While being careful not to openly challenge Nazi standards, they somehow, for some reason—maybe because they recognized the painting's quality—maybe some other reason—did not destroy that wonderful work of art. Eileen found the painting hidden in the back of a closet after she and Jordan moved into the house in 1946. She immediately rehung it in its rightful place."

Lillian smiled as she looked at her seatmate. "You must forgive my passion, Lucy. The things we speak about today—they touch my own life experience—they bring back memories—painful memories of things that happened to me—of things that happened to people whom I cared for deeply."

Lillian bit her lip. She was silent for a couple of minutes, gazing out the window of the airplane as it soared through the blackness of night. A tear slid down her cheek. She calmly, but subtly wiped the tear away, careful not to allow Lucy to see it. Then she added, "But Lucy, it is a special treat for me—an uncommon privilege—at this stage of my life—to be able—to be able to share thoughts with someone who understands the horror of repressive governments—but who also appreciates the incredible wonder of art. I hope we will continue to be friends, Lucy. I feel so comfortable chatting with you—chatting with you about these things—things that I find people in Wichita do not want to think about."

Lucy looked at Lillian and smiled. "I honored be able say, Lillian Maier is my friend. Your mind, Lillian—it simply beautiful. Thank you being my friend."

*****

Lillian and Lucy each leaned back in their seats. Nothing was said for half an hour. Then Lillian spoke again. "You know, Jung once commented on Hitler's genius. He wrote that Hitler expressed the collected unconscious of the German people and brought those perspectives to the German conscious. Jung was correct. Hitler was not an intellect who anticipated what the German people wanted to hear. His secret was his belief in himself. Hitler had the ego of a zealot and was willing—no, driven—to express his feelings as facts rather than beliefs or impressions."

Lillian leaned forward with an intent look on her face. "The unconscious feelings of the German people were similar to those of Hitler. That is why they responded so fervently to his message—it reflected their own fears—their own desires. They were given confidence by a leader partly because that leader stated his beliefs—their beliefs—with such absolute certainty. The German people felt a need to find someone to blame for the difficult challenges they were forced to face. Hitler had that same need. And his diabolical social policies, responded not only to the common folk's unconscious feelings with words, but also with actions."

Lillian looked down and shook her head sadly before saying, "Perhaps all of this just demonstrates why, in times of uncertainty, populist leaders often arise from the masses and are listened to as if they are messiahs. Historians often give those leaders credit for anticipating the feelings of the common people. But they haven't anticipated anything— they've merely shared the unconscious sentiments of the people. Populist leaders are, in reality, a part of the cultural and social mass—not visionaries. They give words to the collective unconscious of frightened and inarticulate people.

Historians often remark that Hitler was emotional in his speech delivery. Why wouldn't he be? He was sharing his own beliefs. Wouldn't one expect the manner in which he expressed his beliefs to reflect his feelings? And Hitler was smart enough to recognize that when something he said resonated with others, well, it was worth repeating—again and again."

It seemed that Lillian was done speaking and was going to take a short nap. She turned to the window and closed her eyes. However, she must have still been processing the thoughts she had just shared, because a moment later her eyes opened and she turned back to Lucy saying, "I guess the moral of this story, Lucy, may be that when leaders of a nation are not responsive to the unconscious fears and suffering of their populace, there is a real and present danger that a tyrant—someone driven by unconscious demons—rather than by wisdom—will rise to power."

*****

A couple of minutes later, a member of the flight crew walked back to chat with Lillian and Lucy. He informed them that for security reasons, the flight had been diverted to Ramstein Air Force Base in Southeast Germany. Lillian asked him to clarify. He responded that that was all he knew. Forty-five minutes later, the flight landed at Ramstein.

Alex awoke from his sleep long enough to exit the Boeing 707 and board another airplane waiting to fly the threesome back to the United States. Once they were seated on the next flight, Alex closed his eyes and went right back to sleep. Alex woke up half way across the Atlantic. He groggily stood up, then walked down the aisle to use the bathroom.

After he returned to his seat, Lucy asked him how he was doing.

"You would not believe the dream I just had."

With that he closed his eyes and went back to sleep.

*****

The flight landed early Thursday morning at Andrews Air Force Base near Washington DC. Alex woke up and looked around—thrilled to be back in the United States—glad the flight was over.

Lillian addressed him. "Alex—Lucy said you had a strange dream. Would you mind telling me about it?"

Alex chuckled. "Lillian—I consider you to be wonderful—a very interesting and much trusted friend. But I have become older and wiser. If I never tell another living person about one of my dreams, it will be too soon. And Lucy—if I do offer to tell my dreams to anyone—under any circumstances—I want you to grab me and get me out of there—like a bat out of hell."

The three of them laughed. Then they grabbed their bags and departed from the airplane.

*****

Half an hour later, Alex, Lucy and Lillian were standing in a receiving room near the runway. A uniformed Air Force clerk walked up to Lillian and told her there was a phone call for her. The clerk directed her into an empty office to take the call. She motioned to Alex and Lucy that they should follow. For the next few minutes, Lillian just listened to whoever was on the other end of the line, adding an occasional *Uh huh* and *OK*. Alex and Lucy watched closely, wondering if the call was good news or bad.

After about five minutes, Lillian hung up the phone. "Well, doesn't that about take the cake? That was Jordan. I think you will enjoy hearing about all that has transpired. First of all, Schmidt and Beckman as well as two other Stasi agents were arrested by American military police outside Jordan and Eileen's home early Wednesday morning. They were searching for you Alex. They aren't searching for you anymore."

Lillian smiled. "When the US military police turned Beckman and his friends over to the Stasi, they informed the Stasi of Schmidt and Beckman's activities over the prior few days. Turns out that the Stasi were already investigating these clowns. Schmidt, Beckman and the two other Nazis had been involved in a series of illegal activities including smuggling Nazi loot out of Berlin and selling it for personal profit. Apparently, the East Germans feel no warmer towards Nazis than the West Germans do. Schmidt, Beckman and their two associates are now in the custody of the Stasi. We won't need to worry about them again. Jordan told the Stasi the United States had been investigating Beckman and Schmidt—that the CIA knew the two of them believed in a legend that somebody had travelled through time to visit Hitler—that while that legend was obviously absurd, it represented an opportunity to catch Beckman and Schmidt. The US was not going to pass that up. So, Jordan told the Stasi that the CIA lured Beckman and Schmidt into a trap using Alex—an American student—as a decoy—a counterfeit time-traveler."

"End result? Church covered your tracks. Then he used the same story to protect you within the State Department. Sometimes a lie is so much more reasonable than the truth. You've just got to love a good lie. And there is more good news, the State Department is helping us out one more time—thanks to Jordan. A special flight to Wichita will leave shortly. We'll be on it."

Alex and Lucy each gave Lillian a hug.

*****

Alex felt light, unburdened. He and Lucy were out of Berlin and had escaped the plot of Schmidt and Beckman. Now, he was on his way home. He couldn't wait to tell Papi about every detail of his adventure. But he would start out by telling him about his visit to Frankfurt.

Lillian looked Alex in the eye and took a deep breath. Then she said, "Alex. I have something awful to share. I chose not to speak about it sooner because you had too much to worry about already. However, what I am about to explain is a major reason for my coming to Berlin. It is the primary reason I pushed so hard to get you to return to the United States as quickly as possible, to get you back to your home in Wichita."

An ominous silence followed her statement. Alex hadn't known Lillian long, but he had gotten to know her well enough to know Lillian was about to share something of consequence.

"Your father was so excited that you were pursuing his history, that you wanted to better understand what had happened to him in his youth..."

"Lillian. No preludes please. Just tell me. Has something happened to Papi?"

Lillian sighed. "I am sorry, Alex. But there is no good time—no good way. Your father had a stroke a week ago. The doctors said it was massive. When I left for Berlin, he was comatose—and not expected to survive. Your mother and I have never been close friends. But we spoke several times in the last week. She thanked me for my support. I told her I was going to Berlin to find you. I promised to bring you home. She assured me she would keep me updated on your father's condition. The State Department promised to make sure her communications got through. When I spoke with Jordan, he gave me the bad news. Alex, your father has died. Your mother is strong. But she needs you. She will meet us at the airport in Wichita when we arrive this evening. I am so sorry Alex. I know this is devastating. I wish I could find something positive to say other than just telling you that your father was proud that you were pursuing understanding...."

Alex held up a hand, indicating to Lillian that he wished she would say no more. Lillian and Lucy just looked at Alex. Alex looked down at the ground, pursed his lips, and said nothing.

Moments later, they boarded the flight that would take them to Wichita.

Chapter 21: Wichita

Alex and Lucy spent the evening sitting at the dining room table with Alex's mom. Lucy had heated up a casserole a neighbor had brought over. None of them had eaten much. Mutti spoke about her memories of a younger Papi—reminding Alex how proud his father had been of him, telling Lucy stories about Alex's childhood.

"Mutti—you need sleep. The doctor told me you didn't sleep last night. He is concerned about your health. Go to bed. Tomorrow will be a hard day. Tomorrow, we bury Papi."

Alex's mother said, "I will go to bed when I am ready." And she sat helped Lucy clear the dishes.

The three of them moved into the living room. An hour later, Mutti fell asleep in her chair. When she woke up a little while later, she said, "OK. I will go to bed."

*****

Alex did not sleep well that night. He tossed and turned. As the first daylight began to creep through his window, Alex got out of bed. He was ready to face what promised to be the one of the hardest days of his life. Mutti was already up, preparing a breakfast of scrambled eggs, bacon and toast.

Afterwards, the three of them climbed into the Ford Fairlane and drove the three miles to the cemetery for the grave-side service. Only a handful of people were there. Among them, standing toward the back, was Lillian. Alex noted that Lillian appeared uncomfortable—almost nervous. Mutti walked up to Lillian and thanked her for bringing Alex and Lucy home. They briefly embraced.

The rabbi, whom Alex hadn't seen in years, asked Alex if he would like to say a few words about his father.

"Rabbi—I wouldn't know what to say. I have so many special thoughts about my father. But today is a day during which I will remember Papi in silence."

The Rabbi began the service with a Hebrew prayer. Then he spoke about Klaus Schwarz's life. "Klaus loved his childhood in Frankfurt Germany. But the hate and violence perpetrated by the Nazis made it necessary for him to leave his homeland and family. His parents and brother, who were unable to leave Germany, perished in concentration camps. Klaus made a life in this country. He was respected by his professional colleagues and by this community for his great intellect—for the principles which governed how he lived—and for the wisdom that had led him to those principles. Klaus will be missed by his loving wife and son. We shall all miss him."

*****

The Rabbi led those at the grave-site in the Kaddish. Then the wooden coffin disappeared into the freshly dug grave.

Alex looked around at the grave-site. His mother was still in shock. Lucy was looking up at him, clearly concerned about how he would respond to his father's burial. Standing by herself at the back of the assemblage, Lillian looked lost.

No one spoke. The only sound was the light rain on the grass, trees and stone monuments of the Wichita cemetery. Alex looked down. He shook his head from side to side in disbelief. He wished he had had the opportunity to tell his father about the past year. Alex would have asked him for forgiveness for never having fully understood his father's grief.

Alex took his mother's hand in his and led her toward the car. As they drove away from the cemetery, Alex suggested that Mutti, Lucy and he go out to get something to eat.

"Alex—I'm just not hungry. You and Lucy go out if you wish. I prefer to go home and be alone. I am tired. I feel so empty."

*****

When they got home, Mutti told Lucy and Alex that she was going to take a nap.

About three or four hours later, she got up from her nap, came into the kitchen where she and Lucy put together a salad and heated up a brisket and kugel brought to them by members of the Temple Sisterhood. The three of them ate their dinners in silence. When they finished, Mutti announced that she was still tired and would return to bed.

Alex and Lucy put away the leftovers and washed the dishes. Then they went into the living room. Alex opened his father's liquor cabinet, took out two beautiful crystal old-fashioned glasses and a matching carafe. He poured a glass of brandy into each of the glasses.

"Papi loved these glasses. I remember him taking out the carafe and glasses when we had a special visitor. He told me that holding one of these glasses in his hands brought back good memories. Their heaviness, the quality of the cut-glass workmanship, reminded him of a set of glasses his father had had in Frankfurt."

They sat in the living room, sipping brandy. Nothing was said for some time. Then Lucy broke the ominous silence. "How go it, Alex? You not speak any feelings. You not cry. You say little. You look sad. Alex. How you feel?"

Alex heard her question, but remained silent.

Minutes later, he responded. "Lucy, I just don't know what to say. I was so happy to be going home—so proud to be able to tell my father about my trip. I especially looked forward to telling him about seeing his home in Frankfurt. Papi would have been so interested in hearing about Mary Becker. He would have been impressed with Mary's integrity. And he would have been pleased we went to Dachau—that I had come to better understand the horror he knew so well."

Alex took a sip of the brandy and looked up at the picture of his father's family that had been taken thirty-five years ago. He took a deep breath, then exhaled. "I was so eager to share my dream-visions with him—each one in great detail. Papi would have found them fascinating—on so many levels. He would have asked thoughtful questions—and expressed his fears for my safety. He would have chastised me and congratulated me at the same time for each moment of danger. Most of all, I wanted to tell him about Hitler being able to see me. He would have laughed and told me I was a fool. But he would have been proud of me for standing up to Hitler. He would have roared with laughter when he heard Hitler fell on his face. And he would have thanked me for addressing that son-of-a-bitch on behalf of his brother and parents; on behalf of himself. I wanted that conversation so much, Lucy. It would have meant the world to him—and to me. Instead—I just feel empty—guilty. It was wrong for me to leave my mom and dad. It was selfish of me. I will never forgive myself. I feel so awful. My life will always be empty in that respect."

Alex was quiet for a while, then he added, "Papi experienced great loss, grief and pain in his life. Yet he cared so much for me. And he died without knowing how much I really loved him, how much I respected him, how much I cared for him."

They sat there in the living room, saying nothing.

After half an hour, Lucy spoke.

"I sorry Alex. I wish something I could say. But I not know what that be. You love your Papi much. I know he love you. But I sorry. I not know what else say. I tired now too. I go bed. You come soon. Yes? Sleep important. Sleep be magic. It erase sadness. Come bed soon. Please."

Lucy kissed him on the forehead and left the living room.

*****

Alex sat there. Time passed.

The pendulum clock on the wall next to the china cabinet chimed twelve times. Alex leaned back on the upholstered sofa, looking at the family pictures on the living room walls. There was a photo of Papi, his brother and his parents taken at the Palmengarten—probably around 1930. The photograph next to it showed Mutti with her parents. The next picture, a snapshot, showed a grinning Alex on a pony at a State Fair. Papi and Mutti were standing next to him looking equally pleased.

Alex looked at the glass and porcelain pieces in the mahogany china closet. Each item had a story behind it. Alex had relished hearing his parents tell their stories about those objects when he was young. He reflected on one of the porcelain figurines—a boy with lederhosen. Alex's grandparents had given it to his Papi on his fifth birthday.

There were so many memories.

Alex looked at his father's overstuffed chair—remembering the wonderful chess games—his father leaning forward, sitting across from Alex who sat on a dining room chair—with the black and white chess board and the familiar chess pieces resting on the footstool between them.

It seemed so strange to be here—for his father to be gone—forever. It just seemed so strange.

Alex was tired. He closed his eyes.

*****

Alex awoke to a familiar voice.

"Alex, what are you doing here? Mutti and I just read your letter—from Florence. How can you be here now?"

Alex looked up at his father. Klaus Schwarz was looking intently back at him.

Alex was confused—but for only a moment. Then he recognized what had happened—what was happening. This was a dream-vision—or was it a dream? If it was a dream, Alex decided he would treat it as a dream-vision. He had the chance to speak to his father one last time. Even if this was a fantasy, he was going to take full advantage of it.

And if it was a dream-vision, well, it was the most special one.

"Papi. I have much to tell you. I must start by sharing something extraordinary. It will shock you. Papi—I am speaking to you in a dream-vision. You just read the letter from Florence. The time I am speaking to you from is about a month after you received that letter. Much has changed, Papi. Much has changed. You and I have always been very honest with one another, Papi. The result wasn't always pleasant."

They both laughed. But Alex could see his father's laugh was nervous. His father was anxious to hear what came next.

"I was honest with you before I left. I will be just as honest now. Lucy and I returned from Europe a couple of days ago. Lillian met us in Berlin. She helped us Papi. She is a good person. Lillian helped us a lot. Now I need to tell you the most difficult part of this. Papi. Today was a hard day. Today, Mutti, Lucy and I went to the cemetery—to say goodbye to you."

Klaus had been sitting upright. When he heard his son say this, he closed his eyes, took a deep breath through his nose and leaned back in his chair. After he released his breath, he spoke to his son. "Alex. I don't know what to say. I've been having headaches—a lot of them. But this—?"

Klaus rubbed his chin as he always had when he was striving to absorb a complex or challenging idea. He took another deep breath, exhaling slowly. "This—this is too much. I have always believed that Shakespeare was right when he wrote there are more things between heaven and earth than are found in our philosophies. You told me some incredible things when we went out to lunch last winter. But this—this is—how do I say it? This takes the cake. But if this is my last hurrah, then I shall take advantage of the opportunity. Let's talk, son. Let me hear what you have to say, Alex. Speak to me."

Then Alex began to converse in his father's native language. He described the strange insight he gained from meeting Frau Baumgarten. He told about meeting Mary Becker—her bravery and her sadness. He described his joy at seeing the beauty of the Palmengarten and of imagining his father there as a child. He told his father that he had seen Dachau and about the overpowering sadness of the visit to the concentration camp.

Then he shared each of his dream-visions—his adventures in Florence, Paris, Munich and Berlin. He described them in great detail. Papi sat forward as he listened, figuratively and literally on the edge of his chair.

There were many questions. Papi asked about present-day Frankfurt and Mary Becker, about Dachau and about each of the dream-visions. Alex slowly and carefully responded to every one of his father's questions.

The conversation seemed to last for hours.

Finally, Klaus told Alex, he was getting tired. He told his son he needed to close his eyes for a few minutes.

Alex stood up. It made no difference at that moment whether this was real, a dream, or a dream-vision. Alex walked over to his father, and kissed him on the forehead. "I love you Papi."

Klaus opened his eyes and smiled at his son. "Goodbye son. My life has included a great deal of loss and pain, a lot of sadness. But it also included moments of great joy. No moment in my life has given me such a sense of fulfillment as this. Thank you, son. I love you too."

"Goodbye Papi. Thank you so much. You have been a wonderful father."

"And you have been a wonderful son."

*****

The pendulum clock chimed four times Alex opened his eyes and looked at the clock. He surveyed the room. He was by himself.

Alex stood up, gave a long look at the empty overstuffed chair that, only moments before, had seemed to hold his father.

It was time to go to bed.

Made in USA - Kendallville, IN
74748_9781956920024
01.27.2022 0940